'What is it you want of me, Becky?'

'I—I could not sleep.' Her fingers twirled nervously with her hair. 'I came down for a drink.'

'You're lying, Becky. I'm in no mood for games. Tell me what you are doing downstairs!'

She swallowed, her tongue moistening her lips, a gesture at once provocative and revealing the extent of her nervousness. 'I wanted——' She broke off, too ashamed to speak of the need which had driven her to seek his company.

She tried to back away, but Jake's hold tightened, his eyes glinting savagely. 'We are married, Jake.'

His expression remained closed, giving her no encouragement.

Her chin came up. 'How can you be so insensitive?' she burst out. 'I have been a poor wife until now. But obviously you are too used to dealing with whores to know the effort my coming down here has cost me! I was wrong last night and the other nights to refuse you. I...I wanted our marriage to be more than a hollow shell.'

For as long as Pauline Bentley can remember, she has been captivated by history. She finds reliving the excitement of the battle of Crecy or a medieval tournament more exciting than the current news of the day. Born in Essex, she was trained as a legal secretary, but always came away from visiting castles or manor houses with the desire to write about them. She now lives in Sussex and finds inspiration and relaxation during long walks over the South Downs with the family and dogs. She is married and has two children and a growing menagerie of pets.

Previous Titles

SONG OF WYCHAVEN
CAVALIER'S MASQUE
LURE OF TREVOWAN
SHADOW OF PENGARRON

WOMAN OF CONFLICT

Pauline Bentley

MILLS & BOON LIMITED
ETON HOUSE   18-24 PARADISE ROAD
RICHMOND   SURREY   TW9 1SR

First published in Great Britain 1990
by Mills & Boon Limited

© Pauline Bentley 1990

Australian copyright 1990
Philippine copyright 1990
This edition 1990

ISBN 0 263 76759 0

Set in Times Roman 10 on 10¼ pt.
04-9003-89006 C

Made and printed in Great Britain

CHAPTER ONE

'PULL your hood further over your face, woman,' Oliver Ashleigh snapped. 'I would not have us recognised.'

The harsh voice of Rebecca's grandfather grated on her ears. Obeying his command, she pulled the drab brown cloak closer about her slender figure, unable to control a shiver of apprehension. From the moment they had arrived at the river port of Bridgwater, both her grandfather and Squire Hardwycke had been acting strangely, almost furtively.

'What's amiss, Grandsire?' Her violet-flecked eyes narrowed uneasily as she studied his wiry figure in its sober black cloak and sugar-loaf hat. The wide brim hid his expression from her, but, despite the chill mist covering the port which robbed the late April morning of warmth, his long, thin upper lip was beaded with perspiration.

'Nothing which need concern you,' he responded sharply. 'We're here to collect the Squire's wine.' As he spoke he drew back behind stacked wool bales waiting to be loaded aboard ship.

Her unease deepened. Oliver Ashleigh feared nothing but God. Why then was he so tense—so intent upon being inconspicuous as they stood on the crowded quay? He was staring at the merchant ship moored close by.

Following his gaze, Rebecca scanned the busy decks. The sailors were lifting the hatches in preparation to unload their cargo. All looked innocent enough. So why was her grandfather so nervous, if he was here merely to collect a consignment of wine?

Rebecca frowned, her pleasure in this unexpected outing fading with the realisation that all was not as it seemed. She looked across to where Squire Hardwycke waited by the coach, its leather blinds drawn against in-

quisitive eyes. Her grandfather and his friend were be-
having like conspirators. The knowledge caused her heart
to jolt. That was exactly how they had been acting all
morning, ever since Squire Hardwycke and his son, Tom,
had arrived at the Ashleighs' home at Coombe Grange
and insisted that Rebecca join their party travelling to
Bridgwater.

She had thought at first that Tom had made the
suggestion in order to spend some time in her company,
but throughout the journey he had been quiet and distracted. She looked up at Tom, who was standing unusually silent at her side. His long, curly chestnut wig
hid his profile from her, but his lean body was stiff with
tension as he too studied the merchant ship.

'Why all this furtiveness, Tom?' she whispered.

Absently, he turned to her, his handsome, squarish
face unusually pale. 'It is necessary.'

'So my presence *is* meant to make this look like a
family trip.' Her eyes widened as her anxiety mounted.
'What are you and Grandsire doing here? Just what is
at stake?'

Tom went even paler. He took her elbow and drew
her a few steps away, out of her grandfather's hearing.
'Old Ashleigh guards you well, even though we are to
be betrothed next month. Of course, I seized this opportunity for us to be together, my dear.' A strained smile
parted his lips, but did not ease her suspicion that he
was lying. 'There is nothing happening here to trouble
your pretty head over.'

'I'm not a fool, Tom, so do not treat me as one. This
is no innocent trip,' she pursued, her glance returning
to the merchant ship, where a cloaked figure was di-
recting several men who were hoisting wooden vats from
the hold and swinging them down to the quay. 'Rumours do reach Coombe Grange, and our servant Lizzie
has an active tongue.'

Tom chewed at the drooping edge of his narrow brown
moustache, his blue eyes becoming guarded. 'Since when
did you pay heed to servants' gossip?'

'Since there has been talk of rebellion,' she persisted, her stomach tightening with unease. 'I know Grandsire has no love for our Papist King James. Does not the exiled Duke of Monmouth—for all he is King Charles's bastard—plot to take his uncle's throne?'

Tom glanced furtively from side to side. 'Keep your voice down. Such talk is treason.'

'I am aware of that!' Her troubled gaze searched his face for some sign of reassurance and found none. 'That's why I want to know if you and Grandsire are involved.'

'Odsbones, Rebecca, what do you take us for?' Tom blustered.

'Men who have sworn to tolerate no Catholic upon England's throne,' she accused. 'I've heard enough talk when Grandsire's godly companions gather at the Grange. Tell me, Tom, is this delivery of wine a cover for arms to be smuggled into the country?'

'It's not a woman's place to know of such things—let alone speak of them,' Tom said irritably. 'We're collecting wine today, nothing more. Your grandfather is beckoning me; I must go.'

His relief at getting away was so obvious that it fanned her suspicions. She watched him hurry to the side of her grandfather, who spoke quickly. A moment later Tom left him and was instantly swallowed up among the porters and seamen working on the quay.

Rebecca shivered. Conspiracy was almost tangible in the air. She could understand her grandfather's religious fervour, but she thought Tom too shrewd to dabble in treason. Since Tom's return from studying in Utrecht, he had become a frequent visitor at her home. After the years of seclusion at the Grange, since the death of her parents when she was a child, his presence had been like the brightness of the sun after a long, dreary winter. Throughout her seventeen years her life had been governed by the strict religious doctrine of her grandfather, whose friends were as dour and stern-faced as himself.

She had known Tom, who was two years older than herself, since childhood. Then he had been a shy, nervous boy, dominated by his overbearing father. His years from home had changed him, and from their first reunion she had been dazzled by his company. If the extravagance of his compliments often made her laugh, they had also stirred her heart.

Glancing anxiously at Oliver Ashleigh, she saw him glaring at the ship, his weather-hewn cheeks flushed crimson with anger as he watched the cloaked man stride down the gangplank.

'There's treachery afoot!' he ground out thickly. 'What's a *Masters* doing on that ship? I'd know their arrogant features anywhere. I'll have no dealings with that devil's brood.'

Rebecca followed his incensed stare. The mist no longer distorted the image of the man approaching. Above medium height, he was not unduly tall, but his assured step was that of a man used to command. Beneath a black plumed hat he wore no wig, nor needed one, for his long light brown hair, its tips streaked golden by the sun, waved thickly past his broad shoulders. As he neared, he tossed his cloak back over one shoulder, revealing a dark grey velvet suit trimmed with black braid. The fall of Venetian lace at his throat emphasised his bronzed complexion, proclaiming him a man who spent most of his time out in the open, working on the land or—more likely from the worn silver decorations on his sword-belt—as a soldier.

Such a man could not be a Masters! For years she had listened to her grandfather's ranting on the wickedness of the Masters family, especially of Sir Charles Masters, whose land bordered upon the Ashleigh estate. Those lean, clear-cut features were not those of a man steeped in debauchery—as her grandfather had described all the Masters men.

'Get in the coach, Rebecca,' Oliver Ashleigh snapped.

She hesitated, her attention drawn to the stranger as he swept off his hat and bowed to her. He looked to be in his late twenties, but his cool self-possession would have been the envy of a man twice his years. As he straightened she caught a glint of interest in the hazel eyes which swept admiringly over her. Her heart gave a curious twist. His rugged, clean-shaven face was strikingly arresting: not handsome in the way that Tom's smooth, almost boyish looks were symmetrically beautiful, but with lean, chiselled planes which were potently masculine, both sensual and threatening. When he replaced his hat, she saw that tucked into its band, alongside the black ostrich feather, was a sprig of greenery. Oliver Ashleigh wore a similar sprig in his own hat. The stranger's arched brows lifted with wry amusement as he encountered her grandfather, bristling with hostility.

'Jake Masters at your service, Mr Ashleigh. I see the family likeness has not escaped you. I did warn His Grace that it could present difficulties. He would send no other—for I know both the country here and his mind.'

'You may wear the emblem of our cause, but I'll see you dead before I put my trust in you!' Oliver Ashleigh flared. 'There was no talk of a Masters being sent. Sir Charles is King James's man.'

'Sir Charles is not me. I am not my kinsman's keeper,' Jake Masters returned fiercely, and Rebecca detected in his voice a faint accent which she could not place. The cleft in his chin whitened at the effort it was costing him to control his temper.

'I'll deal with no thieving, murdering Masters,' Oliver Ashleigh persisted with mounting rage.

The stranger tensed, green sparks glinting in his tawny eyes. 'Sir Charles has mentioned his dispute with you over the water rights on the borders of Ashleigh and Masters land, which is at present before the courts. That is a matter between you and my kinsman. My business here concerns a more weighty cause.'

'Fine words!' Oliver Ashleigh spat out. 'But then all Masterses have slippery tongues.'

Rebecca held her breath. Her grandfather was being deliberately insulting and, judging from the stranger's rigid stance, he did not take insults lightly. His gloved hands flexed and unflexed over his sword-hilt, his voice steely.

'I'm not ignorant of the feud between yourself and my kinsman, nor of the fact that it goes back to the time when our families fought on opposing sides when the first King Charles ruled. *You* prospered during Cromwell's Commonwealth. It was some years before my kinsman could return to England and be rewarded for his loyalty.'

'And, brigand that he was, Sir Charles made full use of his powers.' Oliver Ashleigh's gaunt face blazed with hatred. 'He revelled in imposing those extortionate taxes on my estate after the Restoration. But he didn't break me then, nor ever will.'

'Your stubbornness matches Sir Charles's.' Jake Masters' lips tilted in mocking humour. 'For myself, I serve my own conscience, as I believe you serve yours. Would you have me return to The Hague, and inform His Grace that those he thought loyal have turned against him?'

Rebecca gasped at the mention of The Hague. That was where the Duke of Monmouth was in exile. Surely then her grandfather was involved in the plots of rebellion?

At the sound of her indrawn breath Oliver Ashleigh rounded on her. 'I told you to return to the coach, girl. And remember you have heard nothing...nothing!'

'Is she kin to you?' Jake Masters demanded, his cutting tones stopping Rebecca in her tracks.

'My granddaughter—orphaned by the drunken stupidity of another of your kinsmen!' Oliver Ashleigh snarled.

Rebecca flinched at the violence of her grandfather's hatred. It had been thirteen years since her parents had been killed in a coaching accident, when their vehicle had collided with one driven by Edward Masters, Sir Charles's son. Edward had escaped with nothing more than bruises. She stayed where she was while Jake Masters signalled to four sailors to load two wine vats on to the waiting wagon, and was startled by the sympathy in his tone when he again addressed her grand-father. 'The death of your son and his wife was a tragic accident.'

'They were as good as murdered by that drunken sot.'

Jake Masters' eyes narrowed warningly, his voice low and taut. 'I was not in England at the time and know little of the incident, but I understood Cousin Edward was not solely to blame. Nevertheless, you have my con-dolences for the loss you suffered that day.'

'I don't want your pity!' Oliver Ashleigh's voice began to rise. 'Or anything to do with your devil-spawned family.'

'Grandsire, take care,' Rebecca cautioned, looking anxiously about her. 'We are being watched. I thought you wished to avoid drawing attention to yourself.'

'Your granddaughter is more prudent than you,' Jake Masters replied, his full lips twitching with amusement as he regarded her.

Subjected to his penetrating stare, Rebecca's throat constricted. His bronzed, angular features were disturb-ingly attractive, his unruffled composure and assured self-possession both daunting her and arousing her re-luctant admiration. He had shown remarkable restraint in the face of her grandfather's hostility, for the old man was allowing his hatred for Sir Charles to overrule his judgement. Whatever had brought Jake Masters into contact with Oliver Ashleigh must be important.

'Oliver!' An impatient voice called from the nearby coach. Squire Hardwycke thrust the leather curtain aside, his fleshy face suffused with angry colour. 'What's the delay?'

At the same moment Tom, breathless from running, appeared at her grandfather's side and gasped out, 'Soldiers...along the quay...searching the cargo... Jennings has not turned up.''

'Keep your voice down,' Jake Masters commanded sharply, his expression contemptuous as he rounded on Ashleigh. 'Two old men and a popinjay! Is this the measure of your recruits? Why, the woman's got more sense than the rest of you, especially this mewling youth—there's guilt written all over his face. I came here expecting to meet your leaders, not risk my neck because of the loud-mouthed stupidity of a callow youth.'

'The devil, sir!' Tom blurted out, his hand going to his sword-hilt. 'Take that back or I'll——'

'You'll what?' The challenge was as derisive as it was lethal. 'I've spent ten years soldiering—my sword is not a gaudy toy. I never draw it unless I mean to use it.'

Tom paled and stepped back, his hand falling to his side.

Rebecca felt a stab of shame at the ease with which Tom had backed down. It would have been folly for him to have crossed swords with a trained soldier, but his words had been just empty bluster, as the resentment smouldering in his eyes and pouting expression told her. Disappointment at Tom's manner spurred her anger towards Jake Masters.

'By what right, sir, do you insult us?'

'Rebecca! Be silent,' Oliver Ashleigh growled. 'You forget your place. Get into the wagon. It is loaded and we must leave.'

She scarcely heard her grandfather's words, for her temper soared at the bold way Jake Masters studied her. His grin was sardonic, and her fingers itched to slap the insolence from his face. She clenched her hands to curb the impulse. As though reading her mind, Jake Masters raised an eyebrow, his obvious amusement bringing a stinging rush of colour to her high cheekbones.

He tipped his hat in salute to her. 'Ma'am, you alone here have the fire and courage I expected to find. A pity your loyalty is wasted on so undeserving a creature.'

His lazy drawl sent a shiver through her body. How dared he ridicule Tom? And the way he had singled her out—and was now regarding her—was not only indecent, it was an insult to her virtue. Worse, Tom was allowing him to do it.

Her arm was grabbed by her grandfather, and she was roughly pushed towards the wagon. 'Have you no modesty, woman? Get in the wagon before I take a whip to you.'

'Keep your anger for our true enemies, Ashleigh,' Jake Masters cut in. 'There is more at stake than your petty feud with my kinsman. Either you are prepared to deal with me, or I find someone else to serve His Grace's interest.'

As she settled herself on the hard wooden wagon-seat, Rebecca stared across at the two men. From the stiff way her grandfather held his sinewy frame, she could see he was fighting to overcome his prejudice. Her blood ran cold. She was convinced now that both her grandfather and Tom were involved in the planned rebellion. If Oliver Ashleigh had decided to support so drastic a measure to rid England of a Catholic King, there would be no turning him from his course. But it was treason! If they failed, the scaffold awaited all involved.

The thought of the consequences scoured her. For all her grandfather's strict ways, she loved him. He was all the family she had. If only there were a way to save him from this madness.

Heavy-hearted, she watched her grandfather listening to Jake Masters. He nodded curtly, and the younger man strode away as Oliver Ashleigh moved to the coach and spoke through the window to Squire Hardwycke. Tom joined them, but his stare followed Jake Masters' commanding figure, and his round, smooth face hardened with hatred.

Rebecca's feelings of humiliation returned. Masters had shown Tom for the boy he still was, afraid of confronting a man who taunted him, and because of that Tom had fallen in her esteem. At that moment she almost loathed the man herself for shattering her romantic illusions.

Seeing her grandfather and Tom coming towards the wagon, she hid her concern. It was more than the news Masters had brought which had deepened the haggard lines about Oliver Ashleigh's mouth and brow.

'If Jennings is too craven to take the cargo as planned, we have no choice but to hide it on the estate until other arrangements can be made. The Squire and I travel to

Taunton—we have contacts there. Hide the arms in the barn on the edge of Pheasant Wood.'

He placed a gnarled hand on the driver's seat, and looked up at Rebecca. 'I've urgent business elsewhere. For all it isn't fitting, without a maid to accompany you, Tom will have to drive you home. To still wagging tongues, the Squire and I have agreed that your betrothal will be official as from today and your wedding will be in a month.'

Rebecca started, a dart of panic shooting through her. An hour ago she would have been delighted at the news that she could wed Tom in a month. Now, she was confused. That her grandfather would even consider allowing Tom to be alone with her throughout the two-hour journey back to Coombe Grange showed the danger which was already surrounding them. She was certain now that the wine vats stored arms for the planned rebellion. If they were discovered on Ashleigh land it would mean her grandfather's arrest and certain death.

'God be with you, Grandsire,' she began. Her plea for him to stop this madness, and the words of love she so desperately wanted to say, froze upon her lips as he regarded her coolly. Not once during the long years she had lived in his house had he ever shown affection towards her. It was as though the death of his son, followed a year later by that of his own wife, had drained all the love from him and left him a bitter, unforgiving shell, who grudgingly tolerated her presence in his life.

As Tom climbed on to the seat beside her, he flashed her a self-satisfied grin and took up the reins. Oliver Ashleigh held the mare's bridle for a long moment, his expression haggard as he regarded Tom.

'You had better keep to the side tracks as soldiers will be patrolling the main road,' he advised. 'But, mind you return straight to the Grange—and no stopping. I've not brought my granddaughter up to have her reputation questioned. Dare to lay a finger on her, young man, and, betrothed or not, I'll have you flogged.'

'I hold Rebecca in too high esteem to force my attentions upon her. I will not abuse the trust you place in me, sir,' Tom returned. 'I dared not hope you would permit us to wed so soon.'

'In the circumstances I have no choice.' Oliver fixed him with a stern glare. 'See you do not break my trust.'

Rebecca sat in uneasy silence as the wagon wound its way from the dock and through the town. The excessive number of soldiers outside the taverns or watering their horses at the roadside troughs increased her tension.

'Relax,' Tom warned. 'You don't look very pleased that I managed to wangle these two hours we'll have together. And what good fortune the old man agreed to let us marry within the month!'

'You forget yourself, Tom, and show scant respect to my grandfather,' she said stiffly. 'As he said, he had no choice but to permit our marriage. I know what's in the wine vats!'

Tom untied his dark cloak and tossed it into the back of the wagon, his saffron velvet coat and waistcoat edged with gold braid showing a bright slash of colour as the sun broke through the clouds. 'You need not fear—the soldiers will not suspect a wagon with a woman on board. We'll be safe enough.'

He urged the ageing mare to a faster pace, the light breeze lifting the long curling locks of his periwig as he smiled across at her. No longer did the sight of his handsome countenance and finery quicken her heartbeat. They passed out of the town, and Tom drew a leather flask from the inside of his coat. Uncorking it, he drank deeply, the distinct fumes of brandy disquieting her further.

'Is it wise at such a time for you to be drinking?' she remonstrated as he propped the flask on the seat between them. 'If the soldiers should stop us, you will need a clear head and sharp wits.'

'All the more reason to act as though this is a lovers' jaunt.' He grinned, slipping his free arm around her waist.

She stiffened, uncomfortably aware of a cart approaching from the opposite direction. 'Tom, keep both your hands on the reins. The track is deeply rutted and you'll have us in a ditch. Besides you gave your word to Grandsire that you would treat me with respect.'

'What harm in a cuddle and perhaps a kiss?' Tom's blue eyes darkened sullenly. 'We're to be married in a month.'

'And isn't that all the more reason to guard my reputation against vicious tongues?'

His thin mouth tightened truculently. 'It's rather late to play the innocent after the brazen way you gaped at Jake Masters.'

'That's a lie!'

He took another long draught from the flask, his cheeks flushing with anger. 'I suppose you think I should have stood up to Masters? The man lost his army commission for duelling. He nearly killed his opponent—after first making a cuckold of him.'

'It would have served no purpose to create a scene at the port,' she conceded, strangely disappointed that Jake Masters was both a reprobate and murderer. But then he was a *Masters*—what else should she have expected from Sir Charles's kinsman?

Tom glowered under his thick straight brows at her and again put the flask to his mouth.

'Must you drink so much, Tom?' she cautioned.

'Less than an hour betrothed and already you've turned into a scold,' Tom sneered. 'I thought better of you, Rebecca.'

Brushing back the hood of her cloak as the sun grew warmer, she pushed a stray curl of her dark brown hair back into place under her plain linen cap. She turned her head away from Tom, her heart as troubled as her mind. As I thought better of you, Thomas Hardwycke, she thought bleakly. The last of her romantic illusions were shredded. The brooding petulance was nearer to the Tom she remembered as a youth than to the teasing, light-hearted man who had courted her through the winter. She knew now that she had been infatuated by him because he was so different from her grandfather's friends. Tom had shown her his weakness this day.

Strong-willed herself, she could love only a man she respected.

He tossed back the last of the brandy and continued to scowl, his manner sullen, as he chewed at the drooping corners of his moustache. The miles plodded by and, lost in her own troubled thoughts, Rebecca paid little heed to his brooding silence, or to their surroundings. Vaguely, she was aware that they were approaching a wood a few miles from her grandfather's estate. Suddenly, from over the brow of a hill running parallel to the track, a troop of soldiers rode into view.

Her stomach clenched. What if they stopped the wagon and searched it?

Tom slowed the mare. Sliding his arm around Rebecca's waist, he drew her closer. She stiffened and pulled back.

'For the love of God!' he snapped. 'They'll pay us no heed if we look like lovers.'

'You'd brand me for a whore,' she flung back, slapping his hand away, disgust that he would show such little regard for her reputation sharpening her tongue. 'Is that the respect you would show towards your betrothed?'

The drumming of hooves warned of the soldiers' approach. Tom turned sickly pale; his expression alone would betray them. Biting back her anger, she slid her arm through his and forced a smile. 'I'm as prickly as a hedgepig after all this talk of rebellion—not to mention your, and Grandsire's, part in it. Is not our journeying together supposed to look innocent? Tell me the story again of your days abroad—of the time you and your companions stole the burgher's wig.'

Tom laughed nervously. 'You mean when we tied it around the head of a pig and let the animal loose?' At her nod of encouragement, some of the tension left his body. 'That was a rare sight. The burgher was fit to have an apoplexy. He was flapping about like an enraged crow on his spindly legs trying to catch it. They both ended up in the duck pond.'

Rebecca laughed, her brow touching Tom's shoulder as the soldiers galloped past. From the corner of her eye she saw their commander glance briefly at them, and ride on without slowing his pace. When the last of the troop disappeared around the curve in the track, she let out her breath in relief.

Just as she was about to pull back from Tom, she found herself crushed in his arms, his moustache scratching her cheek and lips as his mouth sought hers. She wrenched her lips free, her body burning with indignation. 'Stop it, Tom! You abuse Grandsire's trust.'

'Come now, my dear. What harm in a kiss or two?' Tom wheedled. The tired mare took advantage of the slack reins to halt and graze at the wayside grass as Tom tightened his hold about Rebecca, his breath reeking of brandy. 'You were magnificent—so brave. These dowdy clothes old Ashleigh insists you wear hide a woman of fire and spirit.'

She pushed her hands against his chest. 'I would be a woman of honour first. I did what had to be done. Let me go, Tom. Anyone could ride along the road and see us.'

'You are right.' His blue eyes flashed with an unholy light. Freeing her, he flicked the reins and turned the mare off the track and into the nearby trees.

'Tom, have you lost your wits?' Rebecca cried. 'You'll overturn the wagon——'

Her admonition died as Tom hauled the mare to a halt and flung himself across her, pushing her down on to the hard wooden seat, his mouth cruel and relentless upon hers.

The wagon swayed as the mare moved a step or two forward while she cropped at the lush grass. Rebecca struggled, her clenched fists beating at Tom's back as she tried to twist her head free.

'Odsbones, Rebecca!' Tom snarled against her ear. 'What's the fuss? No one can see us. A kiss, that's all I ask. We're betrothed, aren't we?'

'No, Tom!' she cried, twisting her mouth free. The touch of his lips repelled her, as did the thought that they would soon be married.

'There's no need for coyness,' Tom slurred, his weight crushing her as he began to fumble with the buttons at the high neck of her gown. 'In a month we'll be wed. What harm? Who's to know?'

'Stop it, Tom!'

His hot mouth smothered her protests, her neck and spine jarring painfully as she was trapped against the hard seat.

'I want you,' he groaned, his hands clasping her breasts.

Nausea churned her stomach, and she clamped her mouth and teeth against his kiss, her body twisting in her frantic struggles to be free. To her alarm, each movement inflamed him further. His brandy-fuddled brain was past reasoning with, and her back felt as if it would snap in two as he forced her down lower on to the seat; her kicking legs, hopelessly hampered by her half-dozen petticoats, prevented her from wriggling free.

'Don't fight me, Rebecca. I love you . . . need you!'

His tongue invaded her mouth, making her gag, and she bit down, tasting the bitter, iron taste of blood.

'Hell's bitch!' he yelped, his face contorted with frustrated desire. The wide white collar at her throat ripped, tearing the black material of her gown as it came away in his hands. 'You damned, teasing little hypocrite! I'll tame you. You want me as much as I want you.'

'No!' Her cry choked in her throat as his lips ravaged hers. When his hands tugged at her skirts, her fingers curled into claws, outrage giving place to fear as she fought to keep her virtue. Her nails broke as they gouged into his cheek leaving a bloody furrow.

With a howl of rage he slapped her, slamming her head down on to the seat with a vicious thud. A rainbow of colours blinded her vision, but still she kicked and squirmed, frantically trying to beat him off.

'Damn you! Don't fight me!' Tom jammed his knee between her thighs and jerked one of her hands over her head while he fumbled with his breeches with the other. 'You're as good as my wife. Come now—there's no need to be a prude. It's just a bit of fun.'

'Stop it, Tom! If you love me, you'll not force me.'

He was past reasoning, his brain fired by their close encounter with danger, by brandy and lust. She struggled harder, knowing he was deaf to her pleas. Suddenly her hand touched a solid wooden handle, and her fingers closed over it, jerking the riding whip from its holder.

'Oh, no, you don't!' Tom fumed, wrenching it from her bruised fingers and flinging it aside. It slapped down on the mare's back, and with a whinny the startled horse bolted, throwing Tom to one side as the wagon lurched and almost overturned.

'Odsbones, Rebecca, you damn fool woman! You'll kill us both,' he growled, making a wild grab at the reins. His face puce with rage, he struggled to bring the mare under control. But the horse was terrified, her plunging gait causing the wagon to rock dangerously from side to side.

Clutching the side of the seat, Rebecca managed to pull herself upright. Every bone in her body jarred as the wheel hit a stone.

'Devil take you,' Tom gritted through bared teeth as he savagely tugged at the reins. 'You need teaching a lesson. I'll show you who is master once we're wed.'

'There'll be no wedding! Do you think I would wed a rapist?'

'You'll marry me all right,' he threatened. 'How else will you save your precious reputation?'

The mare was slowing. Rebecca glanced at the ground flashing past the cartwheels. Once the wagon stopped, she would again be at Tom's mercy. Her frantic gaze scanned the wood. It looked deserted. There was no one she could call on for help. She had to get away.

She stood up, bracing herself to jump.

'*Sit down!*' Tom grabbed at her cloak and, through its folds, her full skirts, while keeping hold on the reins. A thread of fear pitched his voice higher. 'Of course we will marry. It's all arranged.'

'I'd rather marry a cursed Masters than you!' she raged, tugging at her skirts, but his grip held firm, causing the linen ties of her cloak to bite cruelly into her throat.

Somehow she forced her trembling fingers to undo them, and the cloak fell away. At the same moment the mare checked at an approaching curve. Drawing a deep breath, Rebecca jumped. The cloak fell away but her skirts, still held by Tom, ripped at the waist, and a stream of profane oaths rang in her ears as the ground shot towards her. Landing on her hands and knees, she rolled on the thick grass which cushioned her fall, and swayed dizzily to her feet in time to see Tom bring the mare to a standstill a short distance away.

'Rebecca! You fool woman. I meant you no harm,' he shouted, leaping from the wagon.

She whirled, searching for cover. She had to get away. Her faith in Tom was broken. The closely packed trees, as yet uncoppiced this year, were a few yards away. The wagon was too large to find a passage through them and she knew Tom dared not leave the cargo of arms. As she ran, she tripped over her flapping gown, the torn folds trailing behind her and revealing a wide expanse of her white petticoats. Her breath wheezing through her bruised throat, she scooped the hem over her arm, and fled towards the safety of the trees.

'Rebecca!' Tom's shriek rose above the thudding of her heart. 'I'm sorry. Rebecca, stop!'

She ran on. After the way Tom had forced himself upon her, she could not trust him. There was a village the other side of the wood, but with her gown all ripped she could not be seen like this. She would be branded a wanton. The crashing of undergrowth behind her warned her Tom had risked pursuit. Of course—would he not face her grandfather's fury if she returned home upset, her ripped clothes telling their own story? She gulped a reviving breath. She had to get away—hide from Tom. Her mind raced. It was likely Tom would go straight to the Grange to wait for her. It would not be safe to go back to her home until her grandfather returned. There was no one she could turn to. Oliver Ashleigh had kept her so secluded at the Grange that there was no woman, except their servant Lizzie, whom she could call friend. To go to strangers would mean a scandal.

Already her legs were tiring, her lungs burning from lack of air...but she dared not slow her pace. Tom would not follow her much further. He could not risk the wagon being taken or searched. She bit back a cry as hazel branches whipped across her face, their cruel twigs biting into her soft flesh.

'Rebecca!' Tom's frustrated shout was a long way behind her. She ignored it. She was becoming light-headed with exhaustion. The blood booming in her ears like cannon-fire, she splashed through a shallow stream and on to an unfamiliar track.

'Look out!' A deep voice rang out close by.

Too late she saw a horse and rider looming above her. She screamed, and threw up her arms to protect her head, but her limbs had no strength left when she tried to throw herself to safety. Agony exploded through her side and shoulder as she was knocked backwards. A muffled curse, in a sinisterly familiar accent, carried to her. Then nothing. Her head hit the ground and darkness swooped down upon her.

CHAPTER TWO

REBECCA was dimly aware that she appeared to be floating, each dip and sway sending a shaft of fiery agony through her body, the pain building as she struggled to consciousness. Her head felt as if it had been split in two, and there was a nagging pain in her side like something burrowing into it, but even as her mind registered the pain her eyes refused to open. As her body continued its fluid motion, she discerned the steady clop of a horse's walk, and realised that, despite her discomfort, she was warm, the pleasant fragrance of orris root wafting around her. A warning clanged in her dulled mind. It was a manly scent, and with it she detected the faint aroma of tobacco smoke and, stronger now as her senses returned, the smell of warm leather and horseflesh. With a start of alarm she forced her eyes open.

The blurred image of a man's face was outlined against a cornflower-blue sky. The swaying motion could only mean she was on horseback, her body draped across the man's legs and held in place by a strong arm encircling her waist. The pain in her side was the saddle pommel pressing into it. Slowly her vision cleared. Green-flecked hazel eyes ringed by thick dark lashes regarded her solemnly. The sharp pointed nose and rugged contours of Jake Masters' face were inches from her own.

'At last you are conscious,' he drawled, his unusual accent more pronounced. 'We are about three miles from your home. I'm taking you to my hunting lodge where my housekeeper will tend your injuries. It's too far to reach Coombe Grange in your condition.'

'I cannot go anywhere with you!' she protested, and struggled to sit up. The effort left her gasping, while each movement of her battered body was torture.

'Be still,' Jake Masters commanded. 'You're in no state to move. You're lucky to be alive, appearing out of nowhere right in front of my horse.'

'Please, put me down.' Her head spun crazily and she strove against her growing panic. 'If we are seen, I shall be ruined.'

'No one would be that uncharitable!' His tone showed his impatience at the narrow-minded intolerance of their community. 'It's obvious you are hurt and in need of assistance.'

She fought against the dizziness, her mind becoming confused. 'Grandsire will be furious... I must go home... No. Not home—not yet. It's not safe at the Grange while Grandsire is away... Tom! Where's Tom!'

'I've seen nothing of Hardwycke. Was he with you?' Jake Masters frowned. 'Did a patrol stop you? Is that why you were so frightened? Are the weapons safe?'

Jake curbed his stream of questions at seeing the woman's eyes glaze over. She was still too dazed from her accident to reason clearly and, from the state of her dishevelment, it was obvious she had been through some earlier ordeal, which could well have shaken her wits. Her words had puzzled him. His task in Somerset was not an easy one, and Oliver Ashleigh's hostility complicated it further. Somehow he had to win the old man's trust. Could his granddaughter be the key to that?

He looked down at the unconscious woman. He had grudgingly admired the way she had spoken out at the port. Her pallor could not rob her complexion of the olive colour enhanced by hours spent in the open, and her dark brows and high cheekbones were delicately structured. She was a finger's length taller than most women, big-boned, but beneath what remained of her gown her body was honed to supple slenderness. Although she had the natural grace of a lady, from her roughened hands it was obvious she did not shun the hard work involved in making Coombe Grange the prosperous farming estate that it was. His mother was such a woman—she had needed to be, to survive in the uncompromising land where his family had worked for thirty years to clear the forest and build a new future for themselves.

A pang of homesickness caught him unawares. The gentle, rolling hills of Somerset were a tame beauty compared to the wild splendour of Chesapeake Bay, where he had been born. Soon he could return to his homeland. It seemed impossible he had been away for ten years. How those years had galloped past! Years spent in soldiering, in enjoying the delights of King Charles's Court. A life so different from the one he had left behind. Yet so far in those years he had achieved little, for it was in Maryland that he planned to settle. He was twenty-nine—time he put the uncertainty of soldiering behind him and considered his future.

He had come to England to win a land grant from the King, and had been side-tracked by a life of adventure. Now, with plots to put Monmouth on the throne, he had found a way to win land enough to rival his father's acres. Thoughts of the New World reopened a deeper wound, one that still festered after ten years... He had also come to England to forget Anne. A curse was smothered beneath his breath. Would that pain and guilt never leave him?

Rebecca winced, hammered by pain as consciousness returned. Her mind still fuzzy, she was aware Jake Masters had dismounted and was lifting her from the horse. They were in a walled courtyard, with at one end stables and what appeared to be empty kennels, and opposite those a two-storey half-timbered building.

'My housekeeper will tend you,' he explained, while showing no inclination to set her on the ground. 'When you are rested I will take you to Coombe Grange.'

She stiffened in his arms. Her grandfather would be outraged that she had spent any time in Jake Masters' company, no matter what the circumstances.

'First you throw yourself like a terrified rabbit before my horse, and then, when I would help you, you look at me as though I were Lucifer himself.' He raised an arched brow self-mockingly. 'I had thought you a woman of sound practicality. A pity that it would seem Ashleigh has poisoned your mind against all who bear the name Masters. Should I have left you unconscious on the ground, merely because our kinsmen are at odds with each other?'

The sound sense of his reasoning added to her confusion. 'It is a long-standing feud, sir. For that reason I should not stay here.' As she spoke, the cleft in his chin whitened. Even to her own ears her words sounded condemning, and that had not been her intention. 'My grandfather will think the worst,' she hastily amended. 'I thank you for your concern, but I must return home before my reputation is lost.'

'The presence of my housekeeper will safeguard your reputation.' His deep voice resonated with impatience. 'You are in no condition to travel further.'

'Master Jake! Who've you got there?' a red-haired man demanded, appearing from the open door of the hunting lodge to take the horse's reins. As he reached up to grip the bridle Rebecca saw the pink scars knotted round his knuckles where his little finger and the one next to it were missing.

'This is Ashleigh's granddaughter, Simmons. She met with an accident. After you've seen to the horses, fetch Martha from the kitchen—Miss Ashleigh needs her injuries tended before she can be taken home.'

The stocky servant eyed her with disapproval, but as he turned to Jake it was worry which creased his broad, freckled brow. 'Then you've brought a parcel of trouble to your door,' he said gravely. 'Since you left there's been word from Skevington. He'll be here in an hour.'

'I can handle Skevington.' The barest pause warned Rebecca that Jake Masters was discomfited by the news. 'Send Martha to my chamber,' he continued, carrying her into the lodge and crossing a large room, furnished with a long oak table, several stools and a wooden settle by the fireplace.

When he moved on and began to climb the flight of stairs apprehension dried Rebecca's throat, from a sudden suspicion of his intentions. 'My needs can be dealt with in this room, Mr Masters. Please put me down.

I'm quite recovered, and well enough to travel.' She began to struggle as she spoke, her fears deepening as he tightened his grip.

'Hold still. You'll have us both down the stairs.' He grimaced when her clenched fist struck his right arm, his exasperation obvious. 'You can go nowhere until your gown has been repaired. Unless, that is, you would give the gossips' tongues fuel for a year.'

Rebecca glanced at the ripped collar of her gown. The bodice was torn across her shoulder and down across her plain linen chemise which only partially covered her breasts. She snatched the tattered edges together, her cheeks burning.

Ignoring her protest, Jake continued up the stairs. 'Later, when your wits have recovered, I would know exactly what happened on the road from Bridgwater. Tell me first, were the weapons entrusted to Ashleigh discovered?'

She shook her head, too miserable at the memory of Tom's treatment to speak.

They reached a railed platform at the top of the stairs and he kicked open the single bedchamber door. Immediately her gaze was drawn to the tester bed, hung with dark green and silver hangings, which dominated the room. She tensed as he approached it, her body ready to fight if he tried anything untoward. As he bent over to lower her on to the velvet cover, the soft waves of his brown-blond hair touched her cheek as intimately as a caress. His gaze held hers for a timeless moment, the hazel depths blazing with a topaz fire as he stared down at the defiance sparking in her own. Her breath was stifled in her throat; she was at the mercy of a man who was kin to her grandfather's sworn enemy.

His hands slid from under her, and he drew back abruptly as though he had read her thoughts. A faint sneer curled his upper lip. 'You have my word you are safe here. I do not ravish innocents.' He moved across the room, absently massaging his right arm where she had struck him.

'You have been very kind,' she said, disconcerted by his consideration. 'Did I hurt your arm? I'm sorry. Tom said you had been wounded in a——' She checked as he spun round, his full lips compressed, the whitening cleft in his chin evidence of his anger. How could she have been so indelicate as to mention the duel which had cost him his rank and position in the army? Or to imply that the incident in question had been over a woman? Hastily, she amended, 'Tom said you had recently been wounded. And you need not fear I shall cause you any trouble. Once my gown is mended I shall leave. There's no reason why my grandfather need know I was here. You, of course, have my gratitude for your kindness.'

His forthright stare increased the heat in her cheeks. 'I've never yet met a woman who did not stir up trouble—nor an Ashleigh!'

Rebecca opened her mouth to deliver a stinging retort, but then her eyes rounded in alarm and she clutched at her churning stomach, her flesh turning cold and clammy.

Jake snatched a glazed pottery washbasin from a coffer, and in two strides was standing over the bed. 'Here, use this,' he said, thrusting it into her lap. He sat on the bed, his arm steadying her shoulders as her stomach heaved and she vomited into the bowl. His hold tightened as the spasm passed and she began to shake uncontrollably.

'I'm sorry, I could not stop myself.'

'It's a natural reaction after a shock, or knock on the head.' He put the basin on the floor and gently pressed her down on to the pillows. 'The sickness will last an hour or two. That is why you cannot travel.'

That much was now obvious to her; she felt as shaky as an hour-old foal. His hand still rested on her shoulder, the warmth of his touch sending a curious tingling through her body. 'After the way my grandfather treated you at Bridgwater, I do not deserve your kindness, Mr Masters.'

He looked at her levelly, his thumb thoughtfully rubbing the furrow in his chin before he spoke. 'Old prejudices die hard—but unless Ashleigh and I can work together the man we have both sworn to serve is the one who will suffer.'

He stood up as a plump, middle-aged woman in a starched white cap and grey gown entered the bedchamber.

'Martha, Miss Ashleigh met with an accident on the highway,' Jake explained. 'She is my guest. Will you see to her needs? Since I have a meeting here shortly, it would be best if the young lady remains in my chamber until my visitor has gone. Then I will return her safely to her home.'

'I would rather leave before your guest arrives,' Rebecca proposed. 'Should my grandfather learn I was here, he would take it amiss.' That, thought Rebecca, was an understatement. An involuntary shiver sped through her. Oliver Ashleigh would be likely to take a whip to her, and have Jake Masters arrested and pilloried as a seducer.

'I regret that will not be possible, Miss Ashleigh.' The smoothness of his voice cut as mercilessly as a scythe through corn. 'Besides, you are not fit to travel. Here at last you're free from whatever demons possessed you to flee through the wood this afternoon. For now, I leave you in Martha's care.'

Instead of leaving, he crossed to an oak coffer banded in studded brass and threw back its lid. From under several layers of clothing he took a pewter pot and tossed it on to the coverlet, saying, 'Miss Ashleigh will have need of that. It will ease her discomfort.' He strode to the door and paused to look back at her. 'While you are my guest, you will stay within this room. Heed my words and no harm will befall you. Disregard them, and I cannot be answerable for the consequences.'

'Am I then to be your prisoner?' Rebecca fumed, wincing as she swung her legs to the floor. Another spasm of nausea cut short her protest.

'You are no prisoner. If you are wise, you will do as I say,' he said tersely, and left.

Martha waited until the retching had passed before speaking. 'Master Jake means well. You mustn't let his manner upset you. Like all military men—and he was until recently a Captain—he is used to having his orders obeyed. Best do as he says.' Martha smiled. It changed her round, matronly face, showing that before indulgence had fleshed out her features she had been beautiful. 'You look exhausted. Take off your cap. I'll wash it for you and you can borrow one of mine when you leave.'

Rebecca sat still while the housekeeper untied her cap, and she was dismayed to see it was crumpled and streaked with dirt. She must have looked like a slattern when Jake Masters helped her.

'Now, let me see where you are hurt,' Martha said, undoing Rebecca's bodice and slipping the gown over her head. 'What kind of accident were you in to rip your dress like this?'

Rebecca looked away from the housekeeper's inquisitive stare. 'The wagon overturned and my gown was caught under a heavy load.'

'Why, you're covered in bruises!' Martha gasped. 'And your gown... it looks like a man has... With respect, Miss Ashleigh, no overturned wagon gave you those marks on your neck and breasts.'

'I would rather not talk about it,' Rebecca evaded. 'The experience was far from pleasant... I was more frightened than harmed. Indeed, if my dress can be mended, I would rather nothing was mentioned of the incident.'

'As you wish. I'm not one to spread gossip. I've seen too many lives made miserable because of it. I'll sew your dress while you rest. But first we must use this cream on those cuts and bruises. It will ease the pain. Don't I know the wonder it performed on the Captain's arm?'

'So he *was* wounded in a duel?' Rebecca could not stop herself asking, intrigued by the mystery surrounding Jake Masters.

'That's for the Captain to speak of, not those who serve him,' Martha silenced Rebecca's questions. She proceeded to apply the salve. 'Now you take your rest. I'll return shortly and sit with you while I sew.' Martha picked up the washbasin and left her alone.

Rebecca lay back on the pillow which smelt faintly of orris root, reminding her that this was Jake Masters' bed. It was impossible to shake his image from her mind. He was so different from what she had expected any member of the Masters family to be. Yet she must not be deceived by his kindness and consideration—there was also the ruthless streak she had glimpsed at the port. In matters of importance he would stop at nothing to gain his own ends. Was it not likely he sought to win her trust, or even to use her to break through her grandfather's prejudice? She stared mutinously at the carved wooden tester above her bed. She did not like the thought of being so used, but her head hurt too much to try and understand this man who was supposedly her enemy.

She looked round the bedchamber. The light oak furniture was ornately carved and waxed so that it gleamed golden in the afternoon sunlight shining through the latticed window. The walls were hung with green and autumn-coloured tapestries, all depicting scenes from the hunt. A battered fourteenth-century wooden shield hung over the fireplace, bearing the red and gold chequered chevrons of the Masters coat of arms. Beside it was a polished steel breastplate from this century. Rebecca shivered. It was a reminder that the feud between the two neighbouring families had begun in the 1640s when her grandfather had supported Parliament, and Sir Charles's father the King.

She closed her eyes against the memories of the more recent years of conflict. Her lids grew heavy and she struggled against sleep, reluctant to trust this place or its occupant. Reason told her to remain on her guard against Jake Masters, while another traitorous part of her wondered about the man himself. How closely related was he to Sir Charles? And what was his involvement with the Duke of Monmouth? He had spoken at Bridgwater as though he knew him well.

She dozed, lulled by the warmth of the afternoon sunlight. Several times her sleep was broken by bouts of sickness and Martha was always at hand, holding the bowl and talking soothingly as she bathed Rebecca's face and hands before returning to her sewing by the window.

When next Rebecca awoke the room was lit by a crimson glow. She sat up, appalled to see through the window the scarlet and saffron clouds surrounding the setting sun. She had been here for hours. Throwing back the cover, she eased herself from the bed, her muscles stiff and aching. Thankfully her dizziness seemed to have passed, but that was a minor problem compared to the possibility that her grandfather would already have returned to the Grange. How could she explain her long hours of absence? And what of Tom? Her throat convulsed with dread. Tom would have made some excuse to her grandfather, and very likely had seen fit to depict his innocence at the expense of her own.

The sound of several voices rising in dissent reached her from the room below, jolting her thoughts back to the present. Jake Masters still had company. They should have left hours ago. She reached for her mended gown lying across the foot of the bed and hurriedly dressed. Fastening the front buttons, she noted with satisfaction the neatly stitched collar and the rents cleverly disguised by two rows of plain black braid. Fortunately, the high neck of the gown hid the bruises about her throat. No casual observer could have guessed the ordeal she had suffered, she thought, and her confidence returned. By the side of a starched linen cap was a brush and comb. Unpinning her hair she shook the long dark braids free to fall past her hips. She brushed quickly, tugging impatiently at the tiny twigs and brambles which snagged the brush, until at last her hair was rebraided and the cap in place. If only she could return to the Grange before her grandfather, she might yet be spared awkward questioning.

She moved to the door. An angry snarl came from below, followed by Jake's calm, reasoning tone, and although she could not hear his words it was obvious that the meeting was not going smoothly.

'By Christ's entrails!' a voice bellowed, and there was the crash of a stool overturning. She pressed her ear to the door. 'Would you see us all hang? Fainthearts have no place here. We act now, or all will be lost!'

'No!' Jake cut in. 'That is not the way. It is too soon.'

'And while we wait we risk betrayal!' another voice shouted.

The voices fell into an angry drone, the words again escaping her. She strained her ears and opened the door a crack. Still she caught only a disjointed string of words. 'Numbers are swelling... Monmouth will land soon... deal with all traitors...'

Suspicion nagged at her. What if her grandfather was right and Jake Masters was King James's spy? This could be her chance to discover the truth.

She eased the door open and squeezed through. The top of the stairs was in deep shadow and only two candles had been lit to chase the gloom of the evening dusk from the room. Edging to the wooden railing, she froze, realising that two of the men seated at the table were facing her. Even as she ducked back into the shadows a glowering, skull-headed man with lank grey hair looked up.

'Who's there?' he shouted.

Her heart hammering wildly, Rebecca stayed where she was, praying they would think she was the housekeeper attending to her duties.

'Is it a spy we have among us, Masters?' the same voice rang out.

'Come down, my dear, and show yourself to my guests.' Jake's silky tones sounded threatening to her taut nerves. Had he not warned her that she would face the consequences if she left the safety of his bedchamber?

Swallowing against her rising fear, she walked down the stairs. Six men, all strangers to her, sat at the table, but her gaze centred on Jake standing by the fireplace. He had removed his jacket and the grey velvet waistcoat emphasised the slimness of his waist and hips. Across this he still wore his sword-belt—a sign that he did not count himself entirely among friends. As she approached, his expression was carefully guarded, showing unruffled calm at her discovery. One gleaming, wide-cuffed boot was propped on the fire-dog and a slender hand, half hidden by an extravagant fall of lace, rested negligently on his hip. Her chin tilted defiantly. The rogue appeared indifferent to her plight. A glance towards the table as she passed the men showed her the remains of a meal, and each of the six men, dressed soberly in black, had the same fanatical light shining in their stern faces as marked so many of her grandfather's companions. When they did not show her the courtesy of rising in her presence, she straightened her back proudly, refusing to show her growing fear.

'You said you were alone, Masters.' The man who had seen her on the landing stood up to confront Jake, his tall, emaciated body reminding Rebecca of a snake rearing up ready to strike.

'A gentleman always protects a woman's reputation, Mr Skevington,' Jake drawled, moving to Rebecca's side. Taking her hand, he bowed over it and raised it to his lips. Briefly their gazes met. Emerald lights flashed in his hazel eyes. Were they threatening, or warning her to stay silent?

'My dear,' he said smoothly, 'as you see, I have unexpected guests who wish to discuss a business venture with me. You still look tired after your journey.' He took her arm and led her away from the company to the foot of the stairs. 'Return to your room and rest. I will not be occupied much longer.'

She could not believe her ears: the wretch had as good as proclaimed her his mistress. A rush of heat flamed in her cheeks. He had deliberately humiliated her. Her eyes smarting with suppressed fury, she glared at him, her voice cool. 'It is almost dark. I cannot stay. Perhaps your manservant, Simmons, could escort me home, since you are occupied.'

'The wench goes nowhere!' Mr Skevington rapped out. 'I take it this wench is not your wife, Masters. Who is she?'

Jake spun round, the icy glitter in his eyes giving the lie to his amicable smile. 'The lady's name need not concern you.'

'Does it not?' The older man bristled, rubbing a bony hand across his sweating temple, thin wisps of grey hair falling across his brow as he did so. 'How do we know we can trust her?'

'Do I not trust her with my life?' Jake declared, staring hard at each man in turn. Only Skevington held his gaze.

Rebecca caught her breath. There was truth in Jake's words—but they were also a challenge defying any man here to question his actions. Had not her grandsire already condemned his silvery tongue? Her conscience pricked her. Now it was she who was judging him unfairly—until now he had shown her unexpected kindness. He had warned her to stay in the bedchamber, and of the consequences if she left it.

'But can we trust a man who has been favoured by John Churchill?' Skevington accused. 'Especially since Churchill is so close to our Papist king?'

Jake stepped in front of Rebecca, his body shielding her from the men. 'You forget, gentlemen, that it is because of Churchill's displeasure that my career in the Royal Dragoons was abruptly ended. And you will also know that, before His Grace the Duke of Monmouth was forced into exile at James Stuart's insistence, I was honoured by his friendship. Now that James Stuart rules England, are we not all here pledged to restore the exile— a true Protestant to rule in his uncle's stead?'

'Fine words, Mr Masters,' Skevington persisted. 'Yet you alone among us have interests on both sides.'

A fist crashing on to the table forestalled Jake's reply, and Rebecca moved to look round his shoulder at the burly man who had leapt to his feet, his round face scarlet with rage. 'Indeed, how can we trust any kinsman of Sir Charles Masters, who is King James's Justice of the Peace and a favoured courtier? I warned you he would betray us. I was right! He would put his lechery before our cause. By his own words he makes no secret of having been thrown out of the army because of his debauchery. He deceived us by bringing his doxy here!'

Rebecca bit her lip to stop her heated protest at the insult. Who would believe her if she tried to defend her innocence? Jake's reputation went before him. If she kept silent, it was possible that in their anger these men would force Jake to reveal more of his motives than he intended. That information could be useful to her grandfather. To her surprise Jake appeared unmoved by the accusations, but his tone was low and dangerous.

'I'm answerable to no man, least of all to my kinsman. If any man wishes to question my loyalty, my sword is at his disposal.'

'But the wench?' Skevington snapped. 'Why should we trust a common harlot who would sell herself to the highest bidder?'

'Devil take you, Skevington!' Jake's eyes flashed green fire. 'I'm not one of your congregation, for you to sermonise at. One more slur upon this lady's honour and I shall forget you are a preacher and make you eat your words.'

The five men at the table leapt to their feet, rounding on Jake like wolves closing in for a kill. One drew a pistol and levelled it at Jake's head, his voice cruel. 'I've heard enough of your arrogance. Tell us the wench's name, or I'll shoot you for the spy you are!'

Jake did not move or speak. Rebecca was stunned that he was protecting her name at the risk of his life. That he, a virtual stranger, had chosen to defend her honour, when Tom had so cravenly failed to do so, caused her heart to thump erratically.

'Gentlemen,' she began shakily, stepping forward to Jake's side, 'I am Rebecca Ashleigh. My name should be proof enough why Mr Masters wished to protect me. I am sure you have heard of my grandfather, Oliver Ashleigh. You cannot doubt the loyalty of so devoutly religious a man.'

'You are Ashleigh's granddaughter?' Skevington's cold stare swept over her. 'Impossible! He'd allow no strumpet in his home. Do you take us for fools, Masters?'

'Until this moment I had not done so,' Jake mocked. 'But the probability you would believe the worst of her is why I kept silent. The circumstances of Miss Ashleigh's presence here are simple. She met with an accident on the road and was knocked unconscious. My housekeeper tended her injuries to enable her to return to Coombe Grange. Your unexpected arrival prevented her from leaving as soon as she had recovered.'

'A likely tale!' the burly man scoffed.

'But the truth,' Jake said firmly.

'Yet if Ashleigh's granddaughter is here,' another interrupted, 'surely it is proof that Masters serves us in good faith.'

'The hour grows late, gentlemen, and tempers are high,' Skevington cut across the murmurs of agreement. 'These matters are best discussed with cool heads.'

'Either you trust me, or I find others more willing to serve His Grace,' Jake declared. 'It is for you to decide— my time in Somerset is short. Now, if you will excuse us, gentlemen, it is already dark, and I must escort Miss Ashleigh home. Her grandfather will be worried as to her safety.'

'I'm for Masters!' Two men spoke in unison.

'Ay—so am I,' a third agreed. 'If he's convinced Ashleigh to trust him then he's the leader we need.'

'Gentlemen, we would do well to sleep on it before we make our decision,' Skevington silenced the outburst. 'We will do our cause no good by quarrelling among ourselves. We will meet again tomorrow. Return to your homes, and God bid you safe journey.'

As the men filed out Jake rang a bell, and Martha came out of a side door which Rebecca supposed led to the kitchen.

'I shall be taking Miss Ashleigh home now. Ask Simmons to saddle my horse, and Miss Ashleigh will need a cloak.'

He picked up his grey velvet jacket, and looked askance at Skevington, who gave no sign of leaving. For a long moment the two men studied each other, an undercurrent of tension rippling in the air between them.

Clearly Skevington resented Jake's role of leader in the district.

The older man's pale eyes glittered with menace. 'I too will be riding to Coombe Grange. I have matters to discuss with Mr Ashleigh.'

'My grandfather may not be at home—business took him to Taunton,' Rebecca blurted out, realising with shock that she could only delay her grandfather's learning that she had spent several hours with Jake Masters. If she could only speak to her grandfather first there might be a chance she could reason with him. Her heart sank, knowing that was unlikely. Oliver Ashleigh's hatred was too intense.

'Nevertheless, I shall accompany you,' Mr Skevington proclaimed, jamming his high-domed hat firmly on his head. 'I shall await you outside.'

Rebecca bowed her head, defeated. 'When Grandsire learns I have been here he will believe the worst.'

'Where's the courage you showed at Bridgwater?'

Her chin was taken in Jake's hand and tilted to meet his gaze. The candlelight turned his hazel eyes golden and softened the harsh planes of his handsome face. He had every right to be furious—yet there was not even resentment in his voice. But, then, until her appearance the meeting had been heated, with many of the men distrustful of him. It had been her connection with Oliver Ashleigh which had calmed their suspicions concerning Jake. Had she played into his hands by leaving the bedchamber?

'I think you knew I could not let those men kill you to save my reputation,' she answered coldly. 'Obviously, Skevington does not trust you—nor does my grandfather—but you led these men to believe that he did. I do not like being used, Mr Masters.'

He dropped his hand to his side, his smile taunting. 'You misjudge me. The moment you left the upper chamber the damage was done. We must make the best of it. I would try and dissuade Skevington from visiting the Grange, but you have seen how suspicious he is. You must understand my task here is difficult, especially since

Oliver Ashleigh is set against me. I cannot risk further complications, but I promise you Ashleigh will be made to see reason.'

She shook her head sadly. 'I doubt that is possible. If Grandsire is at the Grange he will already have heard tales against me. You've seen how strict his ways are. He trusts no one. Why, even though it had been agreed Tom and I would be betrothed next month, he insisted that, since today we had to travel alone together, the wedding itself would take place within the month.'

'You are to wed that apology for manhood for the sake of propriety?' Jake fumed. His arched brows drew downwards. 'Was it he who attacked you?'

'I have known Tom for years. It was a misunderstanding,' Rebecca evaded. 'He had been drinking and——'

'So it was him!' Jake cut in savagely. 'He should be taught a lesson in manners.'

'What purpose will that serve?' she replied, stung. She had protected Tom out of loyalty, but the way Jake was defending her caused her heart to race in the most unaccountable manner, and left her at a disadvantage which she resented. 'My reputation is lost, but if you do not take care it will be you who will be named ravisher.'

He turned as Martha entered, carrying a cloak. Taking it from the housekeeper, Jake wrapped it around Rebecca, his hands gripping her shoulders as he spoke bleakly. 'Then I shall take pleasure in clearing both our names.'

CHAPTER THREE

JAKE reached down from his horse to help Rebecca mount behind him on the pillion saddle Simmons had attached to his own, hiding his misgivings behind an encouraging smile. He could feel the woman's tension as she settled her skirts and lightly placed her hands on his waist, to steady her balance, as they set off. Outwardly calm, she was clearly apprehensive about facing her grandfather—and, aware of Oliver Ashleigh's religious zeal and intolerance, he could understand her anxiety. That she controlled her fears roused his admiration. The last thing he needed was a hysterical woman bewailing her fate. Her resilience, her honesty in speaking out before the Dissenters, knowing her reputation would be questioned, even her misplaced loyalty to Tom Hardwycke, were all qualities he respected. The woman intrigued him.

Skevington rode abreast of him, cutting short his reflections. 'You have explained Miss Ashleigh's presence at the lodge, but I would know why you support Monmouth, since you were once high in favour at Court?'

'My dismissal from the King's service is proof I have fallen from favour,' Jake answered tersely. 'I came to England with the intention of winning a land grant in Maryland. I did not receive it through ten years of loyal service. How better to achieve it than by serving the best interests of His Grace the Duke, who has given me his friendship? I have nothing to lose.'

'Except your life.'

'I'm a soldier, used to living with death at my shoulder.'

'Cynical words, Mr Masters, but, since you regard the New World as your home, why interfere with English politics?'

The darkness hid Skevington's face from Jake, and served to accentuate the malice in his voice. With both Skevington and Oliver Ashleigh suspicious and distrustful, Jake knew he would never succeed in his task here. At any cost he must win their trust.

'Whoever rules England is also King of my country.' He was too experienced at intrigue to allow his own antagonism to show. 'Many of the settlers' families left England to be free to worship as their hearts dictated. They have no wish to see a Catholic on the throne. The fires of Bloody Mary still smoulder in many of their minds.'

'Only in God's cause can one sanctify rebellion,' Skevington answered stiffly. 'I pray daily for guidance and our success.'

As the preacher began to pray aloud, Jake felt the ties of friendship shackling him, as ruthless and merciless as iron. Once Monmouth landed, rebellion was certain. Loyalty fought a bitter battle within him. He must not fail. Monmouth's life depended on his success.

His horse stumbled in the darkness, and as the woman was thrown hard against his shoulder he felt her trembling.

'Are you cold, Miss Ashleigh?'

Rebecca pushed her rigid body away from him, annoyed with herself for the strange feelings his closeness aroused. 'No!' she answered quickly, and was appalled at the quivering huskiness of her voice. She had forced herself to remain silent as he spoke to Skevington, but her curiosity was aroused as she recalled her grandfather telling her that Sir Charles's younger brother had sailed to the New World in 1651, after Charles II had been defeated at Worcester and had failed to regain his father's throne. Sir Charles himself had then been an exile, following the young King in his wanderings in France and the Low Countries.

'Then you are frightened,' he said softly, turning in the saddle to look back at her. 'Do not fear, I'll not let Ashleigh cast you out. I will explain everything.'

His warm breath feathered across her cheek. The moon appearing from behind a cloud silvered his angular face, so disturbingly close to her own. With each mile they travelled she became uncomfortably aware of the masculine hardness of his back, of the play of muscles as he skilfully guided his horse over the uneven track. Inexplicably, her heartbeat quickened. How effortlessly he exerted his devastating charm—made all that was complicated seem easy, all that was frightening seem no more than a childish imagining.

'Thank you, but I can speak for myself. You will have more weighty matters to explain.' She nodded meaningfully at Skevington, who was still mumbling a prayer. 'Sir Charles has dealt harsh fines and penalties upon our brethren. You will have to prove yourself, more than most, to win their trust.'

'At this moment I would be content with your trust, Becky.' He smiled incorrigibly.

Not since her mother's death had anyone called her Becky. Her grandfather had regarded the shortening of a good Biblical name as an abomination. The sound of it upon Jake's lips, and the intense light in his eyes, where admiration mingled with something more—an intimacy which had nothing to do with respect—gave wings to her pulse, the rapid beat causing her aching head to throb with renewed intensity.

'It is not fitting you address me so familiarly,' she admonished, the fierceness of her words cut short by a wince of pain. 'I am betrothed.'

'To a man who does not appreciate the prize he has won! He can never make you happy. He is not worthy of you, and I think you already know it, but are too stubborn to own you were mistaken.'

'You are impertinent, sir.'

His amused, low chuckle fanned her resentment. He suddenly fell silent, and stared ahead, his manner halting her retort. The steady beat of hooves warned of riders approaching. There were four of them. When the moon-light picked out a wide white blaze on the nose of the leading horse and the unmistakable white markings on the horse's forelegs, Rebecca's heart plummeted like iron.

'What treachery is this?' Oliver Ashleigh shouted, bringing his sweating mare to a skidding halt. 'Get down from that horse, Rebecca! I never thought to see the day when you would shame me by playing the harlot.'

'Stay where you are, Miss Ashleigh,' Jake com-manded. He dropped the reins, the trained gelding standing motionless as his master drew a flintlock pistol from his saddle holster. 'You do your granddaughter a grave disservice, sir. She met with an accident on the highway. My housekeeper has been tending her injuries.'

'For seven hours!' Oliver Ashleigh raged, paying no heed to the flintlock Jake rested on his thigh. 'You expect me to believe her still innocent—after seven hours in the company of a known reprobate? You Masterses are all alike. You think you can take any woman for your sport, then cast her off without a second thought. That lecher Edward Masters has a half-dozen sharp-featured bas-tards scattered about the district.'

'I could not return earlier, Grandsire,' Rebecca hastily cut in. 'I was knocked unconscious and was vomiting for hours when I came to my senses. I could not travel.'

'Silence!' Her grandfather's voice was filled with such loathing and contempt that Rebecca felt her flesh shrinking on her bones. 'Do not add lies to the sins already on your head. Your conduct speaks for itself. I can understand you were frightened when those soldiers stopped the wagon. And you did right to run off when two of them dragged you from Tom's side. But what possessed you to ride off with Masters? I would have thought he would have ridden back to Tom's aid. But for Tom, the arms could have been lost.'

Rebecca bristled. So those were the lies Tom had spread. Before she could answer, Jake blazed out, his contempt matching her grandfather's. 'Where is Hardwycke?'

'My son's injuries from fighting off the soldiers single-handed are too great for him to travel,' Squire Hardwycke pompously declared, edging his horse forward from behind the head groom and bailiff employed at Coombe Grange. He leaned his bulky figure forward in the saddle, his fleshy face, pale and grotesque in the moonlight, twisting with hatred. He too had no love for Sir Charles Masters. Since the Restoration Hardwycke Hall had fallen into decay, over half its estate sold off to pay the taxes collected by Sir Charles's henchmen. 'Were Tom not so grievously wounded, he would call you out, Masters, for seducing his betrothed.'

'Hypocrites! Bigots!' Rebecca could no longer control her anger at their injustice, though her head pounded sickeningly with the force of her rage. 'By what right do you condemn me without a hearing? Mr Masters has treated me with courtesy and respect.'

'Your reputation is lost. Have you no shame?' Oliver spat, consumed by an anger which was past reasoning. 'You'll not be so proud after a public whipping and a day in the pillory. Count yourself fortunate that Tom is too much of a gentleman to withdraw his offer of marriage.'

'Perhaps Tom cares more for my dowry than my honour,' she returned, the humiliation she felt at the thought so sharp that the words were spoken before she realised it.

'Jezebel!' the Squire screeched. 'You do not deserve my son's generosity. As for Masters—hanging is too good for this seducer!'

Rebecca was horrified to see her grandfather reach for a pistol stuck into his belt, but Jake moved faster, his own weapon glinting in the moonlight as he levelled it at Oliver Ashleigh's head.

'This has gone far enough!' Jake did not even raise his voice, but the menace in its tone was clear. 'You believe the idle boasts of a mewling boy to save his own hide, while maligning a woman whose courage I have yet to see equalled among your followers. It was not the soldiers who attacked your granddaughter, but Tom

Hardwycke. I warned Monmouth of the risk he was taking dealing with Dissenters. You are too narrow-minded, too quick to condemn anyone who does not act or believe as you do. I've never pretended to be a saint, but I do not force myself upon innocent women.'

'You expect us to believe that?' Oliver retorted. 'Any decent man would have returned my granddaughter to her home immediately. Instead you chose to carry her off to your hunting lodge.'

'It wasn't like that, Grandsire,' Rebecca defended Jake, her skin stinging with embarrassment at such open hostility. 'You must listen to me.'

'I've heard enough,' Oliver flashed back. 'I'll deal with you later.'

'Gentlemen, gentlemen!' Skevington spoke for the first time. 'Regrettable as this incident is, is it worth risking the success of our cause? Mr Masters alone knows Monmouth's plans. I have myself spent the last four hours at Mr Masters' lodge. I did not at first know Miss Ashleigh was there. Indeed, when her presence was discovered it was believed by many that she was a spy. Her very pallor, brought on by her accident, made her look guilty. Does that not prove how easily we can jump to the wrong conclusions? As to the question of Miss Ashleigh's virtue——'

'Who are you, sir,' Oliver butted in, 'that we should take your word?'

'Permit me to introduce myself. I am Bartholomew Skevington. My name is, I believe, known to you. We were to meet tomorrow. In the circumstances I thought it expedient I should accompany Mr Masters tonight.'

'You are the preacher from over Glastonbury way?' Oliver still sounded suspicious and his voice hardened. 'How many others were at the lodge and witnessed my granddaughter's disgrace?'

'Six, and also Mr Masters' two servants.'

'Then, guilty or innocent, she's still ruined.'

'Not if Masters marries her,' Skevington announced.

'I'll see her dead before my name is linked with that devil's brood!'

'Will you, indeed?' In a blast of indignant fury
Rebecca leapt from Jake's horse, and whirled round to
face them all. She swayed as the vicious hammering in
her head increased its tempo, and recovered, breathing
heavily to overcome her weakness. Her eyes blazed up
at Jake, who had remained stoic and silent, the pistol
cocked but now lowered in his hand. 'And what of my
feelings? I will wed no man—not Thomas Hardwycke,
and certainly not Mr Masters—just to save my reputation from malicious gossip. I am innocent!' She turned
to face her grandfather. 'If you believe I hold my father's
name in so little regard that I would be any man's whore,
then I will leave your house tonight, never to return.'

'And where would you go?' To her surprise it was
Jake who broke the stunned silence which followed her
words.

She glared back at him, her fists clenched against the
chilling fear which drained the fury from her. Where
could she go? She had no living relative except her
grandfather. Her head came up proudly, refusing to acknowledge defeat. She would go to the hiring fair held
at Ilchester next week. Better to be a servant than forced
into an unwanted marriage.

'Mr Masters, what have you to say?' Skevington asked,
a trace of the antagonism she had heard at the lodge
returning to his voice. 'Are you even free to save this
woman's honour by marrying her? We know little about
you.'

Jake looked at the men, unmoved by the hatred
deepening the lines and hollows of their stern faces. Each
had his own axe to grind against himself or his family.
Skevington, for all his piety, wanted the power of lead-
ership. What chance did Monmouth stand of success if
these men were the measure of those who would fight
for him? His friend would be placing his head on the
block the moment he landed. If plans went awry, his
own life would also be forfeit. Six months ago he would
have welcomed death. For too long he had sought to lay
Anne's ghost by chasing pleasure where he found it. And
where had it led him? To a pointless duel over a faithless

trollop and the wounding of a man he had once liked and respected.

His glance flickered over the woman, her beauty and defiance touching a chord within him. Skevington did not know the boon he was offering. An alliance with Ashleigh would bring an end to the distrust the Dissenters felt towards him, as kinsman to Sir Charles.

'I have no wife.' He pushed aside the blaze of remorse that a vision of Anne rekindled. 'And, believing Miss Ashleigh to be a woman of impeccable virtue and courage, I would be honoured if she'd consent to be my bride.'

When Rebecca shook her head, he swung down from his horse to stand at her side. Disregarding the astonished stares of the men around him, he took her hand and smiled at her in a way which had never failed to melt a woman's heart, adding softly, 'Your courage deserves better than the fate they would condemn you to.'

'There'll be no marriage!' Ashleigh pushed his horse towards them.

Jake put his arm around Rebecca and drew her behind him, the pistol coming up. 'Get back, Ashleigh.'

'Oliver, do nothing hasty!' Hardwycke protested.

'Gentlemen, this is not the place for such a discussion,' Skevington intervened with false solicitude, which made Jake's finger on the trigger itch to fire at him. 'I suggest we ride to Coombe Grange. Have you forgotten why we were to meet? It was not to discuss your granddaughter's nuptials!'

'Skevington's right.' The Squire shot Ashleigh a warning look. 'It's been a long and frustrating day. The arms are safely hidden. Rebecca is safe, when an hour ago you feared for her life. And in this, at least, Masters had done right by Rebecca. Wouldn't be right in the circumstances for Tom to marry her now.'

Jake led Rebecca to his horse, sensing her distrust and the humiliation she was suffering. She looked pale and drawn, and he suspected her head must be aching as though the devil were dancing on it. Yet still she had faced them like an enraged tigress. He holstered the pistol. His gaze swept admiringly over her trim figure, and he raised her hand to his lips, her fortitude moving him to press his suit.

'My offer was not given lightly—or because convention dictated it.' He felt her pulse quicken beneath his fingers as he bowed over her hand. When he lifted her on to the pillion saddle a barely perceptible tremor passed through her slender body. His blood quickened with sudden desire. So, beneath her cool composure, she was no woman of ice.

Even as he mounted he was aware of the Squire's and Ashleigh's heads bent forward in a hurried whisper. The moonlight barely penetrated the thick foliage of the trees, its pale light spangling the bluebells, reflecting Skevington's silver hat-buckle, the steel rings on harnesses, and, more sinisterly, the polished metal of pistol barrels thrust into Ashleigh's and his servant's belts. The dark tree-trunks surrounding them were uncomfortably like teeth, closing about a giant trap. It was obvious from Ashleigh's rigid stance that he was having difficulty in controlling his temper. What were they planning?

Throughout the journey to Coombe Grange Jake rode in silence, assessing the mood of his companions. Skevington appeared unperturbed by the hornets' nest which had been stirred up. Jake knew the preacher resented his influence with Monmouth, and his knowledge of warfare, which was invaluable to the cause. Once the Duke landed and the army was ready Skevington would not hesitate to be the first to turn against him. Jake glanced across at the preacher, who was speaking in a hushed voice to Hardwycke, and his eyes narrowed. He did not trust Hardwycke—nor Ashleigh, whose hostile stare had turned brooding, while he deliberately ignored the existence of his granddaughter.

Of the three men it was Ashleigh Jake knew he must win over. It was his voice, as that of a respected leader among the Dissenters, which was important. Ashleigh knew the location of stored arms and the names of those who would fight when Monmouth landed. If Ashleigh remained set against him all would be lost. What troubled him for the present was Hardwycke's change of attitude. Why had the sly fox acted as mediator when Rebecca was betrothed to his son? Was it simply a wish to protect Tom from marrying a woman whose reputation was lost? Or was it something else which had made him suggest the marriage? Jake smiled grimly into the darkness. Did they think he was so easily duped?

They crested a treeless hill, the moon illuminating the valley below in a pale ribbon of light, revealing a half-timbered farmhouse, with neat stone and thatched out-buildings spread out before them. The surrounding pastures were filled with the dark shapes of cattle, and as they rode down the hill into the valley, sheep ambled out of their horses' path.

This was Coombe Grange. Sir Charles had not exaggerated when he had told Jake it was rich, fertile land. The old Cromwellian had weathered the Restoration better than most. This was Rebecca's inheritance—a rich prize. Disgust tightened his stomach. It would take more than Rebecca's tarnished reputation to make the impoverished Squire give up the chance to restore the fortune of the Hardwycke estate. Did they seek to sacrifice her in marriage while planning to bring him down? He would not put it past Ashleigh to use his granddaughter as a spy.

As they reached the house Rebecca looked round the moonlit courtyard, her glance sliding over the brick well and a broken ploughshare awaiting repair, her ears attuned to the quiet rustling of chickens and ducks shut in their wooden houses and the stamp of a plough-horse in the stable. An unexpected tug pulled at her heart. If she were to marry Jake Masters the sprawling Tudor farmhouse would no longer be her home. Marriage—the thought left her stunned. She could not believe her grandfather and the Squire truly intended her to wed Jake Masters. It was absurd.

She sat still and tense as Jake dismounted. Why had he agreed to marry her? When he had mentioned that he had no wife she had detected a change in his voice. Was it unrequited love or bitterness which had stirred

Jake from his usual self-control? She folded her skirts more closely about her legs as Jake turned to lift her from the saddle. How did he see her home? Would he see the rich pastures, the well-stocked barns and, of course, the nearby lake which was the cause of the dispute with Sir Charles over water rights? Or did he sense that behind its neat, orderly façade lay a house where laughter was frowned upon and love denied—the home of his enemy?

Over Jake's head she saw her grandfather, who continued to ignore her presence, walk with the Squire into the house. The April evening was suddenly touched with a bleak winter's frost, striking her to the bone.

'I knew Ashleigh was a man of high principles'— Jake's voice was clipped with anger as he reached up to help her to the ground —'but I never thought he would throw his only grandchild to the lions.'

'In his eyes I have betrayed him. He acts as he thinks fitting.' She stood stiffly, aware of his hands still gripping her waist and of Skevington hovering close by. 'As to our marriage, Mr Masters, I do not hold you responsible for my actions. There is no need for you to marry me.'

'Am I such an ogre?' he taunted.

'An ogre I could contend with,' she answered, her confusion deepening as his eyes bored into hers. 'It is your kindness and courtesy, which I so little deserve, that I cannot deal with.'

'Why do my actions surprise you? Because I am a *Masters*?' He grinned wickedly, his teeth flashing like diamonds in the moonlight. 'I act as honour dictates. Do not belittle your charms: your beauty and spirit are worthy of any man's respect—even of so hardened a reprobate as myself.'

'Not so hardened,' she countered, knowing he was mocking her. She was startled that her lips twitched in an answering smile. The rogue had a disconcerting habit of getting below her guard. 'You are a little frayed around the edges, possibly. Also, I do not see you as a man who allows others to shape his future.'

He bowed, hiding his expression from her as she moved past him towards the house, her voice growing cool to combat the charm he so effortlessly exerted over her. 'Mind your head on the lintel. It has cracked many a skull thicker than yours.'

Jake stooped to avoid the low beam as he entered the parlour. He took care to keep his back to one side of the door as, through habit, he scanned the candlelit room, assessing that the door was the only means of escape. His glance fixed on a gold-inlaid musket prominently displayed above the inglenook fireplace. Devil take it! Hadn't that musket once been a prized possession of Sir Charles? How did Ashleigh come by it? he wondered with an inward chuckle.

'The musket was dropped while Sir Charles was trespassing on our grazing land,' Rebecca said, both amusement and a challenge in her voice as she guessed his thoughts.

'And the lack of silver on the dresser?' Jake parried. 'No doubt that was carried off by Sir Charles to pay the King's taxes.'

She tossed back her head proudly, her violet eyes sparking fire in the candlelight. Jake felt his breath catch in his throat. Even the dowdy gown and unflattering, plain linen cap could not detract from the striking beauty of her high cheekbones and dark winged brows, nor mar the sensuous splendour of her tall, curvaceous figure. Experience told him there was a hidden fire within her which no man had yet kindled—a fire which, once fanned, would be all-consuming. With each passing moment the prospect of marriage seemed less of a trial in the service of his master.

'Your kinsman may have tried to reduce us to paupers,' she countered, 'but he did not succeed.'

'Nor did he break your pride, and for that I am grateful,' he replied, surprised to find he was enjoying their sparring.

Skevington pushed himself forward into the centre of the room. 'I see no need for delay. I will conduct the

wedding ceremony, and then we can proceed with the
real matters in hand.'

'No!' Rebecca cried, panic overwhelming her. Her
wide-eyed gaze fell upon her grandfather's back as he
spoke to Squire Hardwycke on the far side of the room.
'Grandsire, you cannot mean for me to marry into a
family you have always considered your enemy!'

For the first time since their arrival at the farm, Oliver
faced her, his voice cold as he addressed the preacher.
'I trust you will forgive my granddaughter's outburst,
Mr Skevington. She shames me by her wanton conduct.
Rebecca, I will speak with you in the buttery.' He opened
an adjoining door, which led through to the storehouse
and buttery built on to the side of the house, and waited
for her to enter.

He had spoken to her as though she were a five-year-
old child, and her cheeks burned with humiliation as she
crossed the parlour. The buttery door clicked shut behind
her grandfather, the only light in the whitewashed room
the moonlight through the tiny slatted window.

'There will be no arguments, my girl. You will marry
Jake Masters.'

'But, Grandsire, he has done nothing untoward. He
merely helped me when I was sick and frightened.'

'Your reputation is lost.' He cast aside her plea. 'Do
you think in any other circumstances I would countenance a marriage between my family and a Masters? They
are rogues and scoundrels all. I don't trust any of them.
Yet it seems that if I am to serve Monmouth I must
work with Jake Masters.' His voice hoarsened with suppressed anger. 'How do I know he does not intend to
betray us all? I would not put it past him. We need
someone close to him—watching his every move.
Someone we can trust. That is why you will marry him!'

She frowned in the darkness, unable to discern her
grandfather's face. Sudden anger exploded within her,
and it took all her will-power to keep her voice low as
she retorted, 'You would use me as a spy... Have you
no heart? You who preach of godliness and high morals?

This is immoral. You would make of me a whore to serve a cause I know nothing about.'

'You will be respectably married,' he snapped indignantly. 'And you will be serving God's cause as well as Monmouth's. We shall rid England of its Catholic King. Or would you rather Masters betrayed us all? He already knows our names and that I am the ringleader of the Dissenters. The gibbet awaits me if Masters turns evidence against us. Is that what you want?'

'How can you even think that?' Appalled, Rebecca stared at her grandfather's shadowy figure.

'Then you will do as I bid and right the shame you have brought upon my house. Remember well that Sir Charles and all his kin have vowed to bring us down. They have already murdered your parents. Would you have us sit by and let this man work his evil without even a fight?'

Rebecca rubbed her brow, her conscience grinding remorselessly as she tried to think clearly through a continuing haze of pain. Was Jake a spy? Skevington was suspicious of him. And there had been odd flashes she had glimpsed at the hunting lodge when Jake, for all his outward calm, was not truly at ease. What was he hiding?

Her own hatred for Sir Charles and the Masters family did not run as deep as her grandfather's, but she had felt the bite of the baronet's spite and vengeance too often not to feel pain at the injustice of it. Yet Jake seemed so different from Sir Charles. Her mind whirled. For his own reasons he was marrying her. Why should he go to such lengths to protect the reputation of a woman he had only just met? Was it merely to forge an alliance with her grandfather? That seemed uncomfortably probable—and rankled.

'What if Jake Masters is *not* a spy?' Her voice seemed to be dragged up from her boots. 'When all this is over I shall still be married to him.'

'If he survives—and rebellion is a cruel reaper—his home is on the other side of the world. There is no need for you to travel with him.'

She shook her head. 'It isn't right, Grandsire.'

'Is it right that he wins his way into our houses by deceit? His years at Court have surely taught him to preserve his own hide by intrigue. Have you considered that the rogue could have seized his chance and deliberately endangered your reputation? What better way to win the trust of others who seek to depose King James than by marrying my granddaughter? He was ready enough with his offer.'

Each sentence drummed into her throbbing brain, condemning Jake and firing her indignation. Had she been so blatantly used—allowed herself to be duped by Jake's potent charm? Might not an accomplished rake have twisted a naïve woman like herself easily around his finger? Her anger churned. It was time he was taught that not all women were gullible. Too often the Masterses had sought to ride roughshod over her family and escape the consequences. This time they would not succeed, even if she had to marry Jake to prevent it.

'I will marry him, Grandsire.' The decision made, a *frisson* of anticipation set her pulse racing. It would need all her wits and guile to play Jake Masters at his own devious game.

Oliver Ashleigh paused with his hand on the door-latch. 'In all your arguments you have not mentioned Tom. Has Masters already turned your head? Your loyalty must be to us—not him.'

'I realised today I do not love Tom,' she evaded, unwilling to bring up events which would only complicate matters. 'Nor am I enamoured of Jake Masters. You have ordered me to marry him, and as a dutiful grand-daughter I am obeying you.' An awesome thought struck her. 'Have you considered that Mr Masters might be suspicious that I have suddenly capitulated? If he suspects that I am a spy he will ensure that I learn nothing.'

'It is such quickness of wit which makes you valuable to us.' His hard stare swept over her, and for a moment mellowed. 'I have sometimes been harder on you than I intended, Rebecca.' He checked himself again, masking his emotions. 'Leave the matter to me. Publicly I shall disown you because of this marriage. That should convince Masters you are no spy. It will also put an end to his using my name to gather information which he could turn against us.'

When they returned to the parlour the Squire and Skevington broke off from discussing possible hiding-places for weapons. Rebecca glanced at Jake, sitting by the fire. He looked unperturbed by the events around him as he idly twisted a gold ring on his small finger. Suspicion spiked her. Was not the conversation between Skevington and the Squire providing him with the information he could use against them? She bowed her head to hide her mounting anger. Yet that single glance, swiftly taking in his graceful, broad-shouldered figure and his sharp, handsome countenance, no longer half-hidden beneath the deep brim of a hat, snatched at her heart. Jake was far too handsome for her peace of mind, and she had felt the potent pull of his devastating charm too often not to feel a spasm of unease at the task which lay ahead. He would not be an easy man to dupe.

'Rebecca will marry Masters,' Oliver harshly pronounced. 'I tell you all now that the thought of uniting my house with a Masters is abhorrent to me. I am forced to allow this marriage to take place because of the shame Rebecca has brought to my family. She has proved herself unworthy of my name. When she leaves this house as the wife of Mr Masters, she ceases to be my granddaughter.'

Rebecca started, for although she knew he was playing out a role his words still rent a raw edge within her. How easily he had been able to say the words to repudiate her—yet not once could she recall he had ever spoken words of praise or affection towards her.

Skevington cleared his throat. 'Gentlemen, shall we proceed? The sooner this business is over the better. Let us pray.'

Jake stood up and came to Rebecca's side. When she would have knelt to pray as her grandfather, Squire Hardwycke and Skevington did, her arm was gripped, preventing her movement.

'You make undue haste. Surely the ceremony can wait until the morrow when it can be decently prepared and performed openly?'

'Such is not needful in the eyes of God. Do you think to escape by seeking delay?' Skevington sneered. 'I assure you this ceremony is binding to our faith. There are the required number of witnesses to hear your vows. Kneel, sir, if you please.'

Still Jake did not move, nor did he relax his hold upon her arm, and she could feel the tension building within him. Had he then no real intention of marrying her but had agreed merely to gain time? And once he had made his escape would he leave her to face the censure and ridicule of the community? The humiliation of it drained the colour from her face. The whole day had been like a bad dream. She could not be a part of this madness— it could not be happening to her. But the persistent headache was proof of her accident and its consequences. She stared straight ahead as she sensed Jake watching her. With a shrug, he gracefully bent his knee and drew her down to his side.

Throughout the simple ceremony, he stared at Sir Charles's musket above the fireplace, his expression devoid of emotion. There was no hesitation in his responses and, when her own voice shook, a warm hand gently squeezed hers in encouragement, disconcerting her further. The touch of warm metal against her finger made her look down at her hand in bewilderment. A heavy gold ring with a single stone, an almost black emerald, glinted in the candlelight. It was the ring Jake wore on his small finger.

'There's no need for such trumpery,' Oliver Ashleigh sneered.

'Mistress Masters will grow accustomed to such trumpery,' Jake answered haughtily, as he stood up and assisted Rebecca to rise. 'The ring remains.'

'Then God's curses upon you both.' Oliver rounded on Rebecca. 'The marriage is done. Now get your treacherous hide from my house. A servant will bring your belongings to you at the hunting lodge. I want no reminders of you here.'

Jake started forward and, seeing the anger snapping in his eyes, Rebecca put a restraining hand on his arm. He shrugged it off impatiently, his expression chiselled from rock. 'Rebecca is now my wife. As such, any man who insults her insults me. Remember that, Ashleigh, before you speak out of turn again.'

'I speak as the good Lord sees fit.'

Rebecca's skin rose in goose-bumps at the hostility flashing between her grandfather and Jake. 'Pay no heed to his words, Jake,' she urged softly, her courage almost failing as his hazel eyes channelled into hers. 'He is angry—and hurt—believing I have betrayed him. I pray he will forgive me in time.'

'Should not a wife put her husband's wishes first?' The smile lifting his lips did not reach his eyes.

Like a duellist her pride measured swords against his. Had he seen through their ruse? 'I would have peace between my husband and grandfather. Is that so unreasonable?'

'I'll not make my peace with any Masters,' Oliver declared with a violence which shook Rebecca. 'That includes you, Mistress Masters.'

Rebecca turned away, unable to curb a tremor gripping her body at the loathing in her grandfather's voice.

'It is time we left, Becky——' Jake's breath fanned her chilled cheek—but the ceremony would not be complete without the husband kissing his bride.

Taking both her hands, he drew her to him, the bold light in his eyes bringing a flood of heat to her face. His fingers brushed a tendril of hair from her cheek, the light touch sending a quiver of anticipation through her body. The rogue was enjoying himself at her grandfather's expense. He would give no one the satisfaction of believing he resented the marriage forced upon him.

Rebecca's pride rose to match his. She was certain it was Squire Hardwycke who had instigated the whole affair. Did he no longer believe her worthy to wed his own son? She would show him the marriage pleased her.

Her gaze fused with Jake's, and the amusement in his eyes brightened with understanding. He was the one who should be condemning her for allowing herself to be compromised. Instead he smiled encouragement and something more—something beyond her experience— flashed between them, leaving her breathless with expectancy.

Jake moved his hands to her shoulders, his head moving inexorably closer until their lips touched. There was an unexpected gentleness in his kiss, his mouth treasuring hers, moving sensuously and with provocative slowness, while a deepening pressure parted her lips, and she tasted the sweetness of his breath. The clean, masculine scent of his skin mingled with the musky odour of orris root he favoured. Her head spun, as a warmth as potent as brandy spread through her veins, turning her knees weak and causing her blood to pound with a pagan beat. Her fingers curled against the grey velvet of his vest to steady herself and she felt the steady rhythm of his strong heartbeat.

Dimly, she was aware of Skevington's embarrassed cough in the background, and her grandfather's outraged muttering of 'Jezebel'. But in that brief, giddy moment she did not care. Through half-closed eyes she saw Jake was watching her, gauging her reaction. It was like a dousing of cold water. Instantly, she pulled back, resenting the ease with which his expert kiss aroused her response. To satisfy his own pride, he was playing the role of the ardent lover, but what thoughts lay behind those enigmatic green-flecked eyes?

Tucking her arm through his, he led her to the door, where he turned to face the occupants of the room. 'I bid you goodnight, gentlemen. Nothing further can be achieved while tempers are running high. I bid you all sleep on it. If we are to triumph in our cause, old grievances must be laid to rest. Tomorrow I shall expect you all at the hunting lodge at noon. I must have the numbers of men and weapons if I am to plan our campaign and report to his Grace. Time is short. If Monmouth is to succeed we must strike quickly, before King James can despatch his regiments to the West.'

The door shut behind them and Rebecca and Jake were alone in the courtyard. A warm body brushed against her skirts and whimpered softly. How could she have forgotten her spaniel, Tess? Her heart filling with sadness, she stooped to fondle the heavily pregnant bitch's ears. The pups were due any day now, and it would not be safe for Tess to walk all the way to the hunting lodge.

'She is your dog?' asked Jake.

'Yes.' Her voice broke through the knot of emotion lodged in her throat. 'I fear I shall miss her.' She sniffed, fighting back her threatening tears as she threw her arms round Tess's black and white body and hugged her for the last time.

The appearance of her spaniel almost crumpled her resolve. She had not realised how hard it would be to leave the farm and people she had known all her life. She had not said goodbye to Lizzie, their maidservant who returned to her father's cottage every evening. The painful lump in her throat spread its fiery tentacles down through her lungs and twined in her stomach. She walked towards the horses, too dazed to register surprise that her own grey mare was saddled and waiting for her, a generous act on the part of her grandfather.

Again, emotion almost overwhelmed her, and she was grateful that Jake was sensitive enough to her mood to remain silent as he held the mare's head while she mounted from the stone block. When Jake swung into his saddle and they set off she looked across at the man who was now her husband.

Husband! Suddenly the enormity of what she had done—and the consequences she must now face—hit her like a hammer-blow. She was married to a complete stranger. He was not even a true-bred Englishman, but a colonial whose home was in the New World. She was his property, with no rights of her own. Even her body was by law now his to use as he saw fit. He could beat her, imprison her, treat her as his servant, and use her as his whore. Or she could become his helpmeet and confidante, his lover and friend, the mother of his children.

She closed her mind to the latter possibility. Her head hurt too much to dwell upon what might have been. The circumstances of her marriage made such a rewarding, satisfying role impossible. Her lips still bore the imprint of his kiss, and her response had shown her that he was capable of arousing a need in her she had not known she possessed. At least her role of wife in that respect did not repel her. She had to use every means at her disposal to win his trust and become his confidante. How else was she to learn whether he was King James's spy? Since, clearly, Jake was no celibate she must swallow her pride and, without love between them, play the whore.

They were approaching the lane leading to the hunting lodge when Jake finally broke through her thoughts. 'Hardwycke was not the man for you,' he said, as matter-of-factly as though he were speaking of the weather.

'Are you suggesting that you are?' She could not resist the thrust.

'I would not so presume.' The self-assurance of his tone belied his statement. Were his conquests so legion that he assumed any woman would be captivated by his charm? The arrogant scoundrel, she fumed, even as part of her acknowledged there was such an air and presence about him that a woman would have to be made of wood to resist. 'Take me as you find me, Becky,' he went on, 'and we will deal well enough together.'

CHAPTER FOUR

'YOU may congratulate us,' Jake announced to his two servants as he stepped into the main room of the hunting lodge. He slid an arm possessively about Rebecca's waist. 'Tonight Miss Ashleigh and I were married.'

Shock registered briefly on both servants' faces. Martha recovered first, her round face lighting with pleasure. 'May I wish you both happy. Why, Master Jake, I never guessed when you brought the young lady here earlier that she was to be your wife,' she babbled excitedly. 'Shame on you for not telling me! I would have made the place more fitting for a bride.'

'There was no time.' Jake laughed easily, taking no offence from the housekeeper's familiarity. He flashed a wry smile at Rebecca. Catching her senses off balance, the erratic thudding of her heart caused the blood to pound through her aching temple like waves crashing on to a shingle beach. 'Ours has been a providential match.'

When he raised her hand reverently to his lips, and she met the full force of the green lights dancing in his eyes, her cheeks scorched with a fierce heat. He was playing the role of adoring bridegroom to perfection, and he was looking at her as though she was the only woman in his life who was important. She checked her wayward thoughts with a start. He was a man who enjoyed the company of women—all women—and that devastating, lopsided smile, whether it were turned upon a lady of fashion or a milkmaid, would make her feel like a queen. She must remember that deception was second nature to the Masters family.

'My dear,' Jake went on smoothly, 'as you see, I do not keep a large household. Until now my needs have been faithfully served by Martha and Ben Simmons. Of course, later you must have a maid. But at the moment to bring a stranger into our household could leave us open to betrayal.'

'I can manage without a maid.'

'Oh, that will not be necessary, Mistress Masters,' Martha assured her with warm sincerity. 'I shall be proud to serve you in any way I can.'

'Thank you, Martha,' Rebecca smiled at the older woman, welcoming her friendliness, and smothered the first bud of remorse at having to deceive the kindly woman.

Her smile faded as she looked at Ben Simmons. The manservant eyed her warily, his freckled brow shadowed by concern. He was not fooled by Jake's explanation of their marriage. There was the air of a seasoned campaigner about the middle-aged servant. He missed nothing, and must know Jake better than anyone. He reminded her of a powerfully muscled bull-terrier, and he would be just as fierce in protecting his master. This man would give his life for Jake. If she was to succeed in learning the truth about her husband's loyalties she must also win Simmons' trust.

Simmons coughed and rubbed the stumps of his fingers, his voice still troubled. 'It's long past the time you should have settled down, Master Jake. I'm right pleased for you. Though what Sir Charles will say when he hears you've wed old Ashleigh's granddaughter, I wouldn't like to say. He had you all lined up to wed another niece of his, like Mistress Anne.'

'Sir Charles has long considered me the black sheep of the family.' A sharpness entered Jake's voice that Rebecca had not heard before. Was it the mention of Sir Charles or of Mistress Anne which had brought it on? And who *was* Anne? Her thoughts were cut short by Jake's again taking charge. 'Bring us wine, Simmons. I have yet to toast the health and beauty of my bride. Neither has Mistress Masters eaten since she left here.'

As the servants hurried out to obey his command, Rebecca moved from Jake's side to stand by the fireplace, where a large log was burning slowly, an extravagance her grandfather would never have allowed upon so mild an evening. She stared at the licking flames and schooled herself to remain calm, while the events of the day chased one another through her mind; and all the time her spine tingled with the awareness that Jake was watching her. The subtle fragrance of orris root seeping into her consciousness warned her that he had moved across the room and was standing directly behind her. There was a rattle of crockery as Martha laid the table with dishes of cold meats, bread and cheese.

Jake laid a hand on her shoulder, the gentle pressure turning her to face him. 'Let me take your cloak, Becky. We can eat by the fire if you are cold.' He unfastened the ties at her throat and handed the cloak to Martha, leaving Rebecca feeling suddenly vulnerable to his gaze. Martha curtsied and left them alone, and, as Jake continued to stare down at her, Rebecca found herself transfixed, unable to lower her gaze.

'You have no need to fear, sweet Becky. I'm not going to force you to do anything against your will—especially tonight when your head must still be aching after being knocked down by my horse.' He led her to the table. 'You will feel better when you have eaten.'

Again, his consideration disconcerted her. 'I am not hungry. But I am aware of my wifely duties.'

'I want no duty-bound martyr in my bed, Becky, but a willing companion.' He shot her a long look which sent a ripple of excitement through her veins. 'Tonight you are hungry, tired, and need time to adjust to having a stranger suddenly thrust upon you as a husband.' He leaned closer, his voice lowering to a confiding whisper. 'Will you not dine with me, so that we may become less of strangers to each other?'

It was a command not an invitation, but even so she could not possibly refuse. 'I would not embarrass you before your servants, Mr Masters. Neither would I give others, such as Skevington and Squire Hardwycke, the satisfaction of believing they had forced an intolerable relationship upon us.'

'Already you prove how well we shall deal together, Becky, providing——' his eyes sparkled with topaz lights

and his voice gentled to a teasing tone as he led her to
the table '—you remember that my name is Jake. And
one other thing would please me greatly.' His hands were
pulling at the ties of her plain linen cap. He whisked it
from her head and tossed it on to the fire. 'You will
never wear such a hideous thing again.'

'Oh, that was Martha's cap!' She stared in dismay at
the blackening material.

'Then Martha shall have several to replace it. While
you will wear only the finest lace.' His deep, sonorous
voice wove its enticing spell over her. 'In London a
seamstress will provide you with a fashionable wardrobe
worthy of my wife.'

He sat her at the head of the table and drew up a stool
to sit at her side instead of the far end. Martha had removed two of the candlesticks and the room was lit with
a cosy glow—a romantic setting for an intimate supper.
As she watched the firelight play over the angular lines
of his handsome face and the soft waves of his blond-
tipped hair, she had the feeling of living through a dream.

She clasped her hands tightly in her lap as she watched
him dip his fingers in the fingerbowl and dry them on
a lace-edged napkin before he selected the choicest meats
and delicacies and put them on a plate for her. The heavy
lace fell back from his sleeve, showing a strong, tanned
wrist, yet his hands, large and lean with long, tapering
fingers, were as delicate as those of any minstrel who
had ever strummed a lute. When his own plate was also
filled, he poured a light golden wine into two silver
goblets and handed one to her.

'This is our wedding feast, Becky.' His eyes grew
serious as he studied her. 'To what shall we toast?'

'To a new beginning.' She attempted lightness, but her
voice sounded breathless to her ears. 'To getting to know
and understand each other. To success?'

'Success in what?' His tone hardened. 'Our marriage—or the cause we believe in?'

She rubbed the side of her neck, her fingers twirling
a stray tendril of hair which had escaped its tight coil.
He was testing her. She had to think quickly. If only her

head did not throb so. Knowing she was a hopeless liar, and despising dishonesty, she strove to find a neutral path, but it needed all her will-power to hold his penetrating stare.

'I would like to think our marriage had a chance of success—that we will find a measure of contentment with each other. Even if love is denied our relationship there could be a closeness, a deepening respect between us.' Her throat tightened as she touched upon the truth of her own hopes, and her voice dropped. 'That will take time. We have first to learn to understand and trust each other.'

'I had not realised I had married a philosopher.' The flippancy was back in his voice, warning her he was being as guarded in his words as herself. She had to beat him at his own game if she was to learn whether he would betray her grandfather and his friends.

Propping her elbow on the table, she rested her chin on her knuckle and regarded him serenely. 'Grandsire taught me to read, write, and keep the estate accounts. He opened my mind to be more than a housekeeper or drudge, but like most men he resented it when I voiced an opinion. Perhaps you now see what a poor bargain you have made?'

He raised his goblet in salute to her, his eyes shining with a provocative promise which sent a shiver through her, though whether from nerves or misplaced excitement she could not tell.

He said, 'Let us drink simply to us. It is not easy to find ourselves married, when there has been no courtship. You shall have your courtship, my dear Becky.'

The wine was sweet and soothing to her taut throat. Jake continued to hold her gaze, blatantly caressing her with his eyes until a flush crept over her neck and cheeks. Somehow she found the strength to drag her eyes away and, lowering her goblet to the table, she absently rubbed her temple which still throbbed.

'If you let your hair fall loose, it will ease your headache.'

When she hesitated, the disarming smile which she found so hard to resist tilted his lips, and of their own volition her hands began removing the pins from her hair. With a shake of her head the thick dark tresses tumbled down over her shoulders and breasts to her waist. He tipped his goblet a second time in acknowledgement to her, saying admiringly, 'I have no complaint with the bargain I made.'

At the way her pulse began to race, Rebecca knew he was gaining the upper ground. He was seducing her with compliments and charm. But what better way was there for him to trick her into a false security than by playing the gallant lover and laying siege to her heart? She was a novice in both intrigue and the art of seduction. It would be all too easy to follow the pull of her emotions and allow herself to fall in love with Jake Masters. She concentrated on her plate for several moments, making herself remember who and what he was.

When her eyes next lifted to meet his, her voice was cool and under control. 'You spoke to Mr Skevington of your family in Maryland. I know Sir Charles's younger brother sailed there in 1651. Was he your father?'

'Yes. He met and married my mother on the ship going out. It was winter before they cleared the land and built the first wooden house. My brother John was born a month later.' Jake twirled the stem of his goblet, then pushed it aside and leaned forward to take her hand as he went on. 'It takes a particular kind of woman to survive there.' A hollowness touched his voice. He checked and went on quickly. 'My mother bore seven children—only four boys survived infancy. The life is hard—the land has to be cleared from a thick forest. It is a perpetual battle and challenge to wrest a living from the land, but in the end the rewards can be great. In all my travels I have never seen anything to rival the raw beauty of the New World. It is that wildness which eats into you, drawing you back to tame it. The land—like a high-spirited woman—is a challenge worthy of a man.'

'Are your brothers still in Maryland?'

'John is. He will inherit Father's land, and they work it together. John has three sons. My other brothers, Nathan and Jeremy, have houses on the upper reaches of Chesapeake Bay.' His voice warmed as he spoke of his family. 'The year I left they had just built their first merchant ship to trade goods and supplies from England. Until then everything was purchased from our neighbours in Virginia. The last I heard, their fleet numbered five.'

'It sounds like a land full of opportunities for those willing to work.'

'It is—but, like all things worth achieving, the cost can also be high in lives.' He eased back on his stool as though he had said more than he intended. 'Nathan is expected to land at Plymouth within the month.'

'Are all your brothers married?' Rebecca's curiosity pricked.

'We all married young. It's expected of one there.'

Rebecca stiffened. 'You have been married before?'

His handsome features set into a chiselled mask. The whiteness of the cleft in his chin was the only sign that she had touched upon perilous ground. He stood up, abruptly ending the intimacy of their supper, and rang the handbell to summon a servant.

'My wife died ten years ago,' he said, with a bleakness which forbade further questions. When Martha, followed by Simmons, entered the room, Jake drew Rebecca to her feet and placed a cool kiss on her cheek. 'The day has been a long one, and tomorrow is likely to be equally so. Martha will attend you. Sleep well, Rebecca.'

The curtness of his dismissal flicked a raw nerve. It proved how shallow his gallantry had been. Beneath that polished charm was a man of finely honed steel. Yet he was vulnerable—the mention of his first wife had shown her that. He must have loved her very much. As she followed Martha across the room she saw Simmons hold out two packages wrapped in oilcloth to Jake, saying, 'These arrived an hour ago from London.'

Her step slowing, Rebecca glanced across at Jake. He turned the packets thoughtfully over in his hands before

breaking the seals to scan their contents. At the foot of
the stairs, she paused, watching Jake as he rubbed the
indent in his chin while he read the first document. His
frown told her all was not well. Then, aware of her
presence, he looked across at her, his raised brow questioning her delay in retiring.

Seeing that Martha had already entered the upstairs
chamber and Simmons had returned to the kitchen, she
said stiffly, 'Goodnight, Jake. I shall leave you to your
plotting. I hold you to your word that you will not force
your attentions upon an unwilling woman.'

His retaliation was swifter than she anticipated. Before
she had mounted two steps he seized her elbow and
swung her round. Her head was on a level with his and
she met the full force of the dangerous glitter in his glare.
'You delude yourself, my dear. You responded eagerly
enough when I kissed you at Coombe Grange. Do not
try my patience too far.'

She tilted her chin back, her eyes afire with scorn.
'The self-delusion of an acknowledged rake does not
impress me, Mr Masters.'

'Then if you have no wish to dance with the devil,
madam, you should not whistle his tune.'

'I shall remember your warning,' she tossed back, her
heart once more locked in a casket of ice, and with un-
hurried dignity she ascended the stairs. In the shadow
of the landing, she hesitated, her glance pulled by invisible cords down to the room below. The sight of Jake
bent over the table, engrossed in studying a map spread
out before him, chipped at her frozen reserve. Her gaze
lingered upon his sharp, clear-cut profile, softened by
the golden halo of his hair falling about his shoulders,
and a sharp pain contracted her heart. How quickly he
had dismissed and forgotten her. She tried to hate him
as his fickle treatment of her deserved, but his subtle,
expert seduction had an insidious power of its own,
working against her resolve. She was playing with fire,
and she knew it. But even when she was angry with him,
as she was now, she still found him the most exciting
and intriguing man she had ever met.

At the sound of the bedroom door closing, Jake lifted his unseeing gaze from the map on the table. The woman had the power to goad him in a way none in recent years had come close to. Her response to his kiss had left him shaken. She was a puritanical icicle one instant; the next she smouldered with a passion which, with an expert's kindling, would flare to a beacon's brightness. It was that dormant passion which inexorably drew him. He had sensed it in her graceful movements—the unconscious language of her body awaiting fulfilment—dignified, elegant, but as sensual as a dancer. He rubbed his finger across his chin. He had no intention of enduring the torture of a woman's cruel, taunting games. He made no compromise. A muscle throbbed along his jaw as he turned back to the map, but his thoughts remained on Rebecca in the room above. He swore under his breath. 'Sblood, I could not have been mistaken. Not a second time.'

Rebecca awoke, as was her custom, soon after first light. She lay very still, listening to the splashing of water. Raising herself on one elbow, she looked through the gap in the bed-hangings. With a start she clutched the sheet closer to her chin, surprised to see Jake, wearing only snug-fitting brown leather breeches, bent over the china washbasin. He straightened, shaking the droplets of water from his long hair as he dried his face and neck with a linen towel, and turned to discover her watching him.

'Good morning, Becky. Did you sleep well?'

She nodded, suddenly aware of the warmth of the mattress at her side and the indentation of the pillow where another head had lain. Jake had spent the night in the same bed as her and she had not even been aware of his presence. Or had she? There was the dim remembrance of the clean, fresh smell of him, of a comforting warmth and hard muscle touching her softer limbs. She had thought it part of a dream brought on by the strong posset Martha had insisted she drink to ease the bruises and stiffening in her tired body.

'I seem to have slept very well. Did you?'

He shot her a wry look as he continued drying himself. 'Well enough.'

The sight of the broad expanse of his chest, covered with a down of curling dark-blond hair, brought a return of fire to her cheeks. She averted her gaze. She was used to seeing her grandfather's emaciated torso when he washed in the wooden tub by the well, and also the flabby paunch of the head groom. She had no idea that the sight of a man's half-naked body, its slenderness refined to a muscular hardness, could, by its very splendour, bring a dryness to her throat and a quivering to the pit of her stomach.

When he moved across the room to select a clean shirt from his coffer and pull it over his head, she saw the long, purplish scar furrowing the muscles on his upper arm. The scar proclaimed him a rake and scoundrel—yet there was more to this complex man she had married than that. He cared deeply about his family in Maryland. Why then had he stayed away so long?

'Does your head still pain you?' he asked, fastening a hip-length tan leather jerkin.

'Just a slight ache if I move too quickly, and I am still rather sore.'

'There is no need for you to rise. It is early yet. I shall ask Martha to prepare a bath for you. The hot water will ease your stiffness.' He picked up his sword-belt from the side of the coffer. 'I shall be away from the lodge this morning and will return in time for my meeting with Skevington at noon.'

'I have no intention of being a slugabed.' She bristled defensively. 'A bath would be welcome, but I know the work involved in carrying heavy buckets of water from the kitchen. If Simmons is to accompany you I shall help Martha all I can.'

He stood at the foot of the bed, his expression softening in a way which set her heart tumbling. 'It pleases me that you would lighten, not add to, Martha's tasks.'

'You forget I am a farmer's daughter, not a grand, pampered lady. I could not endure a life of idleness.' Her lips quivered tremulously as a notion struck her.

'But perhaps my simple ways are not the qualities you would have chosen in a wife. Will your friends in London laugh at my country manners? I would not wish to embarrass you, Jake.'

'You could not do that.' His smile of approval touched her like the first rays of dawn's light, bringing a rebirth of hope for a new day. 'Rather I shall be the envy of every man I meet.'

'Flatterer!' She laughed, dismissing his compliment, but her heart scudded at the sight of his eyes darkening with desire as he moved towards her.

'Temptress! Were there time, I would prove just how potently you arouse a man to madness.' He towered over the bed, and for a moment she thought he would take her into his arms. There was a cough outside from the stairs, and he grinned wryly, his lips briefly brushing her forehead as Martha knocked, and entered on his command, carrying a tray of steaming hot chocolate. Jake winked at Rebecca. 'Until later, temptress mine,' he promised in a low whisper before striding from the room.

Rebecca sighed dreamily, every nerve-end of her body glowing in anticipation of their next meeting. No hard-hearted rake could have treated a woman with the consideration he had shown her. Was her grandfather wrong about him? Every action of Jake's she had so far witnessed had been honourable. She could not believe such a man would play the traitor. Her heart warmed with growing trust and just as suddenly grew chilled. For in the eyes of the Government it was Monmouth who was the traitor, and King James the true King of England. She absently took the cup of chocolate from Martha and sipped it. She did not need to think of the unpleasant side of her marriage—not now, oh, please God, not ever.

CHAPTER FIVE

THE morning passed with a feeling of disembodiment for Rebecca. Refreshed from the bath on which Martha insisted and which eased the stiffness from her limbs, she sat on a stool while Martha brushed and pinned her hair.

'Have you not done yet, Martha?' She felt uncomfortable at keeping the housekeeper from her work. 'The pies must be ready to take from the oven, and there's still the table to be laid. Mr Masters could return at any moment. The lodge must be ready for his guests.'

'Master Jake will be some while yet,' Martha soothed. 'And the pies need another ten minutes at least. You must not fret. Do you not want to look your best for the master? You have lovely hair—it's so thick, and its colour is like polished rosewood. No wonder Master Jake threw that old cap of mine on the fire. 'Tis a shame to hide such glory.'

'It's a sin to parade it before so many.' Rebecca could not shake off her grandfather's teachings overnight. Her eyes widened with surprise as Martha held a silver-backed handmirror out for her to inspect the results. Instead of the neat coils pinned tightly to her head, her hair was piled high in loose curls and several tresses flowed down on to her shoulders. 'I look so different—so...'

'Beautiful,' Martha said with a delighted chuckle.

'But I cannot receive my grandfather's friends without my hair modestly covered.'

'Nonsense. Those days for you are past,' Martha admonished. 'It is your husband's guests you are receiving. He's a proud man, and has a reputation for escorting the most beautiful ladies at Court. Your beauty is a compliment to his good fortune. He will be insulted if you deliberately hide it.'

'And I would be churlish not to do full justice to your hard work,' Rebecca said with a warm smile, but the sadness lingered in her heart. 'It is not easy for me to face my grandfather. You must know he has disowned me for marrying Mr Masters.'

Martha laid a consoling hand upon Rebecca's shoulder. 'I wondered why, as a new bride, you had no sparkle in your eyes. But I am sure that given time, your grandfather will come round and forgive you.'

'That he will never do!' She dropped her gaze to her lap, Martha's kindness filling her with self-loathing at the role of deceiver she was being forced to play.

'Then don't let him see it bothers you. You've Master Jake to consider. Don't let an old man's bitterness spoil your chance of happiness. You've married a good man.' Martha hesitated, appearing ill at ease.

Rebecca looked up at her, and after a moment's indecision the housekeeper went on, 'Forgive my forwardness, ma'am, but I am a woman who speaks her mind. I wouldn't like to see you unnecessarily hurt. If you love Master Jake, pay no heed to the rumours surrounding his life during recent years. It was nothing but a devil riding him.'

Rebecca stood up and faced her maid, her expression questioning. 'You make it sound so sinister. What happened?'

Martha shook her head. 'It's not for me to speak of. Master Jake must tell you.'

'He does not seem a man given to easy confidences. How can I understand his moods if his past is closed to me?'

Martha busied herself straightening imaginary creases from the bedcover. With sudden insight Rebecca asked, 'Has it something to do with his first wife?'

'You should not ask me such questions, mistress.'

She was moved by Martha's loyalty. Surely he could not be such a rogue if his servants were so fiercely loyal? But it was more than that which prompted her to pursue the matter. The complexities of Jake's character intrigued her. The smell of the pies cooking took Martha to the door and Rebecca followed, determined to get an answer.

'If I am to disregard rumours, should I not know the truth about my husband?' she persisted. 'I can trust *you* not to distort that. I know so little about my husband. How can I make him happy if I do not know what this devil is which plagues him? Did he love his first wife very much? I can respect that. How did she die?'

Martha said nothing until they reached the kitchen, and even then she kept herself busy while clearly wrestling with her conscience. Once the pies were out of the oven the servant said heavily, 'I know only what Simmons has told me, and he can be very close-lipped where Master Jake is concerned. Apparently it was the death of Mistress Anne which brought Master Jake to England. They had been married less than two years. Poor lass, she died in childbed and the child was stillborn. She was never strong. Her death changed him— Simmons says.' Martha shot Rebecca a look of sympathy and understanding. 'But that's long in the past now. You are right for him. With you he will forget his pain.'

Rebecca smothered the prickings of her conscience at the reasons she had married Jake, and responded with more than a little wistfulness, 'I would like to think I could make him happy. He has shown me nothing but kindness, and I trust I can judge a man by his actions and not be swayed by vicious gossip.'

'Aye, the Captain certainly has a way about him. Yet in many ways he keeps a tight rein upon his emotions. Give him time, ma'am. He's no saint, but, in your heart, would you truly wish him one? A touch of the rogue always makes a man more fascinating!'

Rebecca looked at the housekeeper in astonishment, and her lips moved in answering amusement as they carried the food into the main room of the lodge. 'You are unlike any housekeeper I have met, Martha. How did you come to be in Mr Masters' service?'

'That's a long story,' Martha said, her expression sobering. 'I owe him a great deal—not least of all a respectable position.' She studied Rebecca for a long moment as she put the last of the dishes in the centre of the table. 'Six years ago I found myself in London. I was brought up a merchant's daughter in York. Father was a strict man, very like your grandfather. I was nearing thirty and had never had a suitor—Father made sure of that. Since my mother died I was expected to take her place, be his unpaid servant and shop assistant. I was the youngest of three sisters, and he refused to provide me with a dowry. I was miserable there.'

Rebecca nodded, understanding only too well what Martha must have endured. 'How did you get away?'

Martha sank down on to a stool, her eyes misting with pain. 'In the end I ran away. Quite by chance I met a soldier, and fell hopelessly in love with the handsome scoundrel. Father was furious when he found out we were meeting.' She broke off, pleating the folds in her large white apron before continuing. 'He beat me, calling me the vilest names. I ran from the house and sought out my lover. His regiment was about to return to London and I went with them. Only he did not marry me ... After a few months he tired of me, and threw me out of his lodgings.'

'I'm so sorry, Martha. That must have been an awful time for you.' Rebecca shuddered, imagining the horror of being deserted and alone in such an evil and frightening place as London. Crouching at Martha's side, she took the servant's roughened, restless hands in hers. 'How did you manage?'

Martha shuddered. 'Not very well. I'd never been so terrified in all my life. I'd no place to stay and no money. For two days and nights I lived in terror of being raped or murdered. At night I took shelter in an old barrel lying at the back of a neglected churchyard. On the third day I was so wretched and weak from hunger I stole a loaf of bread. The baker caught me, and called the Watch.' Martha hung her head, ashamed, her voice cracking with the effort it was costing her to speak. 'A crowd gathered. They were like fiends from hell—enjoying my humiliation and fear. Sometimes at night I wake in a cold sweat. I can still hear their cruel jeers. Two old harridans even began ripping the clothes from my back. I was half-naked and about to be hauled off to Newgate when Captain Masters rode past. If he hadn't stopped...' she sniffed and drew a shaky breath '...'tis a fact, I'd not be alive today.'

'Jake saved your life!' Rebecca unsuccessfully tried to hide her surprise. This was another side of her husband's character she had not expected. As a soldier he should have been on the side of law and order. What had made him save a thief? Her heart stirred for the older woman, and also for Jake. She could not have condemned Martha for her crime when fate had dealt with her so cruelly. She squeezed the servant's hand, prompting her to go on.

'The Captain did a great deal more than save my life.' A fond smile touched Martha's lips. 'He demanded to know what all the commotion was about. I fell on my knees and told him my story, while the mob jeered and mocked me. Not Captain Masters. He looked magnificent in his uniform, but I couldn't believe he didn't mean to arrest me. He lifted me up, and in no uncertain terms told the mob to disperse or they would be the worse for it. Then he spoke to the Watch, and paid the baker handsomely to drop the charges.'

Martha checked her flow of words and looked embarrassed. 'My, how I blather on, and the Captain and his guests due at any moment.'

Martha stood up, but Rebecca laid a restraining hand on her arm. Her throat tightened at a sudden disturbing thought. Six years ago Martha must have been a striking-looking woman. Had Jake saved her from the mob and made her his whore?

'Nay, mistress,' Martha hurriedly interrupted her thoughts. 'I can see what you are thinking. Captain Masters had no designs on me.' She shifted uncomfortably. 'It was six years ago, and I'm sure you would not hold it against the Captain if I explain. I was taken to a lady friend of his, an actress, and she, kindly soul, took me in as her maid. It was during those months I met Simmons. He began to accompany the Captain on his visits to my mistress.'

'Was Simmons then not a servant?' Rebecca asked, puzzled that Jake should take his manservant with him when he visited his mistress.

'Simmons has always served the Captain. He came with him from Maryland in 1675. I was accompanying my mistress to the milliner's when we met Captain Masters and Simmons by chance. It was after that that Simmons began his visits.' Martha blushed. 'Even when the Captain no longer visited the house, Simmons would find excuses to call. Sadly, my mistress died the next winter of a fever. Simmons asked me to marry him, and Master Jake agreed I could serve as housekeeper in his London house.'

Martha fidgeted with the folds of her large white apron. 'Perhaps you do not see me as a fitting person to be your housekeeper?'

'You were betrayed and deserted by the man you loved,' Rebecca sympathised. 'You stole out of desperation. Women are at the mercy of men. We often have no redress for the way they would dictate our lives. The loyalty you give Mr Masters is proof that his faith in you was not misplaced.'

'Bless you, ma'am. I knew you had a good heart.' Martha looked towards the window overlooking the courtyard. 'That's the Captain returned. Oh, I keep forgetting, it's Master Jake now. He doesn't like to be reminded of his rank.'

Martha hurried back into the kitchen, leaving Rebecca alone as the door opened and Jake entered, followed by his guests. Her husband came immediately to her side, his eyes sparkling with admiration as his gaze swept over her hair and face, and her heart responded with a wild erratic beat. Ignoring the presence of the Dissenters, he lifted a ringlet which curled provocatively over her shoulder, and said softly, 'Like a butterfly, you are slowly emerging from your chrysalis. Once in London you shall have silk and satin gowns to do full justice to your grace and beauty.'

Behind Jake she saw her grandfather's lip thin with disgust before he turned his back on her. Following him was Tom, looking out of place among the sombrely clad Dissenters in his crimson velvet suit and elaborate curling periwig. His face was the colour of limewash, except for the two bloody furrows where she had scratched his cheek. He ignored Jake, but the expression he turned upon herself was that of a whipped spaniel. Beside him another young man sniggered. Her conscience stirred guiltily. Tom would have told his friends of their plans to wed. Her hasty marriage to Jake had left him the subject of their ridicule, and he did not deserve that. Though she knew now she could never have married Tom it was true that she had been dazzled by him for a time; her own craving for affection, after the empty years in her grandfather's house, had led her to respond to his courtship, and to mistake infatuation for love.

'Good day to you, Tom,' she murmured politely, aware that Jake was watching her.

Tom inclined his head in sullen acknowledgement. 'Good day, Mistress Masters.'

The coldness of his tone hurt her more than she had expected, laying another stone in the wall which was steadily building between herself and the people she had known all her life. They expected her to betray Jake, who had shown her nothing but kindness, yet they were treating her like a leper. The knowledge shook her, making her hand tremble as she poured the wine into goblets for Martha to hand to their dozen guests.

'My dear, you are still not recovered from your accident yesterday.' Jake stayed her movement. 'You should be resting.'

The warmth of his hand upon hers caused her heart to leap. 'I should be at your side, seeing to the needs of my husband's guests. I am stronger than you think.'

'I stand corrected.' His voice caressed her wounded pride. 'But then each hour in the company of my bride teaches me more about her.'

From the corner of her eye Rebecca saw Tom stiffen, and his expression was murderous. Jake chose not to notice, but the tilt of his supple mouth showed her he missed nothing. He was enjoying himself at the expense of the men who had tricked him into marriage. And it was working. There was a glacial hardness in her grandfather's eyes, which made her suspect that he believed Jake was winning her to his side. But then was not the rogue, by his consideration and easy charm, doing exactly that? It was discomfiting to realise that, after less than a day of marriage, her loyalties were torn by conflict. She took a grip upon herself. She must remain neutral, and not let her softening heart betray her. If Jake Masters was King James's spy then he deserved her contempt—not affection.

Once the guests were seated, Rebecca withdrew with Martha to the kitchen, leaving the men to their plotting. Martha laid a sheet across the kitchen table, and, taking the flat iron from the fire where it was heating, she began to tackle the pile of clean washing. Seeing a torn piece of lace dangling from a cuff, Rebecca picked up Jake's shirt.

'I cannot sit here doing nothing. Is that a sewing casket on the shelf?'

At Martha's nod, Rebecca took it from the shelf and sat down on the wooden settle near the inner chamber door, away from the heat of the cooking fire. Within minutes of her starting to sew the discussion from the other room grew heated, and the words carried clearly to her.

'Of course, the whole of England is behind Monmouth's landing,' Squire Hardwycke pompously declared. The pewter dishes rattled as he thumped the table with his fist to emphasise his words. 'No one wants a Catholic on the throne!'

'But, apart from Lord Grey of Warke, Mr Masters tells us that none of the nobility has given his support,' came a stranger's voice of concern. 'How are we to raise money for the cannon we need? And, above all, how are we to raise cavalry?'

'It is the good men of England who will answer Monmouth's call,' her grandfather proudly proclaimed.

'Once His Grace lands and the nobility see the numbers flocking to his banner, they'll support us. And London will rise—it has always been strong for the cause. Until then we have merchants and yeoman farmers ready to give money. There'll be no shortage of men willing to fight to put a Protestant back on England's throne.'

'You cannot fight a trained army with pitchforks,' Jake cautioned. 'The ports will be watched and ships searched if they are suspected of transporting arms.'

'We risked unloading at Bridgwater once,' Oliver said stiffly. 'We will not chance a port a second time. This coast is the haunt of men who are experienced in landing cargoes in secret.'

The talk of arms and rebellion disturbed Rebecca, and now they would become involved with smugglers—ruthless men who used violence to ensure silence about their activities on the coast. She was caught up in the thick of treason, without really understanding what it was all about. The conflict between Charles I and his Parliament had destroyed so many lives. Now, a bare forty years on, how could her grandfather consider plotting another civil war? And just what were Jake's motives?

Rebecca strained her ears to listen. So far Jake had seemed unimpressed by the Dissenters' enthusiasm. But as a trained soldier would he, more than they, know the problems which faced them? None of the others had held a post of command.

'Monmouth has many faults,' Skevington declared. 'But he is a Protestant, and our late King's son. He has a way with the common people, and will bring a stability to our country. King Charles, for all his wicked and licentious ways, brought us peace. The French and Dutch no longer snap and snarl at our back door. Trade is prospering. We are on the brink of a new age with the wealth of the colonies behind us.'

'Ay, a Catholic monarch will bring a return of the supremacy of Rome.' Oliver spoke with acid fervour. 'Only a Protestant with the backing of Parliament will bring a godly prosperity to our country.'

A chorus of optimistic approval greeted her grandfather's remark.

'You think Monmouth will be content to be a puppet king?' Jake queried, the scornful edge to his voice halting Rebecca's hand over the lace she was sewing.

'He's his father's son,' Squire Hardwycke answered. 'Providing he has his pleasures and mistresses, he will be content enough. Before he was forced into exile, he was popular with the people. He's generous and quick to reward his friends.'

'That is true,' Jake said soberly. 'He has a touching, almost naïve faith in those who profess friendship. It does not always serve his best interests. For Monmouth to succeed we must have the backing of the nobility. King Charles named his brother, not Monmouth, as his heir. If James were persuaded to renounce his faith, what chance would Monmouth have then?'

'King James is too pig-headed and stubborn to renounce his faith,' Oliver snapped.

'Many would see that as a strength, not a weakness,' Jake reasoned. 'Would any man here renounce *his* beliefs to save either his life or his inheritance?'

'And what of the documents proving King Charles did marry Lucy Walters, Monmouth's mother?' Skevington said sharply. 'Those papers make Monmouth the true heir to the throne.'

'King Charles always denied the marriage.' Jake's patience sounded strained. 'He loved Monmouth well and raised him high. Those papers could easily be forgeries. Why should Charles deny his son his rightful inheritance, if he were indeed legitimate?'

'Those do not sound like the words of a man who is wholeheartedly behind our cause,' Tom insinuated sarcastically.

'I am not so bigoted or blind that I see but one path.' The lethal quietness was back in Jake's tone. Rebecca recognised it now as a sign that he was at his most dangerous. 'As a soldier I view all angles of possible attack. Monmouth is my friend. If I believe his cause is lost before it has begun, I will do my utmost to stop him from landing. Gentlemen, convince me your numbers are not mere fabrication, and that you have leaders who will not turn their coat at the first wind of failure, and I will advise him accordingly.'

Rebecca bit back a gasp. Her grandfather would see Jake's words as evidence of betrayal. Setting aside her sewing, she picked up a spare wine flagon and took it quickly into the outer room. The hostile atmosphere could have been cut with a dagger. Jake twirled his wine goblet with deceptive calmness. He was the only one apparently at ease; the others were as taut as fighting cocks ready to attack.

'At last you show your true colours, Masters.' Her heart contracted at her grandfather's angry outburst. 'While we risk everything, you wait, playing a neutral game. It is we who will dance with the hangman.'

Jake pushed the goblet away from him and sat back in his chair, eyeing them coolly. His long fingers formed a steeple to tap against his chin. 'I serve Monmouth. Not you, Ashleigh, or you, Skevington. You have yet to prove to me you are capable of raising an army.'

'I'm not staying here to listen to your insults!' Oliver stomped towards the door, his gaunt face flagged with unhealthy red colour.

'Grandsire! Will you not give Mr Masters a chance?' Rebecca cut in. Putting the flagon on the table, she held her hands out to him in supplication. 'He is merely urging caution. Optimism is all well and good, but it does not win wars.'

Oliver whirled to face her. 'Are you mistakenly addressing me, madam? I have no grandchildren.'

The loathing in his voice struck Rebecca like a mailed fist. Snatching back her hand, her nails gouged into her palm as she moved woodenly to the window, too proud to allow anyone to see her pain. Her grandfather was no actor. He had sacrificed her to the cause. He expected her to betray her husband, and though it was at his command, he despised her for marrying a Masters.

Outside she saw Oliver storm past Simmons, who was grooming Jake's gelding, and heave himself on to his mare, his ageing joints stiff with rheumatism. The pain around her heart intensified. He was an old man. Why did he have to be so stubborn? Moments later the horse clattered from the courtyard and she blinked rapidly against the stinging heat of threatening tears. Her eyes focused on Simmons, finding in the rhythmic, commonplace movements of his brush-strokes a semblance of normality while within this room she was surrounded by treachery and distrust. Behind her she was dimly aware of Jake reasoning with Skevington, but she was too upset by her grandfather's behaviour to pay much heed to his words. A creak of a floorboard nearby, and the reflection of a crimson jacket in the windowpane, brought her head up proudly.

'Why did you marry him?' Tom demanded. 'I never meant to harm you yesterday. I love you, Rebecca. How *could* you marry that—that reprobate?'

'Go back to your father, Tom,' she answered wearily, her gaze remaining upon Jake's horse, whose coat shone in the sunlight like polished ebony. 'Your cowardly lies are the cause of my marriage. It was the Squire's urging. You saved your hide at the expense of my reputation.'

He grabbed her arm, his fingers bruising her flesh as he jerked her round. 'How can you think that? We love each other! Masters is nothing to you. We can still meet. Your marriage changes nothing.'

'My marriage changes everything.'

'It's me you love!'

'If I loved you, I would never have married Mr Masters.'

'Don't tell me you love *him*!' The scratches on Tom's cheeks stood out in a fiery trail as his face twisted with anger. His voice rose as a hush fell over the room. 'You can't love a man you only met yesterday.'

Every head turned in their direction, but it was Jake's brittle hazel stare which goaded her to retaliate. Jake did not deserve to be humiliated before his guests. Shaking off Tom's hold, she allowed her voice to carry to the table. 'Can I not, Tom? I married a most exceptional man. He quite swept me off my feet.'

Tom backed away, his face as red as his velvet suit. 'That's a lie. He seduced you.'

Jake stood up, his hand resting on his sword-hilt. 'You will apologise for that slur upon my wife's honour, Hardwycke.'

Tom edged backwards, his throat working convulsively. 'She was my betrothed before she was your wife, Masters.'

Jake took a step forward, and Tom scurried to the door, pausing only long enough to snarl, 'One day, Masters, you'll pay for this.' The door slammed behind him.

To Rebecca's surprise the Squire stood up and cleared his throat. 'I apologise for my son's lack of manners. He's not quite himself at the moment. I would not want this little disagreement to stand in the way of our cause, Mr Masters. You're too valuable a contact with Monmouth and our friends in London.'

Jake bowed in gracious acknowledgement and, picking up the wine flagon, refilled his guests' goblets. Raising his own, he said, 'To success. To His Grace, James Scott, Duke of Monmouth!'

Jake threw down his quill, the movement causing the candle-flame to flicker and cast weaving shadows on the lodge wall as he studied the map he had copied, the hiding places where arms were stored, all marked with a special cipher. During the last two days word had got round that he was married to Ashleigh's granddaughter—it had loosened guarded tongues and given him entry to the houses of Dissenters otherwise barred to a Masters. He had achieved more in those two days than he had expected to in as many weeks.

He took out his pocket watch, opened the gilded case and was surprised to discover it was almost midnight. His gaze lifted to the upper landing and lingered upon the closed door. Time yet for another drink, he mused cynically. Rebecca had already retired when he had returned to the lodge two hours earlier—retired to her virgin's bed. He refilled the goblet and drank deeply. With a jaundiced eye he contemplated spending the night on the hard wooden settle. Better that than face the torment of lying beside her warm, soft body in another sleepless night. The intensity of his desire seared him. She had an uncomfortable habit of slipping into his thoughts, and he found himself remembering the violet brightness of her eyes when she was angry, the proud tilt of her head when defiant, and, most entrancing of all, the sultry promise of her smile when she defended her marriage to him. She was his wife, and he, gallant fool, had promised to woo her before he bedded her.

He rubbed the stubbled roughness of his chin with bleak cynicism. Pleasure and intrigue were not ready bedfellows. And rebellion was the deadliest of servitors. There was precious little time for dalliance, especially with a woman as unpredictable and captivating as Becky. The only comfort he would receive tonight was from the wine cask. He leaned back in the chair, and propped his long legs on the table. Already the wine tasted sour in his mouth.

Rebecca rose from the crumpled bed where sleep continued to elude her, to pace the moonlit floor. She had heard Jake return hours ago, and he had made no attempt to come near her. She should have felt relief; instead she felt abandoned. Her grandfather had made his feelings only too plain—she was now an outcast. Her pride rebelled. He had forced her to marry Jake. Only death would release them from their vows. A wave of desolation swept through her. She had lived for so many years without love, and she could not bear the thought of a loveless marriage. It would be all too easy to fall in love with Jake. But if Jake still loved his first wife, was there room in his heart for her? It was that which made her pull back whenever he began to press his attentions upon her in the last two days. But tonight she was unaccountably restless, disappointed even, that he had not come to their room.

She toyed with the emerald ring on her finger, cursing her perversity. The looseness of the ring worried her in case she lost it. To occupy her mind with thoughts other than of Jake, she ripped a narrow strip of linen from her shift and bound it about her finger so that the ring fitted snugly. The stone caught the moonlight, reflecting green stars on the ceiling like eyes mocking her marriage. There was still no sign that Jake meant to come to her. A tightness formed in her chest as she paced the bedchamber. Whenever she rejected Jake's advances, she somehow expected him to laugh her maidenly protestations aside. For, despite their marriage and her attraction to Jake, it still seemed wrong to give her body to a man she had known only three days. Her stubbornness was unfair to him, she thought guiltily, yet not once had he lost his temper.

She frowned, at a loss to understand the complex man she had married. Then a more awesome thought struck her. What if Jake did not desire her, and the role he played of adoring bridegroom was just that—an act? Her body chilled and on sudden impulse she ran towards the bedchamber door. She had no knowledge of the ways of love, but of one thing she was certain: she would never win Jake by refusing to meet his challenge. And was not tonight the first night of May, traditionally a time for lovers to seek their partners?

A thud outside in the courtyard froze her in mid-stride, then the high-pitched wail of a tomcat launching himself into a fight with a rival filled the night air, and she relaxed. The stables were always the haunt of half-wild cats which kept the rat population at bay. She moved forward, her bare feet silent upon the stairs as she came level with the room below, lit only by a single candle and the glow from the fire. Halfway down she hesitated. At first she thought the room deserted, but then a movement caught her eye. It was the sleeve of Jake's shirt, pale yellow in the candlelight, moving as he rubbed his chin. The candle-flame turned golden the lighter streaks in his long hair and softened the rugged contours of his face.

She watched him leaning back in his chair, his legs propped on the table. He had removed his long grey velvet vest and the Venetian lace stock and his shirt was open at the neck. Despite his relaxed attitude she sensed an undercurrent of tension. For once his expression was unguarded, his full lips set grimly as he thoughtfully rubbed his chin. Clearly he was deeply troubled.

Her heart quivered with a resurgence of guilt, and she moved silently forward. She had been so wrapped up in her own problems that she had not considered his. He too would face the censure of his family for wedding an Ashleigh. But it was more than that which troubled him. His frown was formidable, carrying with it an undercurrent of anger bordering upon self-loathing, which was at odds with the cool assurance he presented to the world. Her instinct was to comfort him, but he seemed so remote, his emotions locked as tightly against her as her grandfather's had always been. Too often in the past her overtures of love had been rejected, and her courage ebbed. She turned to leave as silently as she had come.

Jake tensed, hearing a rustling sound directly behind him. In a single fluid movement he swung his legs to the floor and whirled around, his naked sword drawn from its sheath on the table.

'Good God, Becky!' he voiced his surprise. 'Never creep up on an old soldier. I could have skewered you, believing you an intruder. An assassin stalks his prey through locked doors, and these are dangerous times.'

'I did not mean to startle you,' she returned breathlessly.

Something in the defiance of her gaze stopped his mocking retort. A pulse beat rapidly at her throat, and he saw that she stood before him clad only in her long-sleeved linen shift which doubled as a nightgown. With her hair tumbling in unrestrained curls to her waist, and the thin shift provocatively outlining her full breasts, she was a vision which fired his blood. Then, remembering the scattered documents on the table, especially one incriminating order he should have burnt as soon as he had read it, his desire was doused by suspicion. Had she come looking for just such a document?

'What is it you want of me, Becky?' He steeled himself against the hurt mirrored in her eyes.

'I—I could not sleep.' Her fingers twirled nervously with her hair. 'I came down for a drink.'

She was lying. He did not flatter himself that she had come down to seek his company—not after she had rejected his advances again yesterday. Yet, if she was prepared to marry him to act as Ashleigh's spy in his household, it was time she faced the consequences of her actions.

'A drink, Becky!' he mocked. 'When Martha takes such pains each night to leave a flagon of cider and honey biscuits in my chamber?' He tipped her chin up forcing her to meet his gaze.

Her stare slid from his, a becoming blush colouring her cheeks. His patience exhausted, he caught her to him, his voice gruff. 'You're lying, Becky. I'm in no mood for games. Tell me what you are doing downstairs!'

She swallowed, her tongue moistening her lips, a gesture at once provocative and revealing the extent of her nervousness. 'I wanted——' She broke off, too ashamed to speak of the need which had driven her to seek his company.

She tried to back away, but his hold tightened, his eyes glinting savagely. Her body prickled with humiliation as she held his stare, her desolation growing at seeing the grim set of his mouth. 'We are married, Jake.'

His expression remained closed, giving her no encouragement.

Her chin came up. 'How can you be so insensitive?' she burst out. 'I have been a poor wife until now. But obviously you are too used to dealing with whores to know the effort my coming down here has cost me! I was wrong last night and the other nights to refuse you. I...I wanted our marriage to be more than a hollow shell.'

'Forgive me, Becky.' His hands moved to her neck, gently easing her head back as his thumb traced a lazy circle around the hollow of her throat. 'I know well enough the effort it has cost you. You offer me a gift beyond price, and I allow my cynicism to wound you.'

He laid his sword aside and gathered her in his arms, his eyes, heavy-lidded with desire, staring down into the depths of her soul. He filled her whole vision—his nearness, the musky masculine scent of his skin filling her senses and setting her pulse dancing to a wild exultant beat. Through the thinness of her shift, the heat of his hard body spread a shimmering incandescence through her and she pressed closer, her arms sliding over the breadth of his back as her lips parted, yearning for his kiss. The warmth of his mouth skimmed over hers, the subtle pressure building to a delicious, heady sweetness, to spread gradually through her veins and engulf her in a glowing radiance which robbed her limbs of strength.

His arms bound her closer, and with tantalising slowness his tongue slowly explored the inner softness of her mouth, languidly possessive, treasuring his conquest. When his lips travelled to the hollow of her neck she could not contain a gasp, the long-suppressed woman in her free at last to revel in the embrace of a lover. His mouth moved across her shoulder as he eased the low-necked shift down over her body and his hand covered her breast, his fingers teasing the hardening crest beneath the linen as his head dipped downward towards it. The heat of his mouth circling its peak stole her breath and set her body trembling with excitement. Feverishly her hands wound through his long hair, tethering them together. She was gripped by an unimagined hunger, her inhibitions scattering in her need to be his, utterly and completely.

The loud thud of an empty barrel overturning outside jerked them apart. Jake scowled at the unshuttered window.

'It's just a cat.' Rebecca rose on to her toes, her body pressing against his in her eagerness for him to kiss her again.

His hands gripped her wrists and took them from his neck. 'Aye, you're right—damned cats. And we have all night,' he responded with a husky laugh. Retrieving his sword-belt from the table, his free arm slid down the hollow of her back as he led her purposefully to the stairs.

Inside the bedchamber Jake clasped her to him, distrust forgotten as the devastating effect of Rebecca's scantily clad body roused his passion. With leisurely thoroughness his mouth covered hers, invading, demanding, sensuously arousing, while he guided her hands to tug his shirt from his breeches. The touch of her hands feathering across his ribs spurred his hunger to possess her. Greedily, he kissed her yielding lips which offered the promise of paradise, his body arching with the intensity of his need to make her his own.

He swooped her up, holding her tight against his chest, and with a throaty laugh her arms wound around his neck. Her lips, seeking the hollow of his throat, fired his blood like a torch touching tinder as he carried her to the bed. They sank down together, his kisses drawing soft, ecstatic sighs from her throat. Her answering passion matched the building crescendo of his heartbeat. Easing back, he removed his boots and shirt, his eyes feasting on her hair spread in wild abandon on the pillow, her parted, tremulous lips, and her half-closed eyes enticing as an enchantress. He wanted her more desperately than he had wanted any woman in years. The May evening cloaked them in its sultry warmth as he rolled to bring her beneath him. The single tie at the neck of her shift loosened, he drew the garment down to her hips. All at once she stiffened, her body becoming rigid.

'Jake, wait!' She struggled to sit up, her voice rising with alarm.

Anger speared him at the callousness of her denial, bringing with it a cruel echo from his past. 'Sblood, Rebecca! What devilry is this? Temptress you may be, but I warn you, I'll not stand for your wicked sport!'

'What wicked sport?' She looked at him as though his wits had addled. 'What are you accusing me of now? Can you not smell smoke?' Her eyes widened as she stared up at the oak-beamed ceiling. 'Dear God, the roof is on fire!'

CHAPTER SIX

SMOKE rolled like charcoal clouds down from the roof-beams, the accompanying crackle of flames growing with menace. Jake leapt from the bed, hauling Rebecca with him. 'Stay calm and keep close to me.'

He snatched up his sword-belt from the coffer, an instinctive move for a soldier, while she fumbled with one hand to pull her shift up over her breasts, the thickening smoke already clawing at her throat and stinging her eyes as they raced out on to the landing. The heat hit her like a furnace, the orange flames already licking the oak beams above their heads. The dry thatch was spreading the fire dangerously fast. Her knees buckled, her shaking legs refusing to obey her will to flee.

'Don't falter, Becky,' Jake choked out, his arm supportive about her waist as he propelled her forward. 'The roof will go at any minute.'

The heat was suffocating. Rebecca coughed and her eyes streamed, blinded by the smoke. Her stumbling, terrified gait was slowing Jake down. She shut her eyes, conquering her fear, and her step quickened. Sparks dropping from the roof-beams scorched her arms and neck. She clamped her mouth shut against the pain. The flight of stairs seemed endless as time became distorted by her terror. Not much further. Just a few feet away was the door. The intense heat coated her body in perspiration, making her hand slip on Jake's scalding flesh. The roar of flames was louder, matching the frantic pounding of her heart which seemed to be bursting through her chest. Dear God, they would be burned alive! She could not die—not when happiness was within her reach.

At last she felt the even floor. Another ten steps and they would escape. Her feet skated on the polished floor.

Pain shot through her ankle, as her foot tangled in the leg of an unseen stool. 'Jake!' she screamed as she pitched forward, her mind whirling in panic. The flames roared louder overhead, and an ominous creaking and tearing of wood split the air.

'Becky!' Jake rasped, his powerful hold stopping her from crashing to the floor. 'Just a few feet more. Be brave.'

The timbers creaked louder and, with a roar like an exploding cannon, a beam crashed to the ground by the fireplace. Rebecca screamed, her body ramming into Jake's back as he paused to raise the bar from the door. Another warning crack foretold a second beam about to plummet to the floor. Her nerves strung out like spun wool on a spindle. 'Dear God, spare us!' she prayed, terrified that the roof was about to fall in upon them. Suddenly, an icy blast chilled her body as Jake wrenched open the door, and together they staggered into the night.

Coughing violently, they both sank to their knees on the ground, the fresh air cooling their seared lungs and raw throats. Then Jake's hands were rough upon her, rolling her on to the dew-soaked grass. She flinched back in unexpected pain and cold.

'Be still! Your shift is alight,' he shouted, as he beat the smouldering sparks from the linen.

She fell against him, sobbing, shivering from cold after the intense heat, and reaction at their near brush with death. Jake held her close and, drawing her shift back over her arms, he fastened it at her neck.

'A few moments' more delay and we would have been roasted.' His smoke-blackened face was haggard in the blaze from the flames. 'I owe you an apology. Your quick wits saved us. Forgive me, Becky, for my harsh words.' His throat worked painfully as he gulped for air. 'There's a devil within me that gives me no peace. I have forgotten how to trust.'

'There is nothing to forgive,' she forced out through parched lips. The confession was reluctantly drawn from him and she treasured it, knowing the barriers between them were lowering.

Jake raised her up and led her to the water pump. The cool liquid tasted like nectar to her arid mouth and she splashed her face to cool its stinging heat. Jake thrust his head beneath the gushing water and then straightened and drew her to him. 'Are you all right, Becky?'

She nodded, laying her head wearily against his broad chest. 'What could have started the fire, Jake?'

'Someone with a grudge, I would guess.'

His words startled her, and she lifted her head to stare up at him. 'You mean someone deliberately set fire to the lodge?'

'How else would the roof catch fire? We survived. It's over. And look, thank God, so have Martha and Simmons.'

She saw the two servants stagger round the side of the house, having escaped by the kitchen door. Then a horse whinnied behind them, away from the stables. Rebecca turned, but her view was blocked by Jake's frame. He was still and tense and, when she moved round him, he put out a hand to hold her back. It was then she saw the rider. Holding a flaming torch aloft, Oliver Ashleigh stared at them, grim and unrepentant.

The blazing lodge made the macabre scene as bright as day. Releasing her, Jake strode forward. Even half-naked and barefoot, he was an imposing figure. He halted several feet from Oliver's horse, planting his legs solidly apart. Still holding his sword-belt, he folded his arms across his chest, his arrogant disdain a deliberate insult. 'So, the Ashleighs' have taken to murdering their own.' The quietness of his tone carried a menace more deadly than another man's anger.

'Such a statement I'd have expected from a Masters,' Oliver sneered, his eyes demon-red as they reflected the fire. He stared over Jake's head to Rebecca, his thin face uncompromising. 'I came here tonight to warn you.'

'With a firebrand in your hand?' Jake scoffed. 'If you were twenty years younger you'd answer to me with your sword.'

'Do you think I need you to give me twenty years?' He dismounted and doused the torch in the horse trough, before drawing his own ancient sword. 'I fought under Cromwell.'

Jake made no move to draw his weapon. 'I will not have my wife's grandfather's blood on my hands. Be thankful that no one was harmed this night, or I would not be so lenient. I thought even an Ashleigh had more backbone than to stoop to such a cowardly retribution!'

'Why did you do it, Grandsire?' Rebecca could no longer hold back her pain. 'I know you never loved me. But this!'

The stern lips twisted into a sneer. 'Masters did not take long to taint you. So be it. Regard me as your enemy. I make no excuses to any Masters.'

'Mount up and go, before you try my patience too far,' Jake warned. 'Monmouth's cause has need of every man. That also is something else you have forgotten in your hatred.'

Oliver heaved himself back in the saddle and glowered down at them. 'When Monmouth is King of England, then the reckoning shall be made between us, Masters.' He kicked his horse to a canter and disappeared into the darkness.

''Tis a terrible thing—terrible,' Martha sobbed. 'Thank God no one was hurt.'

Rebecca lifted her head, her cheeks burning with shame as she looked at the two bedraggled servants in their night attire, each clutching a bundle of clothes. Simmons stepped forward and held out a cloak to Rebecca, his voice apologetic as he turned to Jake. 'It's all I could save, Cap'n. Everything happened so fast.'

'It is all my fault,' Rebecca cried, a violent trembling raking her body, as her mind struggled to believe that her grandfather had tried to murder them. She flinched away from Jake's touch. 'We could all have been killed— because of a stupid, outdated feud! Why are you all being so kind? You should hate me.'

'You are not Oliver Ashleigh,' Jake said thickly, placing the cloak around her shoulders. 'Why should I blame you? You've suffered enough.'

'I don't want your pity!' Her pain and humiliation brought her voice to the edge of hysteria. 'I've brought you nothing but trouble.'

'Becca, I did not marry you out of pity.' He drew her towards him. The burning lodge behind him cast a bright halo around his figure and hid his expression from her. 'Would you let this defeat you? Property can be rebuilt. We are safe. That is all that matters for now. We will go to my uncle's house, Fair Winds. Sir Charles cannot refuse us shelter.'

Rebecca strained back from him in horror. 'No, Jake, I'll not go to Fair Winds. I am the last woman Sir Charles would accept as your bride. How can I face him like this? Reduced to wearing filthy rags because of my grandfather's hatred!'

'Sir Charles will accept you.' An underlying anger crackled through Jake's voice. 'But you're right. I will not shame you by taking you there in rags. Simmons will go to Fair Winds at first light and fetch clothes of mine which are kept there. He will explain that the lodge has burned down and my new wife is in need of suitable clothing.' He drew her away from the lodge towards the stables. 'My Aunt Henrietta and Cousin Barbara are staying there and will provide for your needs. Our stay at Fair Winds will be short. Soon I must be in London.' When she nodded her reluctant acceptance, his tone lightened in appreciation. 'Fortunately the night is warm. We will spend what is left of it in the stable.'

She pushed the unpleasant thought of her stay at Fair Winds from her mind as they climbed into the hayloft. 'Do I travel with you to London?' she asked, dreading that he meant to abandon her.

There was the barest hesitation before he answered. 'Of course, but I regret you will be left to your own amusement for much of the time. The people I meet with must be seen secretly. It is better you are not involved.'

His words were reasonable enough, but that slight hesitation nagged at her mind. If the lodge had not burned down she doubted that he would have taken her to London. While Simmons and Martha settled in a far corner, Rebecca took off the cloak, placing it on the thickly piled straw to make a bed for Jake and herself. Lying down, she turned her back on the orange glow in the night sky, visible through a slatted, unglazed window. The heat from the burning lodge had dried her shift but a sea-cold had settled over her body.

'Try and sleep, Becky.' Jake held her in his arms as tenderly as though they were truly lovers.

'How can I sleep? I cannot believe Grandfather would try and murder us. He's a Godfearing man. Does he hate me so much?'

'Hatred can destroy even the noblest men, if they allow it. It becomes a sickness of the mind. You must think of yourself—do not let an embittered man destroy all that is fine in you.'

A painful fist of emotion locked about her throat. Jake's words were balm to her pride. But was his chivalry also a trap to deceive her? She must not forget that his devastating charm was bestowed upon all women—especially when they were in distress. It was his most effective weapon in the art of seduction. How many other women had fallen beneath its spell? The heat of his half-naked body pressed against her stirred her senses. His lovemaking had kindled a longing deep within her which remained unfulfilled, but the presence of Martha and Simmons prevented their now consummating their marriage. She eased herself on to her elbow to stare down at her husband. He lay with his free arm cradling his neck, as he stared up at the roof, apparently lost in thought. Even with his face smeared with smoke, he was devilishly handsome. Her heart tugged painfully.

'Jake,' she whispered, her pulse gambolling as he turned towards her, his eyes glimmering like opals in the moon and dying firelight. 'Do you truly not regret marrying me?'

He smiled that lazy, lopsided smile which made her heart turn somersaults. 'I begin to suspect I've taken on more than I bargained for—but no, as yet I have no regrets.' A wicked light brightened his gaze, and he drew her down to nuzzle her ear. 'How could I, when you have shown me a promise of paradise? If we were alone, sweet temptress—you would have no doubts of my pleasure.'

She lay nestled in his arms, her confused thoughts unravelling. Her hand moved across his warm, firm flesh, idly following the contour of muscles down his arm. Encountering the puckered tissue of his scar, her movement stilled. It was a forceful reminder of how little she knew about his past. Had he fought his mistress's husband? She felt him tense as though reading her thoughts. 'Is it true this scar is from a duel?'

'If I admit that, you will want to know the whole sordid story, I suppose.' The brittleness of his voice warned her to keep silent. Her heart quavered. There had been so many disillusionments tonight that, whatever pain his answer brought, she would rather face it now than later when it would be even harder to bear.

'Should I not know something of the man I married? Tom said you were wounded in a duel. He had reason to blacken your name. Would you rather I believed the worst—that you fought a man you had first cuckolded?'

'I make no excuses for my conduct.'

'I ask for none. I would rather hear the truth. We have little enough foundation upon which to build our marriage. I think you are too chivalrous for so base an act.'

Jake gave a dry, humourless laugh. 'Misplaced chivalry, my dear, earned for me disgrace and dismissal as a captain in the Royal Dragoons. A gallant husband defended a faithless trollop's honour. The Court is all your grandfather believes it to be, and worse. Men have sold their souls for power. Can you conceive of such a world where a Countess has the morals of a farmyard cat, and a young, drunken Earl takes his vanity for chivalry? The Earl challenged me—with just cause—and I fought him. When I drew first blood, honour should have been satisfied. Apparently, I misjudged the besotted fool. Had it not been for my second's warning shout, he would have run me through the back. Army life has its advantages. My reaction was fast enough to parry his blade so that it sliced my arm, but the Earl's wild lunge drove him on to my sword and left him— half a man.'

Jake watched her narrowly, his expression haughty and unapologetic. She might not approve of the life he had led at Court, but he made it clear that it was she who stood on judgement as he awaited her reaction. He had warned her to accept him as he was, and the challenge hung between them still.

She reached up and ran her finger along his stubbled jaw, its roughness making him seem less formidable and daunting. 'Had I not believed Tom had spoken in spite, I would not have married you. Thank you for being honest. The Countess must have loved you very much to risk so much.'

Jake raised a sardonic brow. 'The Countess had a generous heart. I was one of her many lovers. Does that shock you?'

'I'd be lying if I said it did not. But then I am not a worldly or sophisticated woman. I believe in the sanctity of marriage.' She sat up, hugging her knees to her chest, wishing that her stomach did not feel so hollow and empty. 'I suppose our marriage makes a mockery of my ideals. Only when two people love each other can they expect fidelity.'

'The role of cynic ill suits you, Becky.' He turned her to face him. 'You deserve a man far nobler than I. But I would not willingly cause you pain.'

'In the circumstances I can expect no more. Did you not ask me to accept you as you are? I will strive to do that.'

'Blood and nails, did I, in my arrogance, say that?' A light shimmered in his eyes. 'I do not deserve you, temptress mine.'

The gallantry was back in his voice, and, reprobate or not, his confidence cheered her. He was her husband and her first loyalty was to him. Her grandfather's cruel attempt to murder them in their beds had released her from his command to spy on Jake. Her conscience in that respect eased, she lay down at his side and, exhausted, she drifted into sleep. But not to rest: her dreams were disturbed by images of Fair Winds and Sir Charles's sinister, hazy figure, looming up to threaten her chance of happiness.

Jake continued to stare up at the rafters, his mind chasing the ghostly shadows which haunted him. Marriage to Rebecca had seemed an easy means to gain the trust of the Dissenters' closely knit community. Now he was not so sure. He knew it would take little effort on his part to make Becky fall in love with him. He shied away from hurting her. She deserved better. He was already torn by the conflicting ties of friendship, and he did not want further complications in his life. Moreover, his role in London would be more hazardous because of Rebecca's presence.

When this was all over he would return to Maryland with the land grant he had waited so long to achieve. But land was only a part of the future he planned, and he needed wealth to establish the estate in the New World he had always dreamed of owning. Any thoughts of taking a second wife had set the prospect some years in the future, and been mercenary in nature, involving a rich heiress like his cousin Barbara, whom Sir Charles had for the last year been advocating as his bride. He had married once for love and it had been a disaster, leaving him cynical and disillusioned. Never again would he allow his emotions to rule his head.

He frowned, assessing his immediate future. His marriage to Becky was likely to bring an end to the generous allowance Sir Charles had settled upon him while he was in England. Fortunately, over the years he had become an accomplished cardplayer, his winnings supplementing his meagre Captain's pay, and in the last few years he had begun to invest those winnings by entering into a partnership with his brothers. Three times a year his brothers' ships docked in England and Jake procured the merchandise which would bring a vast profit when resold in Maryland and Virginia. Although he would need every penny of those profits one day to stock his

land and build upon it the grand house he envisaged, he
had always been generous to his mistresses—as he intended to be generous in providing for Becky now. When
they returned to the West of England, as he knew they
must, he could afford to rent a house where she might
stay, and his London house, which had been part of
Anne's dowry and which had been retained in England
as an investment, would serve his needs now as it had
in the past.

A familiar ache thrust like a sword through him,
catching him off guard as, unbidden, an image of Anne
returned to haunt him. He shut it out. Hell's breath!
Would she never give him peace? In death the torment
she subjected him to was more cruel than ever it had
been during her life.

She had been an angel of beauty, captivating him with
her vivacious nature, craving love and attention. She had
been provocative and innocent, and at seventeen he had
been wildly in love with her. His parents and Sir Charles
had been delighted with the match, for it was with that
very prospect that Anne, recently orphaned, had been
lavishly dowered and sent to Maryland. Her considerable
fortune meant nothing to Jake. He had married Anne
because he'd loved her. Too late, he had realised that
her childish innocence was no act but cruel reality, com-
mitting him to a private hell.

Rebecca stood in the light oak-panelled hall at Fair
Winds, the cold from the black and white marble floor
seeping through her tight satin shoes. She had not been
warm since she had insisted in bathing in the icy water
of the stream behind the lodge, and it had taken half a
dozen rinses to get the smoke and grime from her hair.
Nervously, she smoothed the bodice of the lilac silk dress
provided by Jake's cousin, her nose wrinkling with distaste. Once the dress had been beautiful, but now it smelt
sourly of stale sweat and a sweet, sickly perfume. The
torn, once white lace at the elbows was grey; and ancient
grease and wine-stains, blackened by mildew spots,
showed the dress had long been discarded from wear by
the owner—and she suspected that even this dirty cast-

off had been sent with ill grace to an Ashleigh. To her further mortification the gown hung loose, and was as unflattering as a flour-sack about her slender figure; worse, it did not even decently cover her ankles.

'I look like a farthing whore.' She could not contain her distress. 'It has been done deliberately to shame me before Sir Charles.'

There was a grim anger about Jake's mouth as he acknowledged the insult shown her, but his almond-shaped eyes sparkled incorrigibly. 'Sir Charles is ever one to appreciate the trimness of an ankle. And Barbara could never have known that this dress exactly matches the colour of your eyes, making them more luminous and beautiful than ever.'

A door opened on their right and a pompous-looking servant in green livery approached Jake. 'Sir Charles will see you now. Alone.'

'Sir Charles will see both myself and my wife,' Jake corrected firmly, and, linking Rebecca's arm through his, strode through the door. She glimpsed a large, spacious salon, its white walls hung with red, blue and gold tapestries, depicting half-naked heathen gods which would have roused the wrath of her grandfather. With no time to inspect them further, Rebecca saw no sin in their opulent beauty, their rich colours making the room cosy and, were it not for Sir Charles's presence, inviting.

Sir Charles Masters waited behind a massive, ornately carved desk. At fifty his slim body was unbowed and although his complexion was pale, his striking, finely drawn face was unlined and still handsome.

'Sir Charles, I proudly present my wife, Rebecca,' Jake announced before the baronet could speak. 'We should have called on you before this, but I am sure you will understand our wish to be alone for our first days of wedded life.'

'Out of Christian charity I have offered you shelter after the fire. That does not mean I will suffer this creature in my presence.'

'If my wife is not welcome, then neither am I,' Jake retorted, the rigid muscles of his arm beneath Rebecca's fingers betraying the effort it was costing him to control his temper.

Sir Charles's lips drew back in a sneer. 'Your concubine, more like. From what I heard that was no true wedding—not by the rites of our Church of England. I know Ashleigh's game. He's in league with those who seek to depose King James, but the wily old stoat covers his tracks well. Once I've proof, he'll rot in gaol for his treachery. Did he truly think I would be swayed by his forcing you to marry this chit? You were tricked!'

Rebecca bit her lip to stop a sharp defence bursting from her lips. If Jake could appear calm then so would she, and her pride needed to know whether Jake would reveal the true reasons he had married her. Sir Charles was the head of his family, and from odd words Martha had dropped about their relationship it seemed they had been closer than he had implied when she first met him.

'I was forced into nothing. I am married,' Jake said, with a quietness which was unnerving. 'Accept it, Sir Charles. Or I leave this house, never to return.'

The grey eyes narrowed as Sir Charles fought to control his anger. Only the pinched whiteness ringing the flaring nostrils of his long, hooked nose showed his inner battle. Whatever Sir Charles's faults, it was clear he loved Jake. Again in control of himself, he turned to Rebecca, his voice silky with false sweetness as he moved to stand in front of her.

'Your pardon, Mistress Masters. Welcome to Fair Winds.' He raised her hand to his lips, but his smile did not touch his winter-bleak eyes, nor did his mouth touch her skin before he dropped her hand. He turned to Jake. 'Now had you not better explain how my hunting lodge was burned to the ground?'

'Who knows how these fires start? It was an accident.'

Rebecca felt a rush of relief that Jake had not involved her grandfather, but the reminder that the lodge belonged to Sir Charles was bitter.

'An accident! Surely not, when Ashleigh was reported in the vicinity by my gamekeeper?'

'He came to bring Rebecca's clothes. Which proved rather unfortunate in the circumstances, since they too were destroyed in the fire.'

'Unfortunate indeed.' Sir Charles's cool glance swept disparagingly over Rebecca's figure. 'It appears your Cousin Barbara has provided rather inadequately for Mistress Masters. She left with her mother within an hour of hearing the news that you had married. Your cousin was distraught. It was wrong of you to treat Barbara so shabbily, Jake. It was as good as arranged you two were to wed.'

Jake stiffened. 'I had agreed merely to consider the matter. That was before I met Rebecca.'

Rebecca twisted the emerald ring on her finger, trying to keep calm in the face of the baronet's hostility. She saw Sir Charles stare at her hand, his lips whitening with anger.

'Indeed!' Sir Charles roared. 'Would you have me believe this marriage is a love-match? I know you too well, Jake. After Anne that would be impossible!'

Rebecca bit harder into her lip, an unexpected stab of jealousy catching her off guard. It was one thing to know Jake did not love her, and that her marriage was a sham, but it was quite another to have Sir Charles throw it in her face.

Jake's hand tightened over hers, his voice low with warning, 'That *you* chose not to marry after the death of the Lady Jane does not mean *I* intend to spend the rest of my days alone. Rebecca is my chosen bride. That will be the last which is spoken upon the matter.'

Hatred smouldered in Sir Charles's eyes as he stared at Rebecca. Her head came up, her pride matching her husband's. Jake had risked his kinsman's anger to defend her. Drawing herself to her full height, she spoke with a gentle firmness. 'Whatever you think of me, Sir Charles, I wish only to be worthy of the honour Jake has bestowed upon me.'

Those wintry eyes touched her with an icy sleet, and with a brief nod he nodded his acceptance. He picked up several papers from his desk. 'More suitable garments will be found for you—Barbara left most of her wardrobe behind since she left in such a rush. Mistress Masters will need to rest after her ordeal. I will speak with you in an hour, Jake. First, I have a report to send to London.'

The interview over, Jake led Rebecca from the salon. A liveried servant approached to guide them to their rooms, but Jake waved him away and, slowing his pace, drew her to a window overlooking the low hedges of the formal garden.

'Did I not say Sir Charles would come round?' He flashed her a smile that caused a tight bud of emotion to unfurl like a rose blossom and fill her with a heady sweetness. 'And you refused to let him get the better of you. That makes you a very exceptional woman.'

'You flatter me. I believe in speaking up for my rights. I will not be daunted by Sir Charles's petty tyranny.' She knew Sir Charles had not accepted their marriage, but she was too happy at Jake's heated defence to wish to spoil the moment by voicing her doubts. She was rewarded by the deepening respect which brightened his hazel eyes. It was that which gave her the strength to face any trial Sir Charles might set upon her.

Uncomfortably aware that the feelings in her heart must be shining in her eyes, she looked down at the ring on her finger, twisting it so that the stone caught the sunlight. The glittering emerald reminded her of the flecks in Jake's eyes when he was angry, but then, as the sun's rays reflected golden upon it, it resembled the warmth of his eyes when he was teasing and at his most charming.

'Does the ring trouble you?' There was a guardedness in his voice. 'Once in London I will have it changed for something more suitable.'

'Oh, no!' she cried, appalled. Though it was cumbersome she would never change the ring. It had become special to her—a talisman. 'It's just a little large,' she answered, and, suddenly recalling Sir Charles's anger when he had noticed her wearing it, she asked, 'But perhaps this ring is special to you, or your family, and

you would rather I did not wear it?' She made to remove
the ring, but Jake stopped her.

'Keep it for now. The ring was my grandfather's, given
to him by Queen Henrietta in reward for his loyal service.'

'Then it is not fitting I wear it,' she insisted, her sense
of right overriding her own attachment to the ring. 'It
has a very special significance to your family.'

He looked sidelong at her, the lean contours of his
face stiffening. 'Must you question my every action?
Your courage has proved you worthy to wear it.'

'Sir Charles does not think so.' Her stare held his
levelly. 'And I do not want to be the cause of dissent
between you. He cares for you very much. Perhaps in
time he will accept our marriage, but my presence here
is a thorn in his side. The wound will heal quicker if we
do not stay.'

Jake saw the strain in the dark circles beneath her eyes,
and relented. To antagonise Sir Charles would only make
matters worse, and staying at Fair Winds would do little
to win for him the trust of the Dissenters. He took
Rebecca's hands and drew her close. 'I will speak with
my uncle and ask for the loan of a carriage. You and
Martha will begin the journey to London today—once
Martha has found a more suitable gown for you, and
altered it accordingly. I will catch up with you on the
road, in a day or two, when my duties here can be left
to Skevington.'

'Does Sir Charles suspect your allegiance to
Monmouth?' Rebecca surprised him by asking. She
missed little with her sharp eyes.

Since the lodge had burned down he had no choice
but to take her with him to London. It was a compli-
cation he could have done without, but he masked his
concern with a wry smile. 'He knows I mean to return
to Maryland. In any event, our family learnt from the
mistake of having all its members on one side during the
Forties. We lost everything until the Restoration. In times
of conflict a wise family covers every eventuality, else
they will forfeit their land. Should Monmouth succeed,
I will be in a position to act as mediator for Sir Charles.

Kings come and go, but the land stays the same, and with the land comes power.'

'And if the rising fails—will Sir Charles come to *your* aid?' A quiver entered her musical voice. 'Or will you face imprisonment and death, as will others loyal to the cause you profess to uphold?'

Jake controlled his temper with difficulty. Did the wench presume to judge him? What could a woman know of politics, or of the pain of siding with one friend against another? 'You forget I could die in battle. Then you will be free of this marriage.' He concealed his misgivings under a cloak of sarcasm. 'I do not contemplate failure. In London I work to secure the throne for our just monarch.'

For a long week Rebecca endured the bone-rattling carriage journey to London. They had crossed the river at Staines, and were now approaching Kensington, only two miles from London itself, and already Rebecca fancied she could see the church spires of London rising like conical wizards' hats on the horizon. Yet still Jake had not caught up with them, though surely a man on horseback could make better speed than the ponderous coach.

'Not much further now, mistress,' Martha said tiredly from the seat opposite.

A wild shout from outside jerked both women upright, their faces paling with sudden fear. The carriage swayed violently as it rolled to an abrupt halt.

'Heaven save us, 'tis a highwayman!' Martha wailed.

Rebecca drew the flintlock pistol Jake had given her as protection on the road, her hand shaking as she eased back the safety hammer. A tall figure wrenched open the door, his body blocking out the sunlight.

'Stand back, sir,' she shouted, her courage seeping as she noted the twin pistols stuck into the tasselled scarlet waistcloth tied over a tan leather jerkin. Ignoring her, the man placed his foot on the floor, preparing to enter. Inside the cuff of the black leather boot, she saw the handle of a dagger. 'Get back, I say. Or I'll shoot.'

'Blood and nails, Becky! Is that any way to greet your husband?'

For a long moment she stared at him in disbelief. His long hair was tied back, his face partially hidden under a deep-brimmed hat. Then he grinned, that uniquely disarming smile, and with a shaky laugh, she secured the safety catch and dropped the pistol into her lap.

'Jake, you gave me such a fright. I thought you were a highwayman about to rob us!'

'And short shrift you would have given me if I were,' he laughed, flopping down on the seat at her side.

Martha stood up from the opposite corner. 'I'll finish the journey with the driver up top,' she volunteered, leaving them alone in the carriage, as she ran to greet Simmons who was astride his own horse while he held Jake's.

Jake put his long legs on the opposite seat, a tired sigh escaping him. 'Very tactful, is Martha.' He had difficulty stifling a yawn, and his eyes began to droop. 'Your pardon, Becky...' His voice was slurred with fatigue. 'I've been thirty hours on the road without a rest.' His chin fell forward on to his chest, the evenness of his breathing telling her he was already asleep.

She smiled tenderly down at him. It was hardly the romantic reunion she had envisaged. She removed his hat and put her arm around him, drawing his head down more comfortably upon her breast. The trees and pastures outside gave way to thickening houses, and after the peace of the countryside the streets of London roared with noise and vigour, like a deafening collage of people.

Rich damask and satin vied with brightly dyed linen and worsted, or appallingly filthy rags. Women paraded in scarlet cloaks and black hoods, the wealthier painted and patched, their elaborate curls topped by wide-brimmed hats trimmed extravagantly with ribbons or feathers. Beside them, the men were just as resplendent, swaggering along on high red-heeled shoes, a long walking cane in one hand and either a large lace handkerchief or scented pomander in the other. But there were also the poor in drab clothes, their bodies running with sores. It seemed everyone was shouting to make themselves heard above the rumble of carts, the cries of the street-sellers, and the hammering of stonemasons and carpenters. While the noise jarred her ears, and the bright colours were garish to her eyes, the stench of urine, unwashed bodies, rotting garbage, and decaying rats and cats left uncleared in the gutters, was nauseating.

Rebecca sank back on to the upholstered seat, holding a handkerchief to her nose. At her side Jake stirred, but did not wake from his exhausted sleep. Outside there was still evidence of rebuilding after the fire which had devastated the city nearly twenty years before. Many of the churches, like the rising walls of St Paul's, were still covered with scaffolding as the masons worked on Sir Christopher Wren's designs.

Yet, despite the noise and squalor, there was a magical excitement running through the crowded streets. London was alive, the pulsating heart of her country, more diverse than any other city in England—where the rich looked wealthier and the poor, God help them, looked even more wretched. She absorbed it all in the slow passage through the crowded streets, until at last the carriage halted by a fashionable row of three-storey gabled houses not far from St James's Park.

Jake sat up, passing a hand across his eyes. 'What a churl you must think me for falling asleep!'

She was amazed at the vitality which was back in his voice after so short a sleep. 'You drive yourself as though you had the strength of five men. You are but human.'

'Human indeed, sweet temptress.' His eyes sparkled with devilment as the driver opened the door for them to alight. Jake took her hands and raised them reverently to his lips, his voice low and conspiring. 'And I have a wife I have, as yet, not made truly my own. The afternoon will be ours, Becky. Then I will send a seamstress to you while I attend a meeting in the City.'

Alighting, he helped her from the carriage, tucked her hand firmly through his arm, and led her up the steps to the open door of the house. Three maids and two male servants lined the entrance hall, their faces no more than a blur as Rebecca was overawed by the size of the house. They seemed to be expected; clearly a messenger had overtaken them on the road. Four doors led off the hall and an ornate, carved staircase rose up from its centre.

Suddenly Jake's step faltered and she heard his sharp intake of breath. Looking askance at him, she saw the usual composure stripped from his greying face, his bloodless lips compressed into an agonised line and his eyes glittering with a feral light. She lifted her gaze to follow his. On the curve in the landing, haloed by sunlight streaming through a glazed window, stood the most beautiful woman she had ever seen, gowned in a misty confection of white lace and silk. Then, with a start, she realized it was not a woman standing there, like the mistress of the household receiving her guests—it was a portrait.

'Why has that portrait been placed there?' Jake rapped out.

A portly butler smiled and came forward. 'It arrived this morning with the messenger from Sir Charles, with instructions to place it where it is. It is his wedding present to you.'

Jake turned his back on the portrait, his voice hard. 'Have it taken down.' His glance flickered coldly over Rebecca. 'You will be tired after your journey. Martha will show you to your chambers.' With a wooden bow he turned on his heel, marched into a book-lined room and shut the door firmly behind him.

Puzzled and hurt by Jake's brusque manner, Rebecca looked again at the portrait which had caused such a change in him. The sunlight brought the young woman to life. She must have been no more than fifteen or sixteen when it had been painted, and it was a portrait of sweet innocence: her willowy figure was as petite as a fairy queen, and her spun-gold hair and cornflower blue eyes would have been the envy of a blessed angel. Without being told, she knew it was Anne Masters. Her heart squeezed, the pain twisting deep inside her. After

so many days apart from Jake, when he had filled her
waking and sleeping hours, she knew she had fallen in
love with him. From such a rival—an unattainable ghost,
at that—could she ever hope to wrest Jake's love?

CHAPTER SEVEN

'IT WAS heartless of Sir Charles to have the portrait hung in the hall.' Martha looked worriedly towards the closed door where Jake had disappeared, and she touched Rebecca's arm, indicating they should go upstairs.

Rebecca studied the image of Anne. 'She was very beautiful.'

'Her beauty was not of this world, so Simmons says,' Martha commented. 'She was a tiny, demure creature, like a fairy flower and just as fragile. This was her parents' house. When they died, Sir Charles, as her guardian, sent Anne to America. It was his wish she marry Master Jake.'

'Do not try and spare my feelings,' Rebecca stressed, needing to know the truth. 'Jake loved her very much, didn't he?'

Martha looked searchingly at Rebecca and nodded. 'From the start all the family knew it was a love-match, so Simmons says. But it's from what he doesn't say that I wonder if all was not as it seemed.' Martha clamped her mouth shut, clearly wishing she had not said so much. 'The Captain has been alone too long,' she stated emphatically. 'He needs a spirited woman to share his life, not a spirit woman. It must have been a shock for him to see Mistress Anne like a ghost greeting him on the stairs, and he so exhausted after being in the saddle for hours. Simmons can hardly stand.'

'I am thoughtless, Martha. Send one of the maids to see to my needs while you tend to your husband.' Rebecca paused on the stairs, noticing two male servants about to lift the portrait from the wall. 'Leave it where it is. This was Mistress Anne's house. Her portrait has a right to be here. I would not have it taken down on my account.'

She followed Martha to the first-floor landing and they entered a bright, sun-filled chamber. The pale lavender brocade bed-hangings and curtains trimmed in heavy lace were softly feminine.

'Was this Anne's room?' Rebecca asked, feeling suddenly uncomfortable.

'No. It was her mother's,' Martha explained. 'That door leads to your dressing-room, which connects with the Captain's room on the far side.'

Rebecca hid her shock that Jake would not be sharing the same room as herself, realising then that the ways of the gentry were not the same as those of country folk, used to whole families sleeping in a single room. In a fine house like this the mode of life was more stately. Martha moved to the door. 'I'll have a bath brought up for you.'

'Thank you, that will be most welcome.' Rebecca looked down at the sage silk travelling gown she was wearing. 'I shall be glad when the gowns borrowed from Barbara Masters can be returned. The seamstress will be arriving later. I want no reminders of Sir Charles's charity in my new life.'

Alone in the room, Rebecca moved to the gilt-framed Venetian looking glass, and ran her hands through her thick, unruly dark hair. The elegant style, swept up off her face to fall in soft ringlets about her shoulders, left her unimpressed. The scratches from her wild dash through the woods had faded and her face had escaped any marks from the fire, but she could never match Anne Masters for beauty. Her eyes were too large, a strange violet-grey instead of a warm and inviting cornflower-blue. And those high cheekbones, accentuated by scandalously long black lashes and full red lips, made her look more like a half-wild gypsy than a gently bred lady. She turned away from the reflection, disheartened. She was the opposite in looks, height and temperament to all that Jake had loved in his first wife.

The arrival of the bath and several servants carrying pails of hot water deflected her thoughts. She bathed quickly, thinking she heard movements from Jake's rooms, and, once dressed, sent the young maid away, while she expectantly waited for Jake to come to her. A tray of food arrived and a table was laid. The sounds in the next room stilled, but Jake did not appear. She waited, her blood congealing, as the spicy sauce on the hot chicken slowly solidified, and the light, fluffy pies crumbled in upon themselves and turned leathery with cold.

Martha came in. 'You've not touched your food! Master Jake sends his regrets, but he has been urgently called away. He said he would be back before dark. The seamstress is below—shall I send her up?'

'I've a headache, Martha,' Rebecca lied, too upset by Jake's apparent rejection to face anyone. 'I could not stand the woman fussing around me. Send her away; she can call another day.'

'The master will be furious. He paid her handsomely to call today, and has ordered a dozen gowns to be made, three to be delivered without delay. The woman is the most popular seamstress at Court.'

Rebecca sighed. It would be churlish to refuse to see the seamstress, and her position as Jake's wife demanded she dress in a manner which would not shame him. 'My husband is generous. Please show her up.'

Jake had not expected to be summoned immediately upon his return to London. That he had, almost within an hour of his arrival, meant his house was being watched. The knowledge did not surprise him, but it nevertheless rankled. He looked round the study he had been shown into, noting the inevitable confusion of maps, papers, dismantled pistols and other accoutrements of war. An inner door opened and a man of medium height entered, his body honed to slenderness from the diligence of his military duties.

'Captain Masters, you are prompt in responding to my request. How is your arm?'

'My wound is healing and will not incapacitate me, my lord.'

John Churchill nodded, his grey-green eyes piercing as a falcons, yet revealing nothing of his thoughts. 'This marriage of yours, Captain. It was rather unexpected, was it not? And complicates your duties in the West of England.'

'It was necessary,' Jake answered warily, his expression as blank as his commander's. Long ago he had seen the effectiveness of Churchill's long silences, which had drawn many a lesser man to indiscreet remarks. There was little Churchill could teach him now, in a game of nerves and intrigue. The pause established between them that Jake would not be drawn, but, since he had nothing to hide, he allowed his guard to drop, his manner assured and confident. 'Does not the success of my mission depend upon my winning the trust of the Dissenters? My marriage into one of their families assured that, but...' He smiled wryly at his commander and acknowledged honestly, 'When you meet my wife, you will see I have made no self-sacrifice.'

'In that, at least, I am glad for you, my friend.' John Churchill relaxed his guard, but his eyes remained serious. 'Yet I sense that the role of His Majesty's emissary sits ill upon your shoulders.'

Jake sheathed a burst of anger. 'I agreed to act the King's informer out of friendship to Monmouth, who, as usual, has allowed himself to be ill-advised. There's no denying that in the West he will raise a willing army— some are already calling themselves the new army of the Lord. And many an old Cromwellian instructs his sons in disciplining troops.' He spoke earnestly, as much to reconcile himself to the task he had been allotted as to convince his commander. The scar along his arm ached, mocking him. But for his wound, he would be serving his King more honourably. 'Although their numbers are swelling, Monmouth's proposed landing is ill-timed. I am convinced he cannot succeed. I would save Monmouth from putting his head in the block in any way I can.'

'Your loyalty to Monmouth is commendable, but take care others do not see it as treason to King James—especially His Majesty himself. Unrest is growing; too many people are suspicious of the King's religion, and His Majesty grows wary.'

'His Majesty is no longer young,' Jake rationalised. 'Without a male heir, his Protestant daughter Mary will soon rule this land.'

John Churchill picked up a silver powder flask which was being used as a paperweight, and frowned at the broken stopper. Outwardly he appeared unconcerned, but Jake sensed he was deeply troubled. 'Our Catholic queen is still young. What if she should produce a son?' Churchill shot Jake a hard look, needing no words to convince Jake that a son born to King James would be a disaster for England. The Popish Plot in recent years still festered in people's minds, their suspicions fed by Titus Oates' insinuations that even King James had been involved in the Catholics' plans to poison the late King; if reminders were needed, Oates himself was on trial for perjury this very week.

Jake watched Churchill put down the powder flask and pace the room. A few years older than himself, his commanding officer was rapidly rising and Jake believed he was destined to greater glory. He was hungry for power, but had the knack of winning a fierce loyalty and respect from his troops. Until now Churchill had been unswerving in his duty to King James.

Churchill stood by the desk, his voice resolute. 'Princess Mary must succeed her father. She and her husband are fierce Protestants. Indeed, William of Orange sees himself as the champion of the Protestant cause in Europe. He may support Monmouth now, to test the feeling of the people in England, but I doubt he would tolerate a usurper sitting upon his wife's throne. Monmouth is an unfortunate pawn...' He looked levelly at Jake, his handsome face pale and grim as he continued. 'If Monmouth lands, I will be commanding the army sent to destroy him.'

Churchill paused. The harsh glare from the afternoon sun, full upon his face, showed Jake the dark shadows beneath his eyes. Did Churchill, like himself, remember the days when Monmouth had been high in favour? As a young cornet newly arrived in England, Jake had first met the Duke when he was fêted as the King's favoured son. He had been gradually drawn into Monmouth's circle, had served under him in France and Scotland, and, as he proved himself a notable huntsman and sportsman, at both of which Monmouth excelled, they had become close friends. In the earlier years, before Churchill had married, Jake knew his commander had also been a rake-hell and a friend of Monmouth, though always loyal to James, then Duke of York.

Churchill cleared his throat and went on gruffly. 'For all his pleasure-loving ways, Monmouth is a brave and courageous soldier. He has always been popular with the people. If he lands—Royal bastard or not—the charm he inherited from his father will have people flocking to his standard—and this time his courage will be charged by desperation. Better the rebellion is crushed before it can begin... and men do not die for a cause which is already doomed. I want you to return to the West Country.'

A knock at the door was followed by the entry of an aide. 'His Majesty bids you attend upon him at the palace, my lord.'

Churchill gathered some papers from his desk and walked with Jake to the door. 'We will talk more on this later. A week is all the time you have to collect what information you can in London. Make contact with any whose names you have discovered this afternoon. It is better if next time we meet it is in secret.'

Rebecca was relieved when the seamstress finally left, her head now throbbing with an ingrained headache from the woman's constant gossiping. Jake had clearly spared no expense in instructing the seamstress to provide a complete wardrobe for her; and a riding habit, a day and an evening gown were to be delivered within two days. Yet Jake's generosity did not ease the pain of his rejection, and, left alone, Rebecca restlessly paced the bedchamber. The room darkened as the sun disappeared over the opposite rooftops. Her pacing continued, her mind too active to settle even though her body began to tire. Time and again the night watch passed beneath her window, crying out the hour. Had he passed once, or twice, since she thought she had heard Jake return? The house had fallen into silence, the servants having retired for the night. But sleep for her was impossible, and with each passing hour her anger grew.

She drummed her fingers on the carved bedpost. She could either accept her marriage for the hollow shell it was, she inwardly raged, or she could fight to win Jake's love. For whatever reasons of his own Jake had married her she had no intention of spending her married life in the shadow of Anne Masters. Rebecca picked up a brush and, releasing the long night braids, she stood before the looking-glass. Her eyes sparkled with determination as she brushed her hair until it shone with mahogany glints in the candlelight. She would await Jake's pleasure no longer.

The reflection staring back at her was far from the demure Puritan maid of a week ago. Over her nightshift she wore a midnight-blue silk dressing-robe Jake had given her, the wide sash of the robe tied high under her breasts, accentuating their fullness and the smallness of her waist. She turned sideways, critically surveying her slender figure, and a smile played over her lips. While covering her completely, the robe moulded to every movement of her body, revealing the outline of her hips and legs as she walked. She could not hope to match Anne Masters in ethereal beauty, but, before the fire had interrupted their lovemaking, Jake had shown her she was a woman capable of passion. She would go to him as she had that night at the lodge and, surely, dressed like this she could not fail to rouse his desire.

You play the courtesan! an inner voice mocked her. She ruthlessly smothered it. Jake was her husband, and tonight she was determined to supplant Anne Masters' ghost in his heart.

Her decision made, she picked up a candle and moved silently through the house, the flickering light dimly revealing the polished floor and carved panelling. Halfway down the stairs she saw that the portrait of Anne Masters

had been removed, and her step quickened with anticipation. A light visible under the library door guided her
like a beacon, her heartbeat wild and erratic, and her
blood racing hot with excitement, even as the idea of
her brazenness sent a *frisson* of trepidation through her.
She was a woman fighting for her rights—fighting to
win the love of her husband.

At the low rumble of Jake's voice carrying to her, her
hand froze on the door-handle. He was not alone. But
who could he be entertaining at this time of night? Her
curiosity was stirred, but she had no wish to confront
Jake and his guest in her present state of undress. The
voices stopped, and with a start she jumped back, her
foot brushing against a pedestal. The marble bust it held
toppled, rattling alarmingly before she managed to steady
it. A sudden rush of air from the library door as it opened
blew out her candle, making her draw further back into
the shadows.

Momentarily Jake was silhouetted against the candlelight behind him. Then he moved swiftly. But her
presence was betrayed by the paleness of her skin reflecting the dim light, and her arm was roughly grabbed,
the sharp jab of a dagger blade pressing threateningly
against her ribs as she was dragged forward into the
brighter light.

'Sblood, Becky!' Jake swore in exasperation, lowering the dagger but keeping a firm hold upon her arm.
'I warned you not to sneak up on me. I thought you
were an intruder—but then I had forgotten you have a
tendency to prowl the house and waylay unsuspecting
men in the dark of night.'

The sharp edge to his tone belied his teasing words,
and the fact that he made no excuses for neglecting her
all day cut her to the bone. Conquering her hurt pride,
she summoned an inviting smile.

'I had not thought I would need to seek you out so
blatantly, my husband, but——' Her voice withered to
a croak when she saw Anne's portrait propped against
a wall in the room behind Jake, the candle burning on
the shelf at its side making a shrine of the life-sized

figure. Her body turned cold and rigid as marble as she strained back from his hold, her tone scathing. 'I see you have shut yourself away to grieve for your first wife. I could forgive you much, Jake—especially your love and devotion for Anne—but I cannot forgive you for insulting me before your entire household. I will intrude no further upon your memories.'

She pulled back, but Jake's arm was a vice about her waist. 'I did not mean to wound you, Becky. Far from it.' His voice was low and sincere. 'Only duty could have dragged me from your side today. Things are not as they appear. Trust me.'

She hardened her heart against his persuasive charm, but the image of Anne Masters mocked her from behind Jake's figure, and goaded her anger past reason. 'I know what is before my eyes. You do not love me, but I had hoped you had the decency not to subject me to this! At the lodge I was fool enough to think our enforced marriage could have a semblance of normality. It's not a wife you need, Jake, but a whore, and for that any woman can serve your needs.'

Jake abruptly released her, his voice low and contemptuous. 'Not all men are slaves to their desire.' His words were cut short by the sound of a footfall in the library. A man adjusting a black silk mask over his face moved into Rebecca's sight. Her heart dropped to the pit of her stomach. Jake had not been closeted alone with his wife's portrait. She had gravely misjudged him.

'I have kept you too long from your bride, Masters.' The stranger's voice was cool and authoritative. 'It is unforgivable of me.'

Behind the half-mask grey-green eyes studied her shrewdly. The elegant brown periwig and dark blue velvet suit, trimmed lavishly with gold thread, proclaimed him a man of wealth, possibly even a courtier, but what struck her most was the same forceful, self-possessed quality as Jake exuded, which made such men natural leaders—men determined to shape their own destinies.

'Allow me to present my wife, Rebecca.' Jake took charge, his tone respectful towards his companion.

'Rebecca, this is...' There was the barest pause, and Rebecca's heightened senses tuned to the air of conspiracy between the two men even as Jake went on smoothly, 'This is John—an old friend from my army days.'

'It is a pleasure to meet you, sir.' She felt uncomfortable, her instincts warning her that this was no ordinary acquaintance of Jake's and her husband was deliberately keeping his identity from her. 'Your pardon for my intrusion. I did not realise my husband was entertaining. I will leave you gentlemen to finish your talk.'

The stranger held up his hand in protest and bowed to her. 'The hour is late. It is I who will take my leave.' He turned to Jake. 'I will not keep you any longer from your lovely and charming wife. It is easy to see why you married in haste.' His taunting voice lowered, carrying what sounded like a warning to Rebecca's tightly coiled nerves. 'I trust that being so newly wed will not distract you from visiting old friends while in London.'

'When have I ever forgotten my friends?' Jake parried the barbed retort as he escorted his companion to the door. He suppressed a flash of resentment that Churchill felt the need to test him, and his voice cooled. 'Shall I summon you a sedan?'

'No.' John Churchill paused by the door, his glance returning to Rebecca. He added softly, 'Your wife has spirit. In view of her grandfather's sympathies, has she any idea of our plans?'

'None. It is better that way.'

Jake was subjected to a long, assessing stare before his commander answered, 'You cannot always keep her in ignorance. Take care, Captain Masters. You wife has that rare quality of innocence and hidden fire which can ensnare a man before he realises how skilfully the web has been woven around him. Are you sure your loyalty is not already torn?'

'Do you doubt my honour?' Jake challenged, affronted. 'My loyalty has not changed.'

Churchill nodded. 'Then I wish you success. I trust your loyalty will not cost that which you most desire. I doubt your heart is as hardened as you profess.' His eyes shone with momentary candour, allowing his guard to slide. 'If you have won the love of such a woman, cherish it. Though, in the circumstances, I doubt not that the road will be stormy and fraught with more strategy than the fiercest battle.'

Rebecca watched the two men bid farewell with misgivings. Why did the stranger wear a mask? And Jake—he had been evasive in his introduction. Distrust flared through her. Was Jake then King James's spy? Her heart cramped. She wanted to believe in him, but how could she when Jake refused to confide in her?

'Wait, Rebecca!'

She ignored Jake's terse command and continued to the stairs. As her foot touched the second step, Jake caught her round her waist and spun her round. 'Let me go!' Her hands formed tight balls to beat against his chest.

He gave her a gentle shake, the metallic ring to his voice warning her of the control he was keeping upon his temper. 'For your own safety, you will hear me out.'

Her nails gouged deep furrows in her palms as she stood still, willing her heart to cease its frantic pounding. He released her and she retreated up several stairs until the dangerous narrowing of his eyes stopped her in her tracks.

'There will be many meetings here after dark, or I shall be attending them elsewhere.' His voice was low and dispassionate. 'It is why I came to London. But these meetings are not without danger. I do not want you implicated. In future you will stay in your room, and you will speak to no one of what you have seen tonight.'

'What could I tell?' she replied in hot defiance. 'You did not trust me enough to tell me your visitor's full name.' Her head lifted proudly, her eyes glittering with scorn at her own self-delusion. 'I will not make the same mistake twice, so you need not fear I will seek your company uninvited again. In public, I will, of course, act the loving and dutiful wife, if that is your wish.'

'You are generous.' Anger clipped his words as he mounted the stairs. Involuntarily, she retreated further. 'Perhaps it is time I taught you your wifely duties.'

Panic seized her. He had spoken out of anger not love. 'No, Jake! You promised me time.'

Lifting the hem of her robe, she turned and ran up the stairs, seeking the safety of her room. He caught her at the chamber door. 'You are mine, Becky.'

The candlelight from her room was full on his face, darkening the taut hollows and showing the eyes heavy-lidded with desire. She willed herself not to respond to his closeness, to his handsome face so heart-stoppingly close to her own. His lips parted in a smile, the promise it held almost disarming her. She locked her heart against its effect upon her senses, too angry to fall prey to his devastating charm.

'No, Jake! A smile and a few conciliatory words will not win me this time, or ever. Would you leave me without a shred of pride?'

The smile did not falter; it broadened, becoming a self-assured threat as his mood changed. His hand took hers, its powerful warmth drawing her inexorably closer until their bodies touched. Through the thinness of her robe, the hard muscle of his chest scorched her flesh, igniting a fuse which sent white-hot sparks darting through her veins.

'Is it pride or stubbornness which makes you deny me? I have neglected you. But I mean to change that. I warned you I would have little spare time in London.' His voice was deeper, but had lost none of its authority. He would never plead for her favours; he was demanding her submission. His hand moved languidly up and down her spine, sending ripples of delight along its length, and it needed all her will-power to continue her resistance. 'I have said I would give you time, Becky—and I meant it. But my patience, like the sands of time, is running out.'

He moved closer, his face hidden now by the shadows, but the subtle male scent of him filled her nostrils, her nerve-ends tingling with awareness of his sensuality. Despite her anger, her pulse leapt, her blood running in heated spirals up and down her spine. 'Your instincts at the lodge did not deceive you. I want you, Becky. And you would not have sought me out this night if you did not feel the same.'

'I will not be used, Jake, by you or any man.' Her voice sounded strangled as she strove to conquer the havoc he was wreaking upon her senses.

'Will you let your pride deny the magic of that night?' His fingers slid into the neck of her robe, his thumbs making seductive circles across her skin as he gently eased her head back, until every nerve in her body betrayed her, tingling with a craving that turned her bones molten and she could scarcely stand. 'I want you now, Becky, with an even deeper intensity than I wanted you at the lodge.' His rich voice was husky with desire. 'I glimpsed then what could be between us—only to have it snatched away by the fire.'

She tried to shut her mind to his persuasion, but it was impossible to deny the clamour of her blood which cried out for the fulfilment it had been denied. Her gaze linked with his, her breath suspended as his head bent over her. Then his lips were on hers and he was kissing her with a thoroughness which scattered her defences. His mouth was like silk against her skin as it moved to her eyes, her cheeks and down to the throbbing pulse in her throat. She was lost, one moment drowning in a sea of sensation, the next burning, his mouth a searing flame setting her afire. His hands slid down the hollow of her back, moulding her body to his, then moved upwards to caress her breast, his fingertips lazily stroking its sensitive peak, spreading shockwaves of pleasure through her body to detonate in her brain. The scent of him intoxicated her, and the knowledge that he desired her shattered her reserve. She clung to him, her mouth opening to taste the nectar of his breath, and she moved restlessly against him, craving the contact of his flesh, her hands tangling in the cool, velvet softness of his long hair, binding him closer.

She answered Jake kiss for kiss, their slow, explora-
tory trail slowly changing to a gathering frenzy. Beneath
its onslaught, she abandoned coherent thought or reasoning, content to succumb to the inevitable. Somehow,
without quite being aware of how, she found herself lying
on the bed, her robe and shift gone and Jake stripping
off the last of his clothing.

The moonlight silvered his body, emphasising the
contours of hard muscle and sleek, lean stomach and
hips. She had never thought of a man's body as being
beautiful, but Jake's body was the perfection God sought
when He created Adam. Her gaze revelled in the
splendour of him, her fingers explored his firm, broad
shoulders, her palms grazing over the dark tracery of
fine hair on his chest and down to the hollow of his hip.
He drew in a sharp breath and reached hungrily for her.

'Sweet temptress.' The words were an adoring caress
as his mouth sought her breast. A liquid heat fanned
through her veins, her throat aching with the fierceness
of her own desperate longing. The sensual pleasure of
his expert touch drove her to seek an answering response
in him, but she was unprepared for the ecstatic won-
derment which came with feeling his body quicken to
the exploration of her unskilled hands. Then he was
above her, and instinctively she arched her hips, their
bodies becoming one. Even the momentary pain was
forgotten as his lips claimed hers in a endless kiss, their
bodies moving in timeless passion, sensations cascading
through her, carrying her upwards to a plateau where
every particle of her body and soul exploded into spasm
upon spasm of sybaritic pleasure. She cried his name
over and over again like a litany, and heard him answer,
his arms cradling her reverently as their breathing slowed
to near normality.

A long time later Jake rolled away from Rebecca, her
even breathing telling him she slept. Even as he moved,
she sighed contentedly, her lithe body moulding itself to
his. Already he wanted her again, and wanted her with
an intensity which left him shaken. He cursed beneath
his breath. He had vowed that never again would a

woman have that power over him. He turned on his side, resisting the urge to kiss her awake, his iron will crushing his need as he threw back the cover to return to his own room. Her hand touched his shoulder.

'Don't leave me, Jake.' Her voice carried sleepily to him, touched with uncertainty. If she had tried wantonly to entice him he would have rejected her, but that uncertainty touched a chord within him and he relented, turned back to her and held her in the circle of his arms, making love to her slowly until, satiated and exhausted, he fell into a dreamless sleep, the like of which had been denied him for years.

Rebecca sat forward in the box Jake had taken for them at the playhouse, her face rapt with concentration as she strained to hear the actors speak above the calls and cries from the stalls below. The play itself was an heroic tragedy, its plot entrancing Rebecca. At the end of the first act, Jake leaned forward, his long gold-brown hair brushing her cheek, and her blood leapt at the possessive way his hand rested on her waist.

'I have no need to ask whether you are enjoying the play,' he teased.

'It is like a magical world,' she breathed excitedly, leaning closer to him. 'Yet so many here are not even listening to the words.'

Jake laughed easily, his manner relaxed, and for once the undercurrent of tension she always sensed beneath his cool self-possession was not apparent. 'It has been performed many times, and the playhouse is a favourite place of assignation and gossip.' As he spoke, the curtain of their box was drawn aside and three men, all laughing, entered. Jake drew back from her, and she felt the cool reserve replacing the easy fellowship of moments earlier.

'Jake, 'tis unlike you to hide yourself away,' declared the shortest of the three men and the one with the most elaborately curled black wig, his crisp voice sounding forced. Rebecca found herself surrounded, their bold gazes sliding over her figure adding to the resentment she felt at their intrusion.

Jake stood up, placing himself protectively at Rebecca's side. 'Your pardon, gentlemen, but—as you see—I was otherwise engaged.'

'And who could blame you?' the short man continued, and grinned lecherously at Rebecca in a way that made her flesh crawl with disgust. 'But 'tis cruel of you to neglect a certain lady-in-waiting who has been beckoning you to her box all evening,' he added, slyly. 'Or have her charms paled since you have a new companion?'

'Gentlemen,' Jake said with chilling formality, 'may I present my wife?'

'*Your wife!*' Two of them chorused their astonishment. 'You jest!'

'Indeed I do not, Francis,' Jake flashed the short man an icy smile. 'My stay in Somerset brought with it unparalleled rewards.'

'My pardon, Mistress Masters.' Francis bowed to her, his small black eyes seeming to strip the clothes from her body. His foppish face was prematurely aged by deep lines of debauchery. 'It is unforgivable to have broached the subject of the Lady Susannah before you. You will not reproach your husband for his past indiscretions, I trust?'

Rebecca felt the smile fix like dried plaster on her face. 'I would not be so foolish, sir.'

'Then you are an uncommonly rare woman as well as beautiful. I doubt there is not a man in the playhouse this night who has not envied Jake his good fortune in escorting you.'

'Uncommonly rare,' Jake echoed, taking Rebecca's hand in a possessive gesture, but a warning edged his voice as he continued, 'And one with more sense than to have her head turned by your suave flattery, Francis.'

For an instant the man's eyes glittered savagely.

'Come, Francis,' one of his companions intervened. 'You don't want to provoke Jake to a duel! Even wounded, he's twice the swordsman you are.'

'I'll not cry craven——' Francis whirled on his hapless friend '—but since I took no offence there'll be no provocation.' With a false laugh he preened the exotic fall of lace at his throat, and looked pointedly at the next box. 'Is that not Major Belthorpe? Wasn't he responsible for your dismissal? Yet I saw you exchange words with him earlier.'

'A curt greeting, no more,' Jake replied, dismissively.

Rebecca tensed, and fidgeted with the pomander hanging from a chain at her waist, trying to quell her rising suspicion. They had arrived at their box at the same time as Major Belthorpe's party, and Jake had been drawn aside by the man while his wife had chatted to Rebecca. Another man had also briefly joined the Major and Jake. When Jake had returned to her, his eyes had been grave and a frown had lingered upon his brow as he had led her into their box moments before the play began.

'You always did play your cards close to your chest, Jake, you scoundrel,' Francis added, preparing to leave. 'But *married*, and none of us an inkling of the forthcoming nuptials! What a sly dog you are.' He grinned lasciviously. 'I shall go and console the fair Lady Susannah.' He bowed over Rebecca's hand, his touch clammy as he squeezed it too familiarly. 'Most charmed to meet you, Mistress Masters. I hope we will meet again and often.'

'Regrettably, we will be travelling westwards in a day or so,' Jake cut in. 'There will be little time for society. Pray forgive us, but the second act is about to begin and my wife is interested in hearing the play.'

A disdainful sneer twisted Francis's mouth. 'The sweet innocence of a country-bred wife must be a refreshing experience for you, Jake. But, then, what needs a backwoods colonial with a refined lady for his wife?'

'You will apologise to my wife for your insult.' Jake's voice dripped ice. 'Or pay for your insolence.'

A sheen of sweat broke out on the older man's brow. 'A thousand pardons, Mistress Masters,' Francis simpered as he backed towards the curtain. He paused at the exit, his smile spiteful as it fixed upon Jake. 'Such ardour, Jake, over an imagined slight. If I did not know you for a hard-hearted rogue, I would swear you were smitten with your bride.'

He left before Jake could retaliate, and his expression remained thunderous until the other two men left the box and he returned to his seat. Throughout the performance he was as attentive towards Rebecca as she could wish, but the relaxed intimacy they had shared during the first act was missing. Her pleasure in the play evaporated, her mind turning over the earlier insinuations planted by Francis. Had they been as spiteful as his parting remarks, or did they hold some truth?

As they were leaving their box at the end of the play a young man whom she had seen earlier in Major Belthorpe's box, bumped into Jake, apparently accidentally. He murmured an apology and hurried on, but Rebecca had seen the sliver of paper he passed to Jake, and the way he surreptitiously tucked it under the heavy lace of his cuff. The crowd leaving the playhouse pressed tightly around them, making it impossible to question Jake. The protectiveness of his strong arm about her shoulders prevented her being crushed by the pushing crowd, and acted as balm to her wounded pride. Even so, her heart felt cased in iron, and she was unable to shake a growing fear. Jake was surrounded by intrigue, and a sixth sense warned her that his first loyalty was not to the Dissenters. Where then did that leave her? A spasm of agony held her in its vicious grip. Jake had played the gallant lover to perfection at the playhouse tonight, but her presence had been a cover to his meeting with Major Belthorpe and she had no reason to doubt an army officer's loyalty to King James. Was that what their marriage was to him—a cover? She shivered, feeling the colour drain from her face, her disillusionment making her stumble.

Immediately, Jake's arm was supportive about her waist, his tawny eyes clouding with concern as he guided her out into the fresh air. 'You look ill. What's wrong?'

She shook her head, unwilling to voice her fears. His anxiety was real and she did not want to face the prospect that he was indeed the spy her grandfather believed. 'It was the heat,' she lied as Jake helped her into their waiting carriage. His arms slid around her, his warm breath ruffling the curls on her forehead as he bent over her. Her heart wrenched. Surely Jake's consideration could not all be gallantry? Last night, when they had made love with such tenderness and passion, must have meant something to him. She had known Jake less than a week. How could she have hoped to understand so complex a man in so little time? His lips sought hers, demanding, insistent, scattering the shadows from her mind. She refused to believe he would treat her with dishonour... but, even as her senses soared beneath the mastery of his lips, she knew that she could forgive Jake everything except betrayal.

CHAPTER EIGHT

ST JAMES'S PARK was a swarming hive of colour and noise: peacock blues clashing with emeralds, pinks, scarlets and brightest gold, as Duchesses jostled against cake-sellers, mincing baronets side-stepped away from uncouth, drink-sodden foot-soldiers. A black-frocked parson harangued a gathering, his voice drowned by heckling apprentices, lovers arranged assignations, men conducted their business, while a few, like Rebecca, just enjoyed the spectacle for the novelty it was.

'I shall never get used to the press of people,' she laughed up at Jake. The wide brim of her hat, tilted above her dark ringlets, shaded the sizzling heat of the butter-gold sun melting in a cloudless, azure sky. There was not a breath of air and the trees dappling the grass with their cool shadows were motionless.

'Then you will not be too disappointed that we must leave London tomorrow,' Jake responded, his voice serious. 'I must be in Dorchester at the end of the week, and have rented a secluded house on the coast for the summer. I hope you'll not find it too remote, for there'll be times when you will have only Martha for company.'

She smiled. 'London is an exciting place to visit, but in my heart I am a country girl.'

Jake shot her one of his cool, assessing stares which revealed nothing of his own thoughts. Her heart stopped. They had not discussed their future, and Jake had spent most of his time in England in London. Fearing she had displeased him, she hastily amended, 'Whether in the country or in London, our home is where you wish it to be. I will adapt.'

'I had every confidence that you would.' Jake looked away to scan the crowd. The messenger he was to meet was late, but his mind was not on the information he

130

was waiting to receive—it drifted back to the harsh, uncompromising land of his birth which was a part of his soul. His words mocked him, leaving him uneasy as he pictured the fertile land which would one day be his, seeing it cleared and prospering by his own back-breaking toil. By a river was the simple log-cabin he would build to shelter him through the first years of settlement, while on a rise behind it he visualised the rising walls of a ten-room mansion which would replace the earlier structure.

The image blurred. That was the future he had planned for his return to Maryland. A future of five or perhaps ten years' hard work before he would have considered taking a wife to share his home. Yet here he was, married. His heart hardened. He had carried that dream with him for too long. There was no place in his life for a woman in those early years—there could not be. He crushed the hollow feeling of guilt. He would see to it that Rebecca did not suffer because of their marriage. Still, his conscience tugged uncomfortably. He was becoming too used to her company, to the peace she could offer him. Blood and nails! he swore under his breath. For her sake he could not afford to weaken. Anne would be alive today if she had remained in England.

Rebecca sensed Jake's mental withdrawal from her, and her pleasure in their walk shrivelled. At the way his gaze skimmed over the crowd she knew that this, like all their outings, was a cover for him to make contact with other conspirators. She quashed the unwelcome notion, her natural resilience refusing to be dampened. During the three days since they had visited the playhouse she had seen little of Jake, his meetings taking place at all hours of the day or night. Their brief moments together were precious—stolen hours which were her only chance to break down the barriers of distrust which surrounded her marriage.

Sometimes it seemed an impossible task, for Jake gave little of his inner self away, but she refused to be daunted. When he returned, haggard-eyed, from a prolonged meeting, she would have an intimate supper awaiting him, and while they dined she would sharpen her wit

against his dry humour until the frown smoothed from
his brow and she drew out his deep-throated laugh. Then
the tension would disappear from his body, and afterwards she would respond to his lovemaking with a
passion which matched his own. Outwardly, Jake was
as attentive as any new bride could have wished, but she
was no nearer to penetrating the reserved barricade
hidden beneath the surface of his easy charm, and it
saddened her to admit that an integral part of him was
deliberately barred from her.

They were approaching the open grounds of the palace
when a horn sounded a warning. Jake led Rebecca on
to the grass as the gravel path cleared before the passage
of a carriage escorted by a dozen Life Guards. In its
darkened interior Rebecca glimpsed a saturnine face with
heavy-lidded melancholy eyes, framed by a dark curling
periwig, and her heart snatched as she recognised King
James—the devil's advocate whom her grandfather
sought to dispose. She noted the obstinate set of his head
and mouth as he stared imperiously ahead. Had he really
learned nothing from the way Parliament had dealt with
his father's stubbornness by cutting off Charles I's head?

'Now you can say you have seen the King,' Jake teased,
but his hazel stare were sharp, assessing her reaction.

'He did not look a despot—merely rather haughty and
burdened from his high office.'

'He certainly lacks his brother's charm and wit——'
Jake broke off, the muscles in his arm beneath Rebecca's
hand tensing as he stared along the path at three advancing riders.

Rebecca followed his gaze and her attention was held
by the man in their centre. His proud bearing proclaimed him someone of importance, even if the def-
erence shown to him by the bowing courtiers, or the
soldiers standing rigidly straight as he rode past, were
not so evident.

'Who is he?' she asked, for the figure was still too far
away to be seen clearly. Jake appeared not to hear her,
and the familiar, accusing voice of Bartholomew

Skevington from close by her shoulder caused the hairs on the nape of her neck to prickle in alarm.

'Captain Masters, does it not cause you regret to see your one-time commander with your fellow aide-de-camps?'

'It is plain *Mr* Masters.' Jake's voice was like velvet polishing steel. 'What brings you to London? I thought you avoided the place you call England's Gomorrah.'

'I would not set foot in this lair of debauchery if the Lord's work did not call me to seek you out. You departed with such haste.' Skevington's eyes narrowed. 'How skilfully you evade my original question. You have not answered me. Were you not once one of Churchill's aide-de-camps? That gentleman has risen high under York's favour. Such could have been your destiny... Of course, that was before your ill-fated duel. Your crippled arm has cost you much.'

'That life is long behind me,' Jake countered. 'There is but one Lord Churchill. I am honoured to have served under him. And, since you ask, my arm has healed well enough to match any man in a fight.'

Skevington glared at the approaching rider who had earlier caught Jake's attention. Rebecca studied him with closer interest. Was this the Lord Churchill they referred to? He was almost level with their group now. She frowned. There was something about the self-assured rider which was disturbingly familiar. When he turned his head towards them to acknowledge a greeting, tentacles of dread slithered up her neck to wrap about her throat. She knew those sharp grey-green eyes and full mouth. It was the masked visitor who had come to their house last week. No wonder Jake had kept his identity a secret from her. It was John Churchill!

The knowledge stunned her, and when Churchill rode past without showing any sign of recognition towards Jake, she felt her world crumbling. Was Jake playing the hare against the hound, informing against the Dissenters to an officer rising in the King's army? Or was it Churchill who was the traitor against his King? A dark cloud settled over her like a funeral pall. She was weary of intrigue—of dishonesty—but, more, she was weary of the distrust which was relentless as a grave-worm burrowing into her flesh, and destroying any hope of lasting happiness with Jake. Skevington's harsh tones mocked her lost innocence as he taunted her husband.

'Your eminent commander scorns to recognise you.'

Jake ignored Skevington, his gaze noting Rebecca's bloodless lips. She had recognised Churchill. He cursed hard and silently, unexpectedly shamed by the pain darkening her violet eyes. She must have guessed something of the truth, and it was in her power to denounce him to Skevington. It would be the end of his mission— all he had worked for in recent weeks. He felt no fear for himself—only frustration that he would be unable to save Monmouth from embarking on a lost cause— and something else . . . a feeling he could not put a name to, as he watched a light snuffed like a candle in her eyes, an opaque shield coming down to erase all emotion.

'Gentlemen, if you must continue this rather pointless discussion, could we please do so in the shade? I begin to feel rather faint.' She sounded bored, but Jake sensed she was hiding a sense of bitter disillusion, and the knowledge unsettled him, destroying his relief that she had not denounced him.

Skevington wiped his own sweating brow. 'Your pardon, Mistress Masters, I shall be brief.' He turned to Jake, his eyes hardening. 'A meeting in St Giles's Fields has been arranged at first dark. A messenger has arrived from the Netherlands with a letter from His Grace which he must deliver to you personally.'

'Then it is best if we are not seen together,' Jake censored.

As Skevington turned to leave, the flush on his crimson hatchet-face darkened with affront. Rebecca held out a hand to detain him. 'A moment, if you please, sir. Have you seen my grandfather since . . . ?'

'Since you betrayed his trust——' Skevington blistered her with his scorn '—I have seen Ashleigh on many occasions. Not once was your name mentioned.'

Rebecca rode the blow to her pride without a flicker of a muscle. She had prayed that by now her grandfather would have relented towards her marriage—evidently he had not. She retraced her steps to the waiting carriage, her silk skirts rustling at her hurried pace. She was angry at the stubbornness of her grandfather, and angrier still at the lack of trust Jake had shown in her by keeping Churchill's identity a secret. But, above all, she was furious at herself for being such a blind fool as to fall in love with Jake Masters and allow herself to believe their marriage stood any chance of happiness.

Her arm was taken, and she was given a rough shake by Jake. 'Have you heard one word I have said, Becky?'

She looked at him coldly, his uncharacteristic display of temper leaving her unmoved. To her surprise she noted that she had been so wrapped in her anger that she had been unaware of getting into the carriage or of it setting off through the streets.

Her rage erupted. 'You treat me as though I were some half-witted child! Very well, keep your secrets...lie to me about your companions. What else should I expect from a *Masters*? I thought you had honour and integrity. Clearly I was wrong. Dear God, what a fool I was! Do you know, I would have died rather than have uttered a word against you? You have left me with nothing—not even my self-respect.' Her eyes met his, violet flames matched against his green flecks of fire. 'Tell me to my face, Jake, that you are not working to bring my grandfather and his friends down.' Her voice rose in an agony of recrimination. 'Tell me! And I will believe you. Dear God, even now, I want to believe you.'

Had she slapped his face the change in him could not have been more shocking. His eyes were green shards of ice and the hollows of his face looked chiselled from granite. 'With respect, madam, you know nothing of which you speak. England is on the brink of another civil war. Is that what you want, along with your pious grandfather? There are many who do not.'

She looked away unable to bear the condemnation in his eyes, her voice equally scathing. 'It is men who seek

glory in war—not women. I care nothing for politics,
only for people.'

The carriage halted and with relief she saw they were
outside their house. Without waiting for the door to be
opened for her, she threw it wide and jumped down on
to the cobblestones, her ankle jarring painfully as she
fled up the steps and into the house without a backward
glance at her husband. Slamming the bedroom door
behind her, she sagged against it, exhausted. That Jake
had not troubled himself to follow her confirmed her
deepest fears. He had married her to gain credit with
the Dissenters, and everything about their marriage was
a lie.

She squeezed her eyelids shut against a wayward tear,
too proud to give in to her misery. Her pride sustained
her. Her head came up, her balled fists relaxed and she
willed the cramping ache in her chest to subside. It eased,
but did not disappear. Her love for Jake refused to be
denied, and she accepted it, but at the same time she
vowed that never again would she be his pawn.

Jake stared after Rebecca's fleeing figure and needed to
exert every particle of his will to stop himself going after
her. He had not meant to hurt her, and he certainly had
not reckoned on feeling guilty because of the role he was
forced to play. Cursing roundly beneath his breath, his
anger grew at the position he found himself in. He could
not afford to weaken in his duty now. The wound in his
arm throbbed and he rubbed it, his lips setting grimly.
Ironically, his wound had provided the cover he needed
when the first rumours of Monmouth's planned rebellion began. The land grant he had been promised by
King James was what he had come to England to achieve
and if he could both have won that and saved Monmouth
from his folly, he had not considered his motives were
dishonourable. That was before he had met Rebecca.

He swallowed hard, his oath of allegiance suddenly
hanging round his neck like a leaden yoke, and fuelling
his anger against himself. Rebecca had given herself to
him unselfishly, with a passion that could have stemmed
only from love. He had not bargained for that, either,

and it tipped his world out of perspective. She was the first woman since Anne to resurrect the ideals of chivalry he had upheld in his youth, and she certainly deserved better than the dregs his embittered heart could offer. If he went to her now a few well-chosen words would win her round... When had they ever failed him?

Yet he hesitated. It was better for her this way, though it meant he would have to run the risk of her denouncing him. In a month or so he would return to Maryland, and his plans held no place for emotional involvement. He turned to the door, knowing he had to get out of the house before he relented, for already a treacherous part of his mind acknowledged that Rebecca was not another Anne—and that the New World would be as much an exciting challenge to her as it was to him.

Rebecca shivered in the early morning chill as she rose from her rapidly cooling bath, her thoughts as bleak as the sooty rainclouds unloading their burden on the slowly awakening city. Jake had been absent from the house for two nights, but had sent no word of his where-abouts. She glanced at the stacked trunks in a corner, packed and ready for their journey to Dorset that morning. An icy finger scraped down her spine. What if Skevington had discovered Jake to be a spy and the Dissenters had killed him? Or he could have been set upon by footpads as he tried to return in the thick of the night? With each passing hour her worries for his safety grew.

'Mistress, you must not fret yourself over Master Jake,' Martha reassured as she helped Rebecca into her petticoats. 'He knows how to look after himself. There's any number of reasons why he has not returned. Is not Simmons still with him?'

'It's the waiting—the not knowing—which is so hard to bear, especially...' Rebecca sighed, and looked over her shoulder at Martha. 'Jake and I quarrelled before he left. He only married me to save my reputation. He does not love me... he does not even trust me... and that hurts most of all. I would never betray him. I could not—because, whatever he is, or has done, I love him.'

Martha slipped a silk robe over Rebecca's shoulders and began to brush her mistress's damp hair. 'Master Jake is not one to wear his heart on his sleeve, but you wrong him. From the first moment I saw you together, it was obvious there was something between you. It was like a hidden source of light shimmering in the air when you looked at each other. That you are capable of rousing his temper, which he always takes such pains to control, proves he's not immune to your charms.'

'Then he has a strange way of showing his affection.'

'He has learned to guard his emotions well—perhaps too well.' Martha took the iron curling-tongs from where they were heating by the fire, her tone confidential as she curled Rebecca's hair into ringlets. 'I've seen a change in him since your marriage. There's a greater warmth to his laughter, a fiercer light glowing in his eyes when he watches you—and he watches you all the time, especially if he thinks he's unobserved. Even Simmons has commented upon it. Give the Captain time. He's a man who will always put duty before pleasure. When his duty is done, then he will see what is so obvious to those who know him.'

'I pray so, Martha. I fervently pray so.'

The sound of a measured footfall along the landing brought Rebecca swiftly to her feet. Jake had returned. She gripped her hands tightly together as the door to her chamber opened.

Jake was hatless, and his long, rain-wet hair clung in tight curls to his brow, the two-day beard stubble accentuating the grey lines of fatigue carved from his nostrils to the edge of his mouth. With a jerk of his head he dismissed Martha, who scurried from the room. He remained framed in the doorway, his eyes hooded as his glance swept over the packed travelling chests before it fixed on herself.

'Good. I see you are ready to leave. We must be on the road within the hour.'

At the lack of warmth in his voice Rebecca tensed. He could have been addressing a servant. When he turned to go, her injured pride stirred her temper like a stiffening wind.

'You look tired, but that does not excuse your rudeness.' She moved closer, her nostrils flaring as she detected the smell of a cheap, sickly-sweet perfume on his clothing. She checked, her rage swirling to gale force. While she had been sick with worry, he had been with a whore. She tossed back her head, the loose pins scattering so that her hair cascaded across her shoulders and breasts. 'I have no need to ask what kept you so long from your home.' Her voice was gritty with disgust. 'You reek of your harlot's cheap scent.'

The cleft in his chin whitened as he raised a mocking brow. 'A shrew's tongue ill-suits you, Rebecca.'

'That is my misfortune.' She ignored the dangerous light flashing in his eyes. 'Your own conduct is hardly unblemished. You are all the foul things my grandfather believed of you—treacherous, despotic, lecherous—an uncaring brute.'

She hugged her robe closer to her figure to combat the wave of pain and disillusionment cramping her veins. When a tear rolled down her cheek, she brushed it furiously away with a whitened knuckle, and walked across the room, placing the filled bath as a barrier between them.

Jake was gutted by her proud defiance. She was hurting inside like a wounded animal and it was his fault. He shrugged off his wet jacket and poured himself a goblet of wine left on the overnight table. The claret was sour from long hours of standing, its bitterness mixing ill with the guilt which settled uncomfortably upon his chest. He passed a tired hand across his brow. Common sense told him it was better she believed the worst, but, even as the thought formed, he found himself drawn towards her. When he reached out to turn her to face him, her body recoiled at his touch. The perfumed freshness of her warm skin filled his senses, and his gaze was mesmerised by a dark lock of hair provocatively curled over her earlobe, which begged to be kissed aside.

The unsettling feeling of loss which had been with him since they had quarrelled intensified.

'Becky.' His hand tightened over her resisting shoulder, forcing her to turn round. Her lips were compressed into a hard line and the contempt in her eyes was like a blow to the stomach. 'I was at the playhouse last evening and there was a reception in the green-room afterwards.' He was surprised to find himself at pains to explain. 'It was business.'

'Business for whom? I dare say you paid your trollop handsomely for her services.'

'Dammit, Rebecca! That's not what I meant.' His anger catapulted at the injustice of her words. He had not been interested in the jaded charms of the actresses when at home he knew Rebecca waited—uncontaminated by debauchery, her body eagerly responsive to his touch.

'Then pray explain,' she challenged, her violet eyes snapping with the heat and beguilement of a sorcerer's fire. 'You make a mockery of our marriage vows. I tried to please you. Am I so hideous...so unsatisfactory a bride, that within a week you must take your pleasure elsewhere?'

'Good God, how can you think that?' He was stunned by her reasoning. He was damned if anything she said made sense, but then understanding the intricacies of a woman's mind had often escaped him—else he would not have failed so miserably with Anne. 'Becky, my dear. You wrong me, but, more unjustly, you wrong yourself.' Catching the glimmer of uncertainty in her eyes, he pressed home his advantage. 'The reception was a cover, enabling me to meet a nobleman who would pledge his support for Monmouth's cause.'

He sensed her wavering and smiled broadly, drawing her closer.

'Don't think you can charm me around your little finger, Jake Masters.' Her fist hit his chest with the unexpectedness of a striking wildcat. Caught off guard, he stepped backwards. The rim of the bath rammed into the back of his knee and before he could recover himself, he toppled backwards. His jaw tightened with shock as the cool water lapped over his hips and chest. A missile thudded into the water sending up a spray to drench his face.

'Wash the stench of your whore from yourself, then I may find it easier to believe your tale.'

Shaking the water from his eyes, he gripped the sides of the tub to raise himself up, and, as he did so, caught the amused glimmer in Rebecca's eyes. The saucy baggage was actually enjoying herself at his expense! Then his own humour swamped his ire, as he saw the absurdity of his position.

Rebecca bit the inner side of her mouth to stop herself laughing. She should be furious at Jake, but the look of astonishment on his face at her retaliation had been too comical to ignore. She doubted if anyone had subjected him to such treatment since he had been a young boy. When his knuckles whitened on the tub as he prepared to lever himself up, she took a precautionary step back. Suddenly Jake grimaced and clutched at his wounded arm, his body sliding backwards until his face was submerged under the water.

She waited for him to heave himself up, but he lay motionless. Cautiously, she edged forward. 'Jake, will you stop acting the fool? I know you're not hurt.'

He did not stir.

'Jake.' Fear gripped her, her voice rising to a yell. 'Jake!'

She threw herself at the tub, her fingers locking into his shirt as she hauled him out of the water. Instantly his arms pinned her to him, his voice throbbing with wicked laughter against her ear. 'I thought you were going to let me drown.'

'It would serve you right if I had!'

'Have you no respect for the dignity due to your husband?' A dangerous gleam lit his eyes. 'It is time you learned some.'

She tried to pull back, but his hold was relentless, drawing her closer, and with a flip of his wrist, he overset her, so that she landed on top of him in the water.

Laughter shook his body and when she met the impact of his hazel eyes, speckled with amused green glints, her anger burst like a spent bubble.

'And what of my dignity?' she chided. 'Only a knave would treat his wife thus.'

Her breath stilled in her throat as Jake rose upwards, lifting her from the water. 'Temptress mine, I need no lesson on how to treat *my* woman. I will teach you obedience.' His voice lowered to a satiny, seductive whisper which shivered across her skin. 'There was no other woman while I was away.'

His lips took hers in fierce possession. He adjusted his stance so that his legs were splayed, the hard muscles of his thighs and the evidence of his arousal pressed against her yielding body, sending flames of desire licking through her like a forest fire. Before the kiss ended their wet clothing lay in a heap on the floor, her body becoming warm and pliant beneath the fervour of his embrace, as she responded to their mutual need. Her anger dissolved and she blotted out the uncertainties surrounding their marriage, savouring the pleasure of Jake's skilful hands which for the moment banished distrust. There was only now, and the exquisite thrill of the dominance of his lips and body upon hers, the joy they received, and gave, building a foundation for their future.

CHAPTER NINE

FOUR days later the coach drew into the busy yard of a Dorchester inn. Outwardly the rambling timber-framed building looked more respectable than some of the accommodation Rebecca had endured without complaint during the journey west. Tomorrow night Jake had promised they would be in the comfort of the house he had rented, high on a cliff overlooking the sea.

Rebecca smiled into her husband's face as he handed her down from the carriage, but his response seemed abstracted. During the first three days of the journey a new harmony had entered their relationship, the frequent and easy mingling of their laughter as intoxicating as the sensual potency of their lovemaking. During those days she had experienced how wonderful, how idyllic her life with Jake could be. But reality had an unpleasant way of intruding upon idylls, and as they crossed the county border into Dorset Jake had withdrawn into himself. Throughout their journey he had refused to discuss his involvement with the Dissenters, or his relationship with Churchill or Monmouth. Her happiness faded, the many-headed viper, distrust, poisoning her peace of mind. The idyll had been the lull before a storm, the harmony a fine layer of gauze covering their unresolved differences in loyalty.

'Good day, sir.' The red-faced landlord waddled forward to greet them. 'Is it a bed your good lady and yourself will be needing for the night? We pride ourselves you'll not find cleaner or more comfortable rooms in all of southern England.'

'A room for us and one also for our servants,' Jake instructed. 'And the use of a private parlour until we leave after breaking our fast on the morrow. But first, landlord, bring the best wine and food your inn has to offer.'

The landlord bowed, rubbing his hand over his ample paunch as he led them past the open door of the public taproom. The smells of stale ale and tobacco smoke invaded the narrow corridor. He opened a door further down the passage and stepped aside for them to enter, saying, 'This is our best parlour. Your servants will be dining in a room at the back.'

Jake nodded for Simmons and Martha to leave them and then removed his wide-brimmed beaver hat, touching the small sprig of greenery tucked into its band and partly hidden by the black ostrich feather. 'I am expecting a visitor.'

The innkeeper nodded significantly, recognising the emblem of Monmouth's followers. 'He will be shown in with discretion, but I must warn you that the militia frequent this inn.' His voice lowered in warning. 'Their commander, Major Tovey, is a pompous ass. And though he hunts down any he suspects of insurrection, he does so merely to further his own career. He has no loyalty other than that to his own self-interest.'

Rebecca walked across the sparsely furnished room to look out of the window. The uninspiring view of the courtyard was obscured by accumulated grime on the pane, and she turned away to sit on the wooden settle. The only other pieces of furniture in the parlour were a dining-table and two stools. By the time she had removed her gloves and hat the landlord had returned with a tray of ale and wine. Jake handed her a goblet, his mood still abstracted as his gaze slid over her head to stare out of the window while he drank from his tankard. A jest withered on her tongue. Jake was troubled, but, more than that, he was erecting barriers between them.

It was as though the last three days had never been. Her mind drifted back over the days since their wedding to the horror of the fire. Despite the evidence of her own eyes she could not believe her grandfather had meant to burn Jake and herself in their bed. Again she went over the events of that night, as she had countless times.

She twirled a ringlet thoughtfully round her finger, trying to recall clearly what had happened. The shock of the fire had blurred her memory, but she could not shake the impression that there had been something very odd about her grandfather's manner. Her frown deepened. What it was continued to elude her.

The door to the parlour burst open, startling her from her reflections. A cloaked figure entered, his hat pulled down over his features. Jake drew a pistol from the sash at his waist, but lowered it when the stranger pushed his hat back to reveal a scarred face and drooping fair moustache and hair.

'The militia were following me.' The stranger struggled for breath as though he had been running. 'I managed to lose them in the back streets of the town but their Major already suspects this inn.' As he spoke he pulled a packet from inside his jacket and handed it to Jake. 'This must be acted on without delay.'

Jake broke the seal and scanned its contents. As he lifted his head to speak, Rebecca caught sight of a flash of scarlet in the courtyard outside the window. Her head shot round, her voice trembling as she cried out, 'The militia are outside!'

'I must go!' The stranger moved to the door.

'No!' Jake commanded. 'It's too late for that. Quick, man, behind the settle.'

Rebecca leapt to her feet while Jake and his companion moved the seat away from the wall. Once the messenger was crouched behind it, Jake dragged it back into place and, pulling Rebecca to his side, sat down. At that moment heavy boots clumped along the corridor.

'Search every room,' a gruff voice commanded. 'That cursed rebel's here somewhere!'

'The packet must not fall into their hands,' Jake said, searching the room for a place to hide it.

Rebecca held out one hand, and with the other unbuttoned the jacket of her riding habit. 'Give it to me.'

'No, Becky, it's too dangerous. If the soldiers are suspicious, they'll not hesitate to search a woman.' Angry voices from the taproom warned them the soldiers were getting closer, and Jake made to conceal the packet inside his own jacket.

Rebecca stopped him. 'If they are suspicious, they will arrest you first—then search you later. Besides, are we not newly married and travelling to the coast to have some privacy away from our family and friends? Why should they suspect us?'

'Then we must convince the soldiers that we are innocent travellers.'

Jake reluctantly handed her the packet, which she thrust deep into her chemise to nestle beneath her breasts, and started to refasten her buttons.

'Search that parlour!' The order came from directly outside their door.

'No. I cannot permit it,' the innkeeper protested. 'The couple particularly asked that no one disturb them.'

'Did they?' The gruff voice sounded triumphant. 'Why should honest travellers demand privacy if they have nothing to hide?'

Jake flung himself across Rebecca. 'Kiss me, Becky. We must convince them we are alone.'

She shut her mind against the fear they would all be arrested and, wrapping her arms round Jake's neck, she bound them closer in a passionate embrace.

'Becky, my love—my heart,' Jake declared ardently as several soldiers burst into the room.

Rebecca screamed and held the edges of her gaping jacket together, while Jake sprang to his feet, an arrogant figure of outraged decency.

'What the devil do you mean by bursting in upon us like that? This is a private parlour!'

'A known insurrectionist was seen entering this inn.' The tallest of the men stepped forward, his tunic heavily decorated with gold lace. He had the meaty arms and barrel chest of a farm labourer, but his high, mincing voice affected a pompous air. 'Everywhere must be searched.'

'It should be obvious that there is no one here but my wife and myself,' Jake countered in stinging tones. 'I would thank you to leave us now.'

Beneath a black wig the officer's coarse face flushed with ruddy colour. 'Sir, you are addressing a Major of the King's militia, not some common lackey.' The Major stared past Jake to Rebecca, who was smoothing her lace stock over her refastened jacket. The packet lay cold against her heated flesh as his pale eyes lingered suggestively upon the straining buttons across her breasts. 'Major Tovey at your service, ma'am. I had no wish to cause you embarrassment. It is my duty to apprehend all rebels.'

'There is no rebel here, Major,' she answered sweetly, swallowing her dislike for his overbearing manner. 'Just my husband and myself, breaking our journey.'

Jake intervened, taking a menacing step towards him. 'And, although somewhat zealous, you may consider your duty done, Major.'

'I take exception to your tone, sir,' Tovey blustered, and with a disdainful flick of his wrist ordered the soldiers from the room. 'I have some questions which need answering. Where have you travelled from?'

'London,' Jake rapped out impatiently.

'And your destination?'

'The coast—where I have rented a house for the summer. My brother's ship is due to dock from the New World in a week or so.'

The Major's eyes gleamed. 'You rent a house to await the arrival of a ship. That sounds somewhat strange, does it not? Or perhaps this ship, which you claim to be your brother's, carries a specific passenger? A visitor who would bring rebellion to our shores!'

Jake smiled, enjoying leading on the pompous Major. 'Then you cannot be referring to my brother's ship. Did I not mention his name is Masters, and he drives a considerable trade with Virginia? I have not seen him for two years, and his stay in England is regrettably short. Hence the rented house.'

Major Tovey visibly deflated. 'Masters? Hasn't Sir Charles Masters some connection with the colonies?'

'He is not himself a merchant, but he is my kinsman. Does that satisfy your curiosity? And I am sure you are

aware that Sir Charles, in his capacity as His Majesty's
Justice of the Peace, is a loyal supporter of King James.'

'Sir Charles's views are known to me.' Tovey did not
trouble to hide his antagonism, now that he felt his prey
had escaped him. 'And, if I am not mistaken, sir, you
are Jake Masters, and once a Captain in the Royal
Dragoons until a scandal cost you your rank?'

'I see you are a man of keen intelligence who misses
nothing,' Jake responded, his voice taking on an icy edge.
'If you have finished your questions, my wife and I
would like to dine.'

The Major flushed at Jake's dismissive tone. Rebecca
held her breath as he scanned the room, his expression
sullen with resentment. 'I am thorough in my duty, but
I doubt that any law have been violated in this room
today...save only marriage vows.'

Jake's hand went to his sword-hilt. 'Apologise to my
wife for that insult.'

The atmosphere in the room bristled with tension. The
Major puffed his chest out to reply, and, fearing the
consequences of the soldier's antagonism, Rebecca
hastily intervened.

'I am sure Major Tovey meant no insult.' She threw
Jake a provocative smile as she moved forward to take
his arm. 'We must have looked like lovers. He is not to
know that we are so recently wed.'

Jake remained glacial-eyed. The Major dropped his
gaze, clearly unwilling to force Jake into a fight. 'Your
pardon, ma'am, I meant no disrespect.' He backed out,
closing the door hurriedly behind him.

Rebecca brushed a shaky hand across her mouth.
'What an objectionable man!' She took the packet from
her jacket and handed it to Jake.

'Your quick wits saved the day. I regret you were subjected to such crude subterfuge.'

'Better my modesty is dented than you languish in a
prison.'

'How calmly you face danger!' He raised her left hand
to his lips, and, before releasing it, detected the slight
trembling of her fingers and ran his thumb across the

emerald ring which had been made smaller for her while they were in London. The admiration sparkling in his eyes made her heart swell with pride. 'Your courage matches that of the original wearer of this ring.' He smiled devilishly. 'And you have proved yourself as devious as any Masters in outwitting an adversary.'

'I suppose you mean that as a compliment.' She laughed, low in her throat. 'But I was not so brave— just very frightened.'

'You did not show it.'

She moved closer to him, drawn by a magnetism strengthening between them. A sneeze from behind the settle broke the intimacy of the moment, and they drew guiltily apart. The messenger had been momentarily forgotten. Outside, Tovey shouted orders to his troop, and as the stranger wriggled out from behind the settle Rebecca looked out of the window to see the soldiers mount and ride out of the courtyard.

The messenger rubbed the dust from his black breeches as he walked to the door. 'That was a close-run thing. Your wife saved the day, Masters. You must be very proud of her.'

'I am,' Jake said, before opening the door to check that the corridor was empty.

A rush of love overwhelmed Rebecca. His simple statement was an answer to her prayers. At that moment she would have walked across burning coals to prove her love for her husband.

'The hall is clear,' Jake said, ducking back into the room. 'Go quickly, friend.'

The stranger tipped his hat respectfully to Rebecca, and disappeared through the doorway. When Jake turned to face her, his expression was grave. 'I must speak with Simmons. Stay here. I'll send Martha to you.'

Alone in the parlour Rebecca sat down, her thoughts whirling in confusion. She had reluctantly accepted that Jake was King James's spy, but his actions in saving the Dissenters' messenger from arrest puzzled her. She stared at the emerald ring, wondering what Jake's role was in the West of England. As usual, there was no ready answer. The overcast light from the window darkened the emerald stone almost to black. Unaccountably she shivered, a feeling of approaching danger darting through her. When her gaze settled on the window, the sense of danger intensified. There had been something wrong about the soldiers who had ridden out. But what? The thought nagged at her until, as she realised what it was, her heart lurched. Major Tovey had not accompanied his troop. She must warn Jake. The Major had resented Jake's authoritative manner, and he had resented even more the ease with which her husband had bested him. Had Jake walked into a trap? Her throat tightened in panic as she ran across the room.

A startled cry rose to her lips when the door burst open, and to her dismay Major Tovey stepped into the room.

'If that isn't a sight to warm a man's heart,' he crowed, blocking her escape. 'A pretty wench all alone and her smile so inviting. Your lover is neglectful.'

'This is a private room, and it is taken by my husband and myself, Major.' Somehow she managed to keep her voice steady. 'Kindly leave.'

'Come now, my dear. You and I both know Jake Masters is not your husband.' Tovey's voice coarsened. 'Masters' reputation as a womaniser precedes him. He's not the marrying type. Besides, no man makes love to his *own* wife in a public hostelry.' His gaze darkened to a leer. 'And you were clearly enjoying his attentions. I know a courtesan when I see one. You, my dear, are too beautiful to be a wife.'

'How dare you insult me so?' Rebecca's rage exploded, and she cautiously put the width of the oak dining-table between them. Why didn't Martha come? And where was Jake?

Major Tovey swaggered forward. 'Now, my pretty dove, no need to be shy. I know how to show my appreciation to a woman. And I can be generous, too—if you please me. Your lover took off somewhat hastily. Had something to hide, did he? I saw that damned

Dissenter running out of the back door. He was in here, wasn't he?'

Rebecca edged further round the table, maintaining the distance between them as the Major stalked her. 'You were in this room and saw there was just my husband and myself.'

'I saw a cosy scene. Or a very clever ruse to put me off the scent. Kin to Sir Charles Masters or not, your paramour is in league with the Dissenters. And when I prove it the arrogant bastard will hang. But I'd not want to see your pretty neck stretched. Far from it.'

Rebecca gauged the distance to the door. She would never reach it before the Major caught her. She opened her mouth to scream for help, but instantly clamped it shut. Did other soldiers lie in wait in the inn? Was this a subtle trap that the Major was laying for Jake? What better way to provoke a man than to assault his wife? Tovey had no proof the messenger had been in this room, and she guessed the Major gloried in his own self-importance and the power he wielded in the district. He was capable of having Jake arrested on the flimsiest pretext.

'Ah, I knew you would be reasonable,' Major Tovey made a dash for her, mistaking her hesitation for acquiescence. 'A kiss, and there'll be no charges against you.'

Her arm was caught in a bruising grip, the Major's speed surprising her in so heavy a man. When his body slammed against hers, the stench of his rotting teeth hit her full in the face, and her stomach rolled with revulsion as his callused hand painfully squeezed her breast.

'Get your hands off me,' she flared, putting all her weight behind her fist to hit his chin. Though her knuckles cracked and the pain jarred her bone to the elbow, the Major did not even stagger.

'Damned hell-cat! I'll teach you,' he wheezed, spraying her with his spittle.

'Jake!' she screamed, knowing she could never fight off Tovey's massive bulk. The flabby flesh on his huge frame was like soft dough as she struck at him. There was no finely honed muscle such as the years of soldiering had sculpted upon Jake's hard body, but Tovey's immense weight was impossible to shove aside. His slap crashed her head back on to the table. A myriad lights flashed across her eyes, the pain stunning her even as she fought to retain her senses. Instinctively, she kicked and struck him, but her legs felt leaden and her efforts made little impression upon his brawny legs or chest. 'No! Stop!' she cried, increasing her struggles. 'No!'

The table dug cruelly into her back as his weight pressed down upon her, crushing the air from her lungs. He pinned her arms above her head with one bear-sized hand. The touch of his callused palm grazing along her stockinged leg to the naked thigh made her flesh shrink into her bones. A red haze of impotent fury mingled with her horror as she fought on, knowing that her strength was fading fast.

Then suddenly she was free of the crushing weight. Dazed, she rolled on to her side, her eyes widening as she stared down at Major Tovey lying spreadeagled on the floor. Jake stood over him, his sword-point pressed to the soldier's throat.

'Mercy,' Major Tovey pleaded, his face draining to the colour of sour cream. 'I was questioning the wench when she tried to escape. I was restraining her and we fell against the table.'

'If you value your worthless hide, don't say another word,' Jake said with deceptive softness. 'It is an officer's duty to set an example to his men. Such conduct, under my command, would have cost you a horse-whipping.' Jake lowered his sword. His expression still murderous, he hauled Tovey to his feet by the front of his scarlet jacket, and pressed him up against the wall with such force that the Major's periwig slipped sideways.

'Jake, I was not hurt,' Rebecca interceded, fearful that if Jake harmed Tovey he would be thrown into prison. 'And if you deal with him as he deserves, there'll be a scandal.'

A muscle throbbed along Jake's jaw. 'I'll not forget this insult to my wife. You deserve to die for forcing yourself upon an innocent woman. But I'll not have my wife's name dragged into the mud because of a piece of human dung like yourself.' Jake dropped his hands from Tovey's figure and stepped back. 'The Deputy Lieutenant of the county is a friend of Sir Charles. He will be informed of your conduct. I trust him to punish you accordingly. Now get out of my sight, Tovey, before I forget myself and kick you out.'

The Major pulled down his crumpled jacket and straightened his periwig. 'Your kinship to Sir Charles will not save you. I know that damned Dissenter was hiding in this room. I'll not rest until I get proof of your involvement—*then* we shall see who is punished.'

The door slammed behind his departing figure.

Rebecca leaned heavily against the table. 'You've made a bitter enemy, and it's all my fault.'

'Nonsense. I can handle that upstart.' Jake drew her into his arms. 'I should have sent Martha directly to you, but she was checking the messenger got away safely. Are you sure he did not harm you? If he did——'

'No. Jake, I'm fine. I'm just sorry to have made things more difficult for you. You struck a poor bargain when you married me. I've brought you nothing but trouble.'

'Tovey is an irritation, nothing more. As to our marriage...' His eyes darkened, his long lashes partially veiling their expression and making it impossible for her to judge his mood. His hands moved along her arms to rest on her shoulders, and she held her breath expectantly, as he carefully weighed his words. 'The other day in the park you showed me unwarranted loyalty. When you recognised Churchill you could have denounced me to Skevington. You believed the worst of me that day, yet you chose to defend me. Why?'

She bit back her natural declaration, Because I love you! Such words would embarrass him since his heart still belonged to Anne Masters. She smothered a rush of sadness that his words of love, spoken to distract the soldiers, had been nothing more than an act. 'A wife's loyalty must be to her husband. You could have thrown me to the wolves; instead you saved my reputation by marrying me. I repay my debts.'

'Is that the only reason?' His hands tightened. 'You make it sound so cold and impersonal. That's not like you, Becky.'

'What more do you want from me, Jake? You've told me you're incapable of loving another woman after Anne. I accept that. Though, if you want the truth, it is cold comfort when I have lived so much of my life without love.'

The arrival of the landlord and a servant, each carrying a tray of food, interrupted their conversation. When they were once again alone, Jake led her to the table and served them both with portions of game pie and slices of roast duckling. Tipping back his stool on to two legs, he leaned his shoulders against the wall, studying her intently. 'Do you regret not marrying Tom Hardwycke? I doubt not that that popinjay effusively declared his devotion.'

The question was fired at her out of the blue, catching her off guard. 'Oh, Tom loved me in his way, but he loved the thought of my dowry more.'

'Poor Becky, you've had a raw deal with the men in your life.' Although the familiar teasing took the sting from his words, for once he did not meet her open gaze, and his face was blank, shutting her out of his thoughts in the way she had come to hate.

'I don't need your pity, Jake,' she flashed back. 'You were honest about your feelings for Anne. I respect that. But I cannot so readily accept your refusal to explain your reasons for being in Dorset. I can only guess why you are here, and sometimes I feel I am trapped in a ring of forest fire which is steadily advancing to swallow me up. I have done all I can to prove my loyalty, yet the distrust remains between us—making a mockery of our marriage.'

'Do you believe I am the King's spy, sent to destroy those insurrectionists like your grandfather? Men who have placed their trust in me.' His emerald gaze shafted through her. The cleft in his chin whitened, warning her that he was controlling his anger. 'Do you think I have tricked them into giving me their trust and then I shall betray them? You talk of honesty, Rebecca. I want the truth from you now.'

She felt as though she were facing the executioner's axe—that it was herself on trial and not him. She braced herself to hold his stare. 'I am a simple country girl and am ignorant of politics. You are an accomplished courtier, with the charm to win both men and women to your side. Yet, even so, I believe honour is important to you, else I would not have married you. I do not think you would betray another's trust. Neither do I believe your role here is all you would make it appear.'

He shoved his shoulders away from the wall and brought his stool down on to all four legs. Leaning across the table, he took both her hands in his. 'You are no *simple* country girl, but an intelligent and loyal woman. It is safer for you to know nothing of my duty here.'

'You mock my loyalty.' Her eyes narrowed. 'If there is danger, should I not know whom to guard my tongue against? What if you are injured? Whom could I turn to for help without endangering your freedom, or life?'

'Dammit, Becky, you ask too much!'

She snatched her hands away and stood up. 'Then it is better if we lead separate lives.'

'Sit down, Rebecca!

'Only if you are prepared to talk.'

Their eyes locked in a contest of wills. Jake nodded. 'I owe you that much at least.'

He rubbed the cleft in his chin as she slowly sank down on to her stool, her back rigid with defiance. 'My allegiance is to King James. But I am also bound by friendship to Monmouth,' he stated flatly, but his stare watched her reaction closely. When she said nothing, but kept her face a bland mask, he went on heavily, 'I have little faith this rebellion planned by the Dissenters will succeed. I have reason to believe that Monmouth will land in Dorset. I would convince him to turn back before it is too late.'

'And if you fail, and there is open rebellion—where do you stand then? Surely you would not fight against him? Your wound is not healed.'

He folded his arms across his chest as he leaned back against the wall. 'I can fight well enough if I have to. Though I pray it will not come to that. If it does...' He shrugged, his eyes hardening as his gaze bored into her. 'Both the King and Churchill know that I agreed to this ruse to stop a rebellion. Whatever the outcome, I will not turn informer on any individual.'

'And what if you find yourself facing my grandfather, or Tom, or any of the men I have known all my life on the battlefield?'

'I am a soldier. I will have no choice but to fight.'

'But you lost your rank.'

Jake shook his head. 'The duel coincided with the first rumours of Monmouth's plans. I still draw my Captain's pay.' When he saw her grip the edge of the table, her knuckles white with strain, he cursed Monmouth, the King, Churchill and all who had caused her so much pain. And he cursed his own helplessness to ease her torture. How could he make her see that her grandfather had abandoned her to her fate? 'Your grandfather has set his own course.' He picked his words carefully, trying to ease her pain. 'He knows the risks. And you can hardly expect me to sympathise with him after he tried to murder us at the lodge!'

'No—he didn't.' Her voice crackled with passionate defence. 'He would not!'

'Becky, you saw him with the torch. He's so embittered with his hatred for Sir Charles that he sees me as the devil incarnate, and you as my handmaiden. The house I have rented is isolated, which is why I chose it. There'll be no meetings with Dissenters because I do not want you involved—it's too dangerous. If this rebellion erupts, any connection with the rebels could mean imprisonment, or death. I want your promise you will do nothing to aid them.'

'Are you asking me to turn my back on my grandfather if he comes to me for help, or is wounded?' Her eyes blazed with outrage.

Jake was aware of the distrust rearing between them. When would she stop fighting him, and realise that he was not her enemy? Couldn't she understand that he was trying to save her life? 'Where rebellion is concerned, no one is neutral. If you aid your grandfather in any way, you will be considered a traitor to the King. For your own safety you must have no dealings with the rebels.'

'Is that an order, Captain Masters?' She stood up. 'I will not ignore a plea from a friend or kinsman. That may be the way of your family, but it is not mine.'

'Those who are prepared to rebel against their Sovereign should be prepared to face the consequences if they fail.' Jake could feel the conflict building between them, but was powerless to stop it. One moment she could be soft and loving in his arms, the next intractable, stubborn to the point of mulishness. In this he had to be brutal to be kind. A hollow frustration gripped him. She had an uncanny way of rousing his protective instincts which was unsettling. He had to convince her of the danger, for if his own plans went without mishap, he might not be in England to save her from her folly.

He crushed a moment's weakness, and the accompanying pang of regret. His plans were made— Rebecca would be well provided for. 'You speak with your heart, not your head.' His tone sharpened. 'Such people have little regard for you, if they would implicate you in treason. They are gambling with your life. I forbid you to have anything to do with any of them. Give me your word, Rebecca.'

She looked at him with an expression of indomitable will, her eyes edged with sadness. 'You ask the impossible.'

'I ask nothing which is not my right—wifely obedience.'

Rebecca flinched. Jake strode to the door. In his eyes was green ice, deep and cold as a frozen sea. 'My brother's ship will be trading between England and the Continent for some weeks. Once my duty in England is done and Nathan sets sail for Maryland, I plan to return with him. In the meantime I have matters of duty to attend to and cannot always be on hand to protect you. Will you give me your word?'

'I cannot, Jake.'

A flicker of pain crossed his handsome face. 'Don't wait up for me tonight. I shall not return for some hours.'

Rebecca stared at the closing door. Just what had he meant by his parting words? Was it an ultimatum? Or a warning, that if she disobeyed him he would return to the New World alone?

CHAPTER TEN

'BECKY! Rebecca!' Jake's voice carried to her from the stableyard.

Rebecca looked out of the parlour window and saw him talking to a man who was climbing down out of a farm cart. He was the first visitor to call at the cottage in the three weeks they had lived there. As she hurried to the door, the room swam dizzily around her, bringing her to an abrupt halt. Holding on to the door-latch, she took several deep breaths until the dizziness passed, leaving only the queasiness which had been with her the last two mornings. When she walked into the hallway she saw Martha anxiously watching her.

'I knew that bloom in your cheeks was more than just sea air. You're with child.'

'I hope so, Martha.' Rebecca smiled. 'But it is too soon to be certain.'

'You *are* with child!' Martha nodded wisely. 'I can always tell. It shows in a woman's eyes, or her smile. When will you tell the Captain?'

'In two weeks or so, when I am certain.' A flicker of apprehension brought her hand to the waist of her sapphire-velvet riding habit. 'Do you think Jake will be pleased? We have never spoken of children.'

'Of course the master will be pleased. What man would not be?' Martha smiled, but Rebecca was puzzled by the troubled look which darkened the servant's eyes.

'Becky!' Jake's tone was now impatient.

Rebecca hurried outside, the vague disturbance she had felt at Martha's worried expression dispelled as she saw her husband. She stared in astonishment as a black and white blur launched itself from the cart with an excited yelp, and flew towards Rebecca.

159

'Tess!' she cried, bending to hug the spaniel as she tore barking round her mistress's skirts, her sleek body quivering from the white tip of her circling tail to the ends of her long black ears. A sudden misting filled Rebecca's eyes at being reunited with her dog, and, laughing, she turned her head aside to evade Tess's tongue lapping her cheek and met Jake's amused gaze. 'You had Tess brought to me. Thank you, Jake.'

She stood up, careful to avoid the spaniel's excited capering, and moved towards her husband.

'How little it takes to please you.' With a laugh Jake reached into the back of the open cart and held up a squirming, black-faced pup. 'This is the last of the litter. Ashleigh had found homes for the other four pups, but had kept this one, who was the largest and most inquisitive.'

Their hands brushed as she took the pup from him, and she had to swallow against her throat tightening with emotion before she could speak. 'Thank you! They are the most perfect—the most precious of gifts. How did you know I missed Tess so terribly? And Grandsire? Is there word from him?'

'No.' Jake's voice hardened. 'He is still bitter about our marriage.'

'But he allowed Tess and her pup to come to me.' She clung desperately to that fact. 'It is a sign that he is mellowing.' She turned to the driver of the cart, whom she belatedly recognised as Dick Shepherd, the eldest son of one of the tenant farmers of Coombe Grange. He hung back, his pockmarked face flushing with embarrassment. 'When you return, will you carry a letter to my grandfather?'

The young man shuffled uncomfortably.

'There is no need to delay your journey, Dickon,' Jake intervened. 'I must meet with Mr Ashleigh later this week, and I shall take my wife's letter.'

'Is my grandfather well?' she could not stop herself asking.

'Well enough.' Dick Shepherd evaded her gaze. 'Though his temper is blacker than ever. We don't see much of him about the farm now. He keeps himself to himself.'

Climbing back into the cart, he nodded significantly to Jake, and Rebecca suspected it was more than Tess and her pup which had brought Dick Shepherd to the house. As the cart pulled away she put the pup on the ground. Immediately, it spotted Oswald the cockerel strutting across the yard and gave chase. When the bird fluttered up on to a fence-post, the incensed pup leapt up and fell over backwards in an effort to reach him.

Rebecca clung to Jake's arm, her laughter mingling with his. 'He's a game little devil,' Jake chuckled. 'What will you call him?'

'Jasper. He looks like a Jasper, don't you think?'

'If you say so.' Jake laughed again. 'Though I doubt if my cousin Colonel Jasper Masters will see the likeness. He was known as Bulldog Masters before he retired from the army.'

'Oh, I did not mean to offend one of your family,' Rebecca said quickly. 'I did not know you had a cousin Jasper.'

Her smile faded with the knowledge that of Jake's family she knew only Sir Charles, and what Jake had told her of his parents and brothers in America. And he was strangely loath to talk more of them.

'Keep the name Jasper; it suits the scamp,' Jake said, as he led her to the stables where both their horses had been saddled. 'He will keep you company when I must leave. There's word that Monmouth is already at sea and has been for some days.'

Her heart twisted painfully. 'How long will you be away?'

Jake avoided looking at her as he adjusted his saddle-girth. 'It is impossible to say. Let's not talk about it now and spoil today. I thought we would ride along the cliff.'

To hide her unease at Jake's changing mood, Rebecca looked across to where Martha was luring Jasper into the house with a bowl of milk and Tess was following after him. That Jake had taken such pains to give her a companion to fill her days, made her suspect he would be away for a considerable time. Her heart was clutched by desolation. They had been happy these last weeks, but how fragile was that happiness?

Jake lifted Rebecca into the saddle and leapt on to his own mount. Touching his heel to his gelding's side, he set off at a canter towards the ruins of a Norman castle a mile along the clifftop. He rode in silence, while his mind rehearsed the words he must say to Rebecca. Whichever way he silently phrased them they sounded callous, leaving him with an unpleasant pang of guilt which he unsuccessfully tried to smother.

Suddenly Rebecca's mare overtook him. 'Hey, sluggard,' she laughed over her shoulder, 'I'll race you to the ruins.'

Jake galloped after her, checking his mount's stride so that Rebecca beat him by a horse's length.

'Rogue, you let me win.' She scowled with mock chagrin as they halted by the crumbling gatehouse.

'Would I do that?' He grinned, lapsing into the teasing banter which had become a part of their life. He leapt to the ground, and held up his arms to lift her down to his side. A shadow lurking behind her violet eyes warned him that she was aware of his preoccupation, and his conscience tugged. He did not want to hurt her, and he respected her too much to deceive her. More than that, the loyalty she had shown him deserved better than the poor reward he could offer.

Briefly, he felt the warmth of her hip beneath his fingers and desire sparked through him, to be ruthlessly crushed. Subtly he felt his control over their relationship was changing. While her passion delighted him, her courage and sense of humour intrigued and fascinated him so that he would find his thoughts straying to memories of their time together part-way through an important meeting with the Dissenters. He could not afford to be distracted. To succeed he must remain single-minded in his duty to the King.

Rebecca sensed Jake's withdrawal from her even before his hands fell to his sides. She turned away, tethering her mare to a thornbush. Momentarily the world spun dizzily and she cursed the weakness which her pregnancy had brought with it. She drew a sharp breath and waited for the horizon to steady, pretending to be absorbed in the seascape below her. As the scene settled to rights, she gazed at the sun shimmering golden on the azure water, the circling green and ochre arm of the bay rising up steeply from the sun-bleached sand. The serenity of the clifftop calmed her, even the screech of the gulls soaring overhead serving to emphasise their isolation. Jake had chosen this place for a purpose. If, as he had said, Monmouth was already at sea, this could be their last day together for some time, and she did not want it ruined because her pregnancy was making her over-sensitive.

Turning to Jake, she saw him watching the distant ships. A breeze lifted his gold-tipped lovelocks from his shoulders. He was coatless, and the wide black leather strap of the sword-belt across his chest was stark against the white lawn of his shirt. It was a sinister reminder of the danger that was all around them, even in this apparently tranquil place. A damp sheen of perspiration glistened on his strong, bronzed throat, a thin trickle coursing downwards, and her fingers ached to follow its path as it buried itself among the darker curling hair beneath the open neck of his shirt. She gave in to the impulse and Jake turned his hazel gaze upon her.

'Is your brother's ship out there?' she asked.

'It is possible—but they are all too far away to tell.' His mood remained distant, plucking at her heart so that she plunged recklessly on. 'You're troubled, Jake. And it has nothing to do with the lateness of your brother's ship, or that Monmouth is at sea. Is it us?'

Her stomach rolled with anxiety as his lashes guarded the expression in his eyes, and she forced herself to persist. 'You do not deny it. So it must be me. Have you tired of your simple country wife already? I must be a dull companion compared to the brilliance of the Court beauties.'

'You are never dull. It is I who am the poor companion.' He tenderly rubbed his thumb along her cheek.

'I have not tired of you. I am here because I choose to be.'

'For now—but for how long?' A tremor passed through her as insight dawned. 'Once you have tried to dissuade Monmouth from rebellion, you will regard your duty in England as done. What then? You spoke of returning to Maryland—but not of our life together. Is that why you had Tess brought to me—so that I had something to love when you left?'

'Tess will, of course, keep you company, as will Martha. I could be gone for days, perhaps even weeks.' His voice seemed to her taut nerves to take on a wary note.

'That is not what I asked, Jake. Your heart is in the New World, not here. I will not bind you to a marriage you do not want.'

A muscle corded in his neck, deepening her fear. He remained silent, his stare on the ships, so that she plunged on. 'Your purpose in coming to England was to win a land grant from the King. Your plans did not include a wife, especially one you had been compromised into marrying.' She could tell by the stiff manner in which he held his body that she had struck a telling chord, and her pride reared up, refusing to let her show her pain. 'You do not have to pay all your life for saving my reputation. Just promise me—if you leave you will tell me the truth, and not just go.'

Jake stared down at her in disbelief. She was offering him his freedom. No tears—no hysterics—no recriminations, just calm reasoning. Why then did he feel no relief?

'You are putting words into my mouth, Becky. Have I given you cause to doubt me?'

'Until now you have always been honest with me, Jake.'

Her magnificent violet eyes were softer, more mysterious than he had ever seen them. Silently those luminous depths promised him paradise. His resolution rocked. She was offering him salvation and a chance of happiness he had believed forever denied him. But at what cost? Memories of Anne haunted him. He would not take Rebecca to a land where death was her reward for loyalty. And how could he expect her to wait the five or so years until a suitable home would be ready for her? It was better the way he had planned.

The lure in her glowing eyes set his blood afire. Since Anne's death he had accepted each day for what it gave him. The future was still uncertain. There might yet be a battle from which he did not return. Today there was Rebecca, and escape from the troubles which plagued him.

'Hold me, Jake,' she breathed provocatively. 'Let today be ours.'

He drew her into his arms, the clean, fresh scent of her hair and skin filling his senses. 'Temptress mine.' He kissed her hungrily, silencing the questions which hovered on her lips. Her response was immediate, her supple body moulding to the hardness of his own as his mouth travelled to the pulse at her throat. 'You have brought light into the darkness which had enclosed my life.'

They sank down on to the warm grass, still locked in each other's arms, the heat of the June sun warming their skin. The lazy drone of the bees and insects mingling with the deep rumble of the sea as it broke on to the beach below them, made a lazy, seductive background to their passion. There was a subtle change to Jake's kisses, a greater tenderness which heightened Rebecca's response and pleasure. When at last he drew back from her, he propped himself on to his elbow, his hazel eyes touched with sadness. 'Whatever the future holds, Becky, I will carry the memory of these last weeks in the cottage through the dark days ahead. Though the home I have provided for you was a poor one.'

He sat up abruptly, as though regretting he had said more than he'd intended, and stared out to sea. Why was he always so guarded with his emotions? Would nothing penetrate the shield which covered his heart?

'I too will treasure these weeks,' she said softly. 'I do not need a grand manor; the house has served our needs. I have been happy there.'

The furrow in his chin deepened as his facial muscles tensed. 'It is no home for a gently-bred woman.' There was a warning roughening his voice.

'You have been kind to me. I did not expect to find such contentment in our marriage. Any place is home when you are there to share it,' she responded. She stood up and walked away from him. Did love always bring with it such agonising pain? Why couldn't she accept just what Jake was prepared to offer? She would only lose him if she demanded more.

'I've wounded you,' he said, joining her. 'That was not my intent.'

'You spoke the truth—I was being unrealistic. We deal well enough together as we are.' She dared not look at him, knowing her eyes would betray her hurt, but kept her gaze fixed out to sea as she deliberately changed the subject. 'Those ships are not making much headway against the wind. Why do we not ride to Lyme? Your brother's ship may be among those, and he will be delighted if you met him when he lands.'

Jake shaded his eyes against the sun. 'None there is my brother's. I can tell that much from the rigging. But it seems I must ride without delay.'

'Do you think Monmouth is aboard one of them?'

'It is possible.'

'Then take me with you, Jake.'

'I will not have your name linked with the rebellion.' He cut across her plea and strode to the horses.

'If Monmouth lands in Lyme Grandfather will be there. I want to see him, Jake. If there is a battle... he could be killed. I want to know the truth about the lodge fire. I need to know the truth. I cannot believe he did it.'

He lifted her on to the saddle and, for a long moment as he stared up into her face, his expression was hard and uncompromising, a far cry from the tender lover of minutes earlier. 'I have tried to reason with Ashleigh. He will not listen.'

'With respect, Jake, do you truly think he would pay heed to a Masters? It is I who must speak with him.'

Her eyes pleaded with him to understand. 'I want the feud between our families to end and the bitterness to be put aside.'

'I'll not quarrel with you, Rebecca.' His eyes were unyielding. 'For your own safety, you will stay at the cottage.'

'No.' She shook her head, her face white with strain. 'You just want me out of the way. Your words earlier meant nothing to you, they were just part of your lovemaking, no more durable than dew evaporating on the morning grass. I'm not a child, so stop treating me like one.' Her voice quivered as she felt the weeks of frustration grind through her. 'I thought I could live with the knowledge you would always love Anne. But I cannot. And I will not cast my grandfather out of my life just because you wish it.'

Jake whirled on her, his mouth twisting with scorn. 'If the purgatory I suffer is from what you idealise as love, I want none of it again. No man could have looked upon Anne and not have been touched by the freshness of her youthful charm, her childlike innocence. Too late I learned the truth...' His eyes snapped with ice, and he looked away. 'She was my damnation.'

She stared at him, her hand going to her throat with shock. 'Jake, I...'

Such a terrible look haunted his hazel eyes that her voice dried in her throat, but when she would have gathered up the reins to ride away he held her hand. 'With you I have found peace, Becky. It is more important to me that you are safe.'

'I need to make my peace with Grandsire. Allowing Tess to come to me was his way of showing he does care.' His brows rose maddeningly. 'I want him to know that I do not believe he started the fire. He's an old man, and every day his support of Monmouth places him in danger. I don't want him to die believing I hate him.'

'Blood and nails, Becky! Why must you be so stubborn?'

She looked down into his face, trying to guess what he was thinking, but his expression was infuriatingly closed to her. 'I thought you would understand the pain of torn loyalties. *He is my grandfather!*'

The cleft in his chin tightened. 'Stubborn jade. If I do not take you, you are capable of seeking him out on your own. But promise me: if he refuses to see you the matter will end there. You will make no attempt to see him when I am not here to protect you.'

She nodded. 'Thank you, Jake. This means a great deal to me.'

They stopped at the cottage long enough to collect what they needed for an overnight stay in Lyme, and within the hour were cresting the cliff-peak of Golden Cap, the highest point on this coast, and travelled on, down through the valley of the mouth of the River Char, over the bridge at Charmouth to climb again on to the cliff path where the Cobb at Lyme came into sight. Three ships rode at anchor and two longboats were heading for the shore. In the prow of the first boat stood a tall man dressed in purple, the sunlight glinting off a diamond star on his chest.

'Monmouth comes openly as the son of a King.' Jake barely concealed his exasperation. 'See how proudly he wears the Garter on his breast. I fear he has already sealed his fate.'

Jake fell silent as he watched Monmouth jump ashore. With a flourish the Duke swept his plumed hat from his long, curling periwig and knelt on the beach in prayer. When he straightened he drew his sword, holding it proudly aloft as he led his small band of followers towards the town.

With a sigh Jake turned his horse towards the port. 'I had hoped it would not come to this. I should have known by the tone of his last letter that Monmouth was determined on this rebellion. He has allowed himself to be swayed by men who would use him to further their own ends. When last I spoke to him he talked of wishing only to live in peace with the mistress he adores and his children.'

'Do you condemn him for that also?' Rebecca asked, half expecting a sardonic reply.

'There was a time, Mistress Masters, when I envied him such peace.' The wide brim of Jake's hat hid his expression from her and his jaw was clamped tight against any further questions.

Ahead of them they could hear the cheering from the people lining the Duke's route. The number of people spilling from their houses slowed their progress through the seaport, and by the time they pushed their horses through the crowd to the market cross the reading of the Duke's proclamation denouncing James Stuart as a Catholic tyrant had almost finished. Looking across the heads of the people, Rebecca could not suppress a shiver at its violent phrases. Who could have advised the Duke to implicate his uncle in the death of King Charles? It was an absurd accusation, and one which would mean the death sentence to any of Monmouth's followers should the rising fail.

'I'll get us a room in an inn,' Jake said, leading her away from the market cross. 'I want your word you will stay there. I have much to attend to and, since Monmouth has allowed his proclamation to be read, time is short. In another hour the streets will be no place for a lone woman, for most of Monmouth's recruits will be drunk from toasting their success. I will discover whether Ashleigh is here and bring you word as soon as I can.'

It was impossible to speak further, for it seemed the whole of Lyme had gone wild as men whistled and yelled, and flung their caps in the air. A fiddler struck up a tune and couples began dancing in the street, causing Rebecca's mare to prance nervously. It was unlike anything she had witnessed before and, against her will, her heart was stirred by the fervent cries of 'À Monmouth! À Monmouth!' What manner of man was the Duke who, after so short a walk among these people, had charmed them into giving their lives to his cause?

Half an hour later Jake rode into Monmouth's camp. At the sight of the Duke standing beneath his standard he hardened himself against the years of friendship. He waited in the background, watching the men press forward to receive a smile and a handshake from

Monmouth. Even from a distance he could feel the pull of the Stuart charm Monmouth so easily exerted. And for once he wished he were wrong, that he did not feel he was witnessing the first steps his friend was making towards the execution block.

His throat felt gripped by iron talons as he marched forward to present himself, and Monmouth's dark eyes lit with recognition and pleasure.

'My friend, my heart gladdens to know you are with me.' Monmouth slid an arm unceremoniously across Jake's shoulders. 'A regiment shall be yours, Jake. And, of course, promotion to Major—nay, let it be Colonel.'

'Your Grace is generous, but I have not come to offer you my sword.'

'Then pray, Masters, tell us why you are here?' an arrogant voice cut in.

Jake shot Lord Grey of Warke a quelling glare. His apprehension rose as he looked around at the Duke's other companions. Grey was the only noble among them. And he was no warrior, although he swaggered forward with the bravado of a buccaneer, impressively armed with a brace of pistols stuck into the sash about his waist.

Jake ignored him and addressed Monmouth. 'I have information which I believe has been withheld from your Grace. I doubt if you have been informed of how inadequate the supplies are here, or how few of the substantial men have committed themselves to your cause?'

Monmouth's proud lips thinned. 'Surely it is you who are misinformed. If I needed proof that my cause is just then it is here in the numbers already flocking to my standard.'

'For years the West of England has been a nestbed of rebellion,' Jake cautioned, and Monmouth's eyes darkened, revealing the anguish and uncertainty beneath his confident assurance. 'I beseech you to listen to me. I do not seek glory from either your rise or downfall. I speak as a man who has long valued the friendship with which you honoured an obscure junior officer.'

'You were never obscure,' Monmouth answered good-humouredly, as he drew Jake out of earshot of his companions. 'With sword or pistol on the battle field there are few men to match your skill. From the start you have always urged caution in this, and I believe that you, unlike others, have had my best interests at heart.'

'Then heed me now, Your Grace. The nobility will not support you, and without them you cannot hope to win. Also, there are few arms to equip your army. You cannot fight a commander such as Churchill with pitchforks.'

'I cannot turn back now.' Monmouth was adamant. 'But I would rather you were with me than against me.'

'I cannot, in honour, forswear my allegiance to King James. Is there nothing I can say to dissuade you?'

'It is too late for that.'

'God be with you, Your Grace,' Jake forced out, against the pain of disappointment crushing his chest.

Monmouth smiled in understanding. 'With you too, my friend.'

The lightness was gone from Jake's step as he walked back to the inn. Already news of Monmouth's landing had spread and men from outlying farms and villages were straggling in twos, threes and fours into the seaport. As he had sadly predicted, most were armed, if at all, only with elderly muskets and scythes. The air was alive with the excitement and undercurrent of expectancy as eager hands helped unload ammunition on to the quay from the longboats. A pulley creaked as the sailors braced their weight against the ropes to drag the first of the cannon up the steep slope through the village from the harbour.

Defeat churned through him. He had failed to stop Monmouth and it could cost his friend his life. He entered the nearest tavern. He needed a drink, and was tempted to get drunk to wash the taste of failure from his mouth, but he paused with the tankard halfway to his lips. Drunkenness would solve nothing. Besides he had promised Becky he would search out her grandfather. The image of her trusting face rose before him. He had been a fool to give in to her pleading, but the wench had an unaccountable way of getting through his reserve. It was unlikely Ashleigh could yet have reached Lyme, and, even if he had, that he would make his peace with his granddaughter.

He pushed the untouched tankard aside. It would not take long to make his enquiries and he would comfort Becky in her disappointment.

An hour later he entered their bedchamber. Rebecca stirred as she lay asleep on the bed and he stood over her. Her face was pale and her dark lashes clung damply together. She had been crying. For the first time he saw her face without its proud defiance, the stubborn streak of courage, or the sensuous lines of passion. Throughout their marriage she had presented to him the face he'd wanted to see. Now, for the first time, he glimpsed her vulnerability. He sat on the edge of the bed and her eyelids flickered. When her eyes opened, drowsy with sleep, he would have had to be blind not to have seen the love shining in their depths as she reached out to him.

Shaken, he said stiffly, 'I failed, Becky. Monmouth would not listen to me, and as for Ashleigh—I'm sorry, he's refused to see you.'

'Where is he? If I went to him?'

'It would make no difference.' He took her into his arms. 'Ashleigh turned his back on me when I tried to insist. I'm sorry, Becky.'

'You did your best, Jake.' Her arms were round him, her lips caressing his ear as she sank against him. 'It is what I feared. While you were away I wrote to Grandfather. If he could read it he would see that the feud between our families must end.'

She looked up at him with such trust that, against his better judgement, he gave in to her unspoken plea. 'We pass where he is lodging on the road from the port. You can leave your letter for him there, but I doubt if it will do any good.'

'I have to try.' She managed a weak smile. 'It was the same with you and Monmouth. You cannot reason with those who will not listen. Your duty is done.'

He steeled himself against the promise of peace her eyes and body offered. His duty *was* done. Therein lay his dilemma. His life in England was over. He had to talk to her—explain why he must return to Maryland alone. Then her lips were on his, her body moving enticingly beneath him, and his body pulsated with the intoxication of her passion, sweeping him beyond the bounds of his control. He needed her as he had never needed any woman. There was a desperation behind her wild kisses, as though she feared this would be the last time they made love together. Her nails scored his back as he covered her, his desire throbbing to heights he had not, even in his experience, thought possible.

He rolled aside, but this time his release had brought him no peace. Becky had drifted into sleep at his side and the words he had planned to speak to her during their morning ride were still unspoken.

CHAPTER ELEVEN

THE seaport was crowded with people from the surrounding villages flocking to Monmouth's banner, and
as Jake, grim-faced, pushed a passage for their horses
through the throng Rebecca touched the deep cuff of
her riding habit where she had placed the letter for her
grandfather.

'Ashleigh lodges here,' Jake said, halting before the
open door of a cottage, the small garden of which was
filled with black-garbed men, their heads bent in prayer.
There was no mistaking Skevington's tall, spindly figure
at the front, and beside him stood Oliver.

Rebecca waited for the prayer to finish, but when her
grandfather looked up and his glance took in her sapph-
ire riding habit lavishly trimmed with silver lace, his
craggy face twisted with disgust. Without a word he
turned his back on her and walked into the cottage.

'Grandsire——' she began, but was stopped by Jake's
hand on her arm. 'Let me go to him, Jake. I must make
him understand. Just a few minutes, that's all I ask.'

'It will do no good. I would spare you the pain.'

'But I must try.' Her voice quivered with desperation.
'If he is alone, he will listen to me. He must!'

At Jake's reluctant nod of assent, she leapt from her
horse and ran into the house. Oliver Ashleigh stood in
the corner of the main room, his hand on a closed Bible.
'Grandsire, please hear me out.'

He turned slowly, his expression uncompromising.
'You sent no word of Masters' movements as we agreed.
You betrayed us. He's won you to his side. You are no
longer my grandchild.'

'I betrayed no one. Least of all a man I have come to
respect. What you asked of me was not possible,

Grandsire. How can a wife, in honour, set out to trap her husband?'

A fierce light leapt into Ashleigh's eyes. 'Then you are saying Masters is here as James Stuart's spy!' He moved to the door, his face working with fury. 'I thought as much.'

'No. You twist my words to feed your hatred.' Rebecca blocked his path, her voice growing urgent as she re-alised that an indiscreet word now could have Jake hanged as a spy. 'Jake is no informer.'

'He made his opinions plain when he spoke to Monmouth.' Oliver's glare blistered her. 'From the start he has been against open rebellion. If he's not for us—he's against us.'

'That's not true.' She took her grandfather's arm, feeling his body go rigid beneath her touch. 'He has always sought the path of reason because Monmouth is his friend.'

His lips thinned with contempt. 'Then why is he not staying to fight? Why is he running like a cur, when all who are loyal are willing to give their lives for our cause?'

'Jake is taking me home. I asked him to bring me to Lyme, so I could speak with you. He does not want me in danger.'

'Bah! A lame excuse. He's a traitor to us and must pay. Then you'll be free of him, Rebecca.' Ashleigh took her shoulders, his expression gentling. 'I was wrong to permit your marriage, to sacrifice you to that—that devil. Once he's dead, you'll be free.'

She recoiled with chilling horror. 'You are blinded by your hatred for his family. Jake is no informer. And I shall never be free... I love Jake Masters. More than that, I carry his child.'

Oliver Ashleigh's face contorted with a spasm of pain, his veined hands, swollen with rheumatism, clenching and unclenching as impotent rage swept through him. 'It was not enough that his family murdered my son, they have now robbed me of you.'

'But that's not true!' Rebecca stared at him, her heart contracting with anguish. Would he never see reason?

Could he not see how his stubbornness was tearing her
apart? 'The child is your great-grandchild,' she reasoned.
'It unites the two families. Surely it will bring peace to
a feud that has festered for too long. Jake bears you no
ill will. Accept my marriage, Grandsire.'

'Never. If Charles Masters thinks I will drop my fight
to maintain my water rights because of this child . . .' He
gasped for breath, his lips turning blue.

'Sir Charles has nothing to do with this.' She checked
at seeing him sag against the wall. He shook off her
supporting arm, the cold, fanatical light in his eyes condemning her to hell. She bowed her head against the
agony of his rejection. 'I love you, Grandsire. But I also
love Jake. Do not make me take sides.'

'Then go to your husband. For I will have none of
him, or you.' His cruel words lashed her like a lead-
tipped whip. 'For the sake of your condition, I shall allow
Jake Masters to ride out of here. But if I learn he has
turned traitor, then he will pay for his treachery.'

He turned his back on her and stormed from the room,
banging a second door firmly shut against her following
him.

'Of all the stubborn, pig-headed men!' she bit out in
answer to Jake's questioning glance as she mounted, and
then lapsed into a smouldering silence as they rode past
the awkward recruits practising the complicated pike-
drill, and through the acrid stench of gunsmoke drifting
across the track from a ragged volley of musket fire. A
mile further on they were forced to climb the grass bank
when a troop of horse showed no sign of slowing as they
thundered towards them, resplendent in the purple and
scarlet uniforms that Monmouth had shipped from the
Netherlands.

'Damn fools!' Jake snapped. 'Have they no thought
of others using the road? They'll kill someone, riding at
that pace.'

Rebecca scarcely heard his outburst for she was staring
at their leader, as she recognised Tom Hardwycke. He,
like all the troop, was dusty and several were splattered
with blood. Dear God! Had the fighting already begun?

To her astonishment, Tom raised his hat to her in salute as he drew level and she saw Jake stiffen. Had Tom forgiven her, or was he deliberately trying to goad Jake? She hoped it was the former.

'So it has started,' Jake said, his face pinched with gravity. He nodded ahead where a second swirling of dust heralded the approach of another troop of horse. 'Once blood has been spilled, the rebels' fate is sealed.'

Rebecca looked back to where Tom's troop had disappeared from sight, and hot needles of fear stung her spine. How would it end? Would Tom, her grandfather, or even Jake be alive at summer's end? She fidgeted with the silver fringing on her riding gloves and strove to master her distress, but her unease grew at seeing Jake take the flintlock pistol from his saddle holster to lay it across his thigh. 'Stay close to me and say nothing,' he warned.

Moments later the troop wearing the scarlet uniforms of the local militia were upon and surrounding them, their expressions hard and menacing, and none more ugly than Tovey's as his coarse face flushed with hatred when he confronted Jake.

'This time I have you, Masters! You come from that nest of rebels. Take him, men!'

'Try it, Tovey, and you die.' Jake levelled his pistol at the other man's heart. 'You cannot arrest a man for travelling the King's highway.'

To Rebecca's astonishment Tovey showed no fear, but then her own throat dried with horror at the cold touch of a pistol barrel pressed against the back of her head by a soldier crowding her mount. Tovey's fleshy lips drew back in a wolfish grin, showing his blackened teeth. 'I've got you this time and you know it, Masters. One move from you and it will be your woman who dies.'

Rebecca bit back a cry, her heart slamming against her ribs as she heard the ominous click of the pistol being cocked. Jake paled, but remained unruffled as he lowered his flintlock.

'A pity you did not learn from our last encounter, or the resulting discipline taken by your superior, *Captain*

Tovey.' His voice crackled with a warning frost. 'You exceeded your powers then, and were lucky to escape so lightly. But the cold-blooded murder of innocent travellers will cost you *your* life. I have papers which prove——'

'Papers be damned!' Tovey stormed. 'You'll not talk your way out of this. You're not two miles from Monmouth's camp, and two of my men are dead after being attacked by his rebels.' As Tovey's hand went to his sword, the muscles of Jake's handsome face locked with the effort it cost him not to counter the attack, which would have led to Rebecca's death. He did not flinch when Tovey's blade pressed against his throat. 'I have all the evidence I need to have you thrown in prison as an insurrectionist. And one move from you and I shall be within my rights to kill you, for trying to escape the King's justice. I said I would not forget you, Masters. I've found out some interesting facts these last weeks—such as the fact that your wife is Oliver Ashleigh's granddaughter. He's been stirring up trouble for months among his nest of fanatics, inciting people to rebel against their Papist King.'

'My marriage has nothing to do with my allegiance to King James.' Jake's voice was low, dangerous, and clipped with years of commanding authority. 'Before you make an even bigger ass of yourself, Tovey, I advise you to check my papers. Though first I would have the pistol removed from my wife's head.'

'Damn your arrogant hide!' Tovey swung back his arm to club Jake with the hilt of his sword.

'No!' Rebecca screamed. 'My husband is no rebel! Have you forgotten he is kin to Sir Charles Masters? And if you have learned anything of our marriage, you will know my grandfather has disowned me because of it.'

Tovey hesitated, his smile lascivious as it settled on Rebecca's defiant figure. 'When I have dealt with your husband, I shall take pleasure in interrogating you, Mistress Masters.'

'This has gone far enough, Tovey!' Jake blazed. 'My papers are signed by Lord Churchill. Are you willing to face King James for hampering his emissary in Dorset?'

Tovey stared at him with red-faced fury as Jake drew a folded document from his jacket and held it out. The pressure of the pistol barrel was removed from her head and Rebecca held her breath as Tovey stared at the seal which validated the words.

'You are free to leave,' he said through clenched teeth. 'Do you require an escort?'

'That will not be necessary,' Jake answered stiffly. 'Again you have abused your rank. Too often I have heard tales that many of the Dissenters arrested by you have arrived at prison half-senseless from your brutality.'

'Those prisoners are rebels and dangerous men,' Tovey protested. 'Sometimes it is necessary to use force.'

'You have proved today how easily you resort to such force,' Jake returned. 'It will be noted in my report to the Lord Lieutenant of the county. Good day, Captain Tovey.'

Jake beckoned to Rebecca to ride on, but as she moved forward she saw the malevolence in Tovey's pale eyes as he glared at Jake's back. Her blood curdled.

'Was it wise to antagonise Tovey?' she asked, once they were out of his hearing. 'He's a loathsome toad, and vindictive enough to seek any means to strike back at you.'

'His type are the scum and scourge of the army. He should never have been given command. I suppose he bought his position by equipping the militia, and now to suit his own ends abuses his power.' Jake shot her a long look, his eyes harrowed with concern. 'Tovey could be a danger to you. Tomorrow I must report to Churchill. It will not be safe for you to stay here alone.' He rubbed his chin, his expression becoming drawn. 'My movements will be erratic for some time until Nathan lands, which could be a matter of days or weeks. I also have matters to settle with Sir Charles. The safest place for you would be Four Winds.'

'No, Jake. I will not be beholden to Sir Charles. But the last thing you will need at such a time is a wife slowing you down, so I will not travel to London with you, either.' The narrowing of his eyes told her that she had accurately read his mind, and that for some reason it discomfited him. She conquered the spearhead of fear slicing through her stomach, and forced a smile. 'Besides, you took the house here to be near Nathan when he arrives—and I have been happy there. Tovey will not harm me, now that he knows you are Churchill's aide.' The effort to appear unconcerned cost her dear, and the nausea of pregnancy returned with a vengeance, forcing her to grip the saddle pommel to steady herself against a wave of dizziness.

'Becky, what ails you?' Jake was off his horse and lifting her from the mare before she could summon the strength to protest.

She clung to his arm as the sickly churning subsided and the landscape stopped swirling around her. 'It is nothing. The confrontation with Tovey must have shaken me more than I realised. I have recovered now.'

'You're as white as sheet. It's not like you to have a fit of the vapours.' His expression froze. 'Good God, are you pregnant?'

She could feel the tension coiling through him, but no flicker of emotion relaxed the harsh planes of his face. This was not how she had meant to tell him. His fingers tightened over her arms and his eyes glittered like fragmented steel. 'Are you with child, Becky?'

'I believe so. I hoped you would be pleased, Jake.'

She felt a quiver pass through his body, before he smiled. 'I had not thought to have our union blessed so soon.' There was a note of pain woven into his voice. 'Of course I am pleased.'

'Are you, Jake?' She strained back from his embrace, seeing through his reassurance to the shock beneath. As she stared into his handsome lean face, her heart ached with her love for him. Though tenderness and concern darkened his eyes, she would not delude herself they stemmed from love. And the news of the child had disturbed him. Did he see it as another shackle binding him to the woman he had been compromised into marrying? 'Your loyalty to Monmouth has cost you your freedom and has now thrust fatherhood upon you in a few short weeks,' she said lightly, though her heart felt it was breaking. 'Yet not once have you spoken of our future.'

He spun her round to face him. 'These last weeks I have lived one day at a time—my wits keeping me one step ahead of men such as your grandfather, or Skevington, who sought to bring me down. If I have not spoken of the future it is because I have not let myself dwell too deeply upon it.' His lips tilted in a lopsided smile and although, as always, its effect disarmed her, she knew he was not being entirely honest with her. 'Once I have reported to Churchill my duty in England is done.'

'But if there is a battle,' she interrupted, crushing her doubts as a more alarming fear struck her, 'will you not have to fight?'

'I have no wish to take up arms against a man I called friend, but my allegiance to King James may force me to.' His fingers tightened over her arms. 'You are my wife, Rebecca—in any eventuality, I have made arrangements that you will be well provided for.'

'Do not even speak that way, Jake.' She clung to him. With a soft laugh he kissed her to silence and then whispered against her ear, 'Temptress mine, I have no plans to end my days mouldering on a battlefield. When I return we will speak of the future. The child changes nothing.'

Jake suppressed the anguish tearing through him as he lifted Rebecca on to the saddle. The child changed everything.

CHAPTER TWELVE

JAKE tensed, straining to discern sound in the mist-barricaded darkness. The sodden earth of Sedgemoor muffled the sound of his horse's walk and also that of any approaching riders. He looked down at the sentry, scarcely able to see his form. 'This cursed mist shields everything,' Jake said softly. 'Use your ears well, for Monmouth must approach across that rhine.'

'Rhine, Cap'n—sorry, Major Masters?' the soldier queried.

'It's what the locals call the ditches separating the fields,' Jake patiently explained, taking no offence at the soldier's error, for his promotion still felt uncomfortable, having the stigma of Judas silver for his peace of mind. 'Before this mist hid the moor from us, we learned that Monmouth was moving his army from Bridgwater. Monmouth knows well the advantage of a surprise night attack.'

Jake continued his inspection of the camp and returned to Churchill's quarters in the village. Now Brigadier, Churchill was seated with Lord Feversham, who had been given command of the army. 'Is there any sign of the mist lifting?' Churchill asked.

'None. Colonel Oglethorpe is checking the roads leading north; I have been with the patrol on the moor, posting advanced sentries. But we heard nothing.'

'Monmouth will not attack tonight,' Lord Feversham proclaimed, his heavily accented voice grating on Jake's nerves. He wished King James had not appointed this self-indulgent Frenchman Lieutenant-General of the army rather than Churchill.

'I was out on the moor myself till past midnight, but this Monmouth, I think, prefers to chase shadows,' Feversham continued. 'He achieves nothing. It is more than a month since he landed and all he does is lead his army in circles.'

'They number five thousand, and they are learning to fight,' Churchill pointed out. 'And they are stiffened by belief in their cause.'

Feversham shrugged with arrogant disdain. 'And have we not seen half-starved deserters skulking back to their farms? He has an army of peasants. *Mon Dieu!* A proper army would be laying siege to London by now, but these *canaille* are camping in a remote field not thirty miles from where Monmouth landed. But no more of this cat and mouse. Soon it will come to battle.'

As Jake watched Feversham strut from the room, he gloomily contemplated Monmouth's position. It must indeed come to a battle at last, one which would decide his friend's fate. He rubbed his hand across the back of his neck to ease the tense muscles. The rebellion had been mismanaged from the start and Monmouth, who loved life so much, was doomed.

'You have misgivings, Major?' He started guiltily when Churchill addressed him.

'The time for those is long past. But I regret it has come to this.'

Churchill nodded. 'Leave me, Masters. Get some rest if you can.'

But Jake had barely got an hour's sleep before a wild drumbeat hammered into his uneasy dreams, and he leapt up to hear the hoarse shouting of his men as they spilled from their tents. 'The enemy is come!'

By seven o'clock with the heat of the risen July sun prickling his skin beneath the weight of his steel breastplate, Jake stared down at the carnage around him. Sickened, he wiped the drying blood from his sword and sheathed it, then massaged the strained, tortured flesh of his scarred arm as his gaze fell upon a trampled green standard with its muddled insignia, 'Fear nothing but God.' Brave words, he mused darkly, but the men who had answered Monmouth's call must now face the wrath of King James.

As he rode back towards the deep and boggy Langmoor Rhine, he recognised several faces among those whose grave it was, but, thankfully, not the one he was seeking. For Rebecca's sake he hoped Oliver Ashleigh was not among the slain, and that he had escaped—as it appeared that Monmouth had done. He picked his way to the plungeon where the rhine could be crossed, noting as he did so a purple-clad figure sprawled in the water. The man's bloody and gun-powder-blackened fingers clutched at the bank to save himself from drowning.

Jake drew his sword, but, as the figure slipped back into the water, he leapt to the ground and, with his free hand, grabbed at the rebel's collar and heaved him to safety. Jake stepped backwards, his sword poised, as the rebel knelt on all fours, gasping for breath with his temple pressed into the ground. With a shake of his short, cropped head, he struggled to his knees and looked up.

'You!' Tom Hardwycke's astonishment echoed Jake's own. 'Damn your eyes, Masters! You should have left me to drown and spared me the hangman's rope.'

'Fate has a strange way of mocking us. His Majesty's Lord Justice will decide your fate, not I.'

'At least I did not turn my coat.' Hardwycke lurched to his feet, his youthful face ravaged by hunger and bitterness. 'Ashleigh was right—you betrayed us.' He fumbled at his sword-belt and, discovering the scabbard empty, swore violently. 'A pox on your treacherous hide! You tricked us, you bastard. As you tricked Rebecca into marrying you after you'd seduced her.' Tom laughed, a harsh sound edged with hysteria. 'But Ashleigh outwitted you. Did you know Rebecca only agreed to wed you so she could be Ashleigh's spy?' A sly light gleamed in Tom's darkly circled eyes. 'How does it feel to wear the cuckold's horns—to have a wife who loves another? You have neglected Rebecca these past weeks... But I was close by to comfort her—as I was those other times you were away. I wonder which of us fathered the child she carries? It's not you she loves. She loves me. *Me!*'

Jake lashed out, his fist crashing into Hardwycke's jaw and sending him sprawling on to the ground. Breathing heavily, Jake stood over him, his hand clenching over his sword-hilt. The blood pounded in his head, and a murderous red haze clouded his reason as rage scalded through his veins, until the throbbing from his duel scar sobered him. He had killed too many men that night. He was sick of bloodshed.

To his right a sergeant and several men scoured the bank to capture any survivors from the battle. It was for the law to deal with Tom Hardwycke, not himself. Jake snatched up the reins, hurling himself into the saddle with such force that his startled gelding reared, but was immediately brought under control. Then sanity returned, and with it the certainty that Hardwycke was lying, and he was amazed at the relief the knowledge brought him.

'You always were an idle braggart, Hardwycke.' He deliberately changed the subject, before his anger at the whelp's lies goaded him to retaliate. 'I have not seen Ashleigh among the slain or wounded. Did he escape?'

'Do you think I would betray him?'

'Or I denounce my own wife's grandfather?' Jake rapped out. 'It is for Rebecca I ask. If you have any regard for her at all, you will spare her the worry of not knowing his fate.'

Tom eyed him sullenly. 'Ashleigh was wounded in the neck and shoulder—but he could have escaped in the mist across the moor.' The soldiers were just a few yards away and, seeing them, Tom straightened, his voice rising with bravado. 'You should have killed me, Masters. Rebecca is not your true wife...she was first plighted to me.'

Those words haunted Jake as he galloped away. The law counted a betrothal as valid as any marriage. And, by the laws of his church, their marriage had been unorthodox.

'Major Masters!' A young ensign cut across his path. 'Major Masters, the Brigadier's compliments, sir. He asks you to attend him without delay.'

Jake nodded. With the rebellion crushed, he would soon be free of his army duties and would be able to return to America. He had received word yesterday that Nathan's ship *The Chesapeake Queen* had landed at Plymouth.

Rebecca put aside her sewing and rubbed her eyes, strained by the dim candlelight, while outside the wind howled along the cliff and the rain buffeted the latticed window. Standing up, she paced the parlour, touching as she passed them Jake's possessions in the room—a broken clay pipe, the silver tankard he always drank from, and lastly a faded red silk sash she had earlier mended, which had been his mother's parting gift when he'd left Maryland. Her hand closed over the sash and she hugged it against her breast in a sudden rush of longing. Another day had passed and there had been no word from Jake.

'Why don't you go to bed?' Martha said gently, as she broke the thread of wool with which she had been darning Simmons' hose. 'I'll bring you a posset to help you sleep.'

'I wouldn't sleep, Martha, and, rather than spend hours tossing and turning, I would prefer to sit here and try and occupy my mind.' She put the sash on the table and smoothed its folds. 'I miss Jake so much. It seems more like five years than five weeks since he rode away after Monmouth landed.'

'But he's sent word,' Martha soothed. 'He survived without harm at Sedgemoor, and he did say your grandfather had escaped. You must try not to worry so.'

'It was a week ago that I received his note. Where is Jake now?' She paced the room, stepping aside from the hearth as Simmons brought in some logs to bank the fire.

'The Major knows how to look after himself.' Simmons put the last log on the fire and stood back, wiping a lock of auburn hair from his freckled brow. 'You must not fret so.'

Rebecca looked at the manservant who was usually so close-lipped. 'You think I'm being foolish. But I cannot help but worry. I do not know what I would do if I lost him.'

Simmons coughed, and looked down at his hands. 'Martha told me you fear the Major will leave for Maryland without you. Forget such nonsense. He never deserts a friend.' He held out his crippled hand. 'I'm a poor valet for him since this, but the Major keeps me at his side.'

'How did you injure your hand?' Rebecca asked, to keep her mind from worrying over her husband, and to feed the curiosity she had always had about the taciturn servant. He shot her a closed look and for a moment she thought he meant to ignore her question.

'On the voyage over here there was a storm,' he said at last. 'Some of the cargo had broken loose and, fearing it would hole the side, the Major and I went below to lash it fast. A rope snapped, and my hand was crushed behind a crate which smashed against the ship's side. Many a man would have dismissed so useless a servant— not so the Major. I'd give my life for him—and I'd stake three years' wages that he cares for you too much to desert you.'

Rebecca moved to Simmons' side, for his words proved that he too had accepted her. 'Thank you, Simmons. You must think me a very foolish creature to doubt Jake.'

He grinned. 'Love makes fools of us all. You've made the Major happy, and I bless you for that.' He turned abruptly on his heel and left the room.

Martha chuckled. 'Did I not tell you, mistress, the Major would return—and soon?'

Rebecca paced on, her mind still troubled. 'I know it is only because I miss Jake so terribly that I worry about him. But what of my grandsire? Jake said he was wounded. He could have been taken prisoner. They've captured Monmouth.'

'Aye, poor man.' Martha shook her head sadly. 'To be deserted by his followers and caught while asleep from exhaustion in a ditch. It will be the block for him.'

Rebecca agitatedly twisted the emerald ring round upon on her finger. 'How do I know Grandsire was not betrayed, or has died of his wounds?'

'You will make yourself ill if you think like that.'

'What am I to think, Martha?' Rebecca had not stopped pacing. 'Every day we hear of new atrocities committed by the army searching out Monmouth's followers. Many of them have been hanged—often without a trial, on the very spot they were taken. Even the families of Dissenters are not spared—wives and children are turned out of their homes and their houses burned. Where is there for the fugitives to go for safe shelter?'

She broke off, seeing Martha frown and look towards the window. Above the whine of the wind and rain was another sound. A rhythmic tap-tap on the windowpane. Yet no trees or shrubs were planted outside that shuttered window. The noise came again, more urgently this time, and, puzzled, Rebecca crossed to the window. Who would have come to the house so furtively?

'Mistress, take care,' Martha cautioned. 'It could be a thief trying to trick his way into the house.'

Rebecca opened the wooden shutters, her startled cry bitten back when she met a pale face pressed against the pane. Shock gave way to a flood of joy.

'It's Grandsire!' she called over her shoulder as she ran out of the room into the dark passage.

'Mistress, I know Ashleigh is kin, but you cannot take him in.' Martha placed a restraining hand on her arm. The servant's face, visible in the faint light from the open door of the parlour, was drawn with fear. 'If the soldiers learn of it, you'll be imprisoned for aiding a traitor.'

'I will not turn my back on my grandfather.' Rebecca shrugged off the servant's hold. 'And I know the dangers. Tovey has searched this house twice, and each time made clear the penalties for harbouring rebels. He's waiting for a chance to strike back at Jake, but I have no intention of becoming Tovey's pawn. I will understand if you and Simmons wish to leave—I could not expect you to help my grandfather and place your own lives in danger.'

Martha drew her stout figure to its full height, her hands locked tightly together beneath her ample bosom. 'The Major left Simmons here to protect you. We will not desert you. For your own sake, Ashleigh must be gone before morning.'

Impulsively, Rebecca threw her arms round the servant. 'You are a good friend, Martha.' Freeing herself, she hurried to the door and pulled it open. The wind tore at her hair, whisking her ringlets across her face, and, as she impatiently brushed the strands away, two cloaked figures emerged from the shadows. When Ashleigh stumbled over the threshold, she instinctively reached out to support him. At her touch, he flinched. Did her touch repel him so? Her joy at seeing him faded, and her hand fell to her side as she led the way to the parlour. If he still hated her, why had he come here?

'Bring some wine and food, Martha,' she ordered.

Ashleigh flopped heavily down on to a chair, and at a groan torn from his lips Rebecca was at his side, her throat clenching with concern. He was bare-headed, his grey hair matted with straw and twigs, and the black worsted of his jacket and breeches was torn and shiny with ground-in filth. In the wavering candlelight his shrunken flesh looked transparent on his bones and his eyelids were squeezed shut as though blotting out excruciating pain.

'Grandsire, what ails you?'

Martha entered with a tray of potted hare, bread, and a flagon of wine. Leaving her servant to deal with her grandfather's companion, Rebecca poured a goblet of wine and held it to Oliver Ashleigh's lips. He gulped thirstily, and only then opened his eyes.

'Why have you come here, Grandsire? You must know it's not safe.'

'So tired...nowhere else to go.' He lifted his bloodshot eyes, their irises dulled with pain.

'And where else should he come, but to his only kin?' a chilling voice proclaimed from behind her.

Rebecca whirled round, her incensed stare falling on Bartholomew Skevington as she straightened to confront him. 'Mr Skevington, while I am obliged to you for bringing my grandfather here, I will offer no refuge to a man who has done all in his power to bring my husband down.'

'Do you think I would stay under the roof of an informer?' Skevington sneered. He drained his goblet and banged it down on to the table.

'My husband was no informer!' Rebecca defended Jake with heat. 'All he learned from his weeks with the Dissenters was for Monmouth's benefit. He advised his friend that this rebellion would fail. Monmouth would not listen.'

The preacher's hatchet face twisted with disgust. 'Masters knew our plans—our strength. Of course he betrayed us! While we rot upon the gibbets, he parades at Court in his finery, his precious land grant in the colonies lining his pocket. If he's such a loyal husband, why isn't he here now with you? I'll tell you why—because you're no longer of use to him. His brother's ship is no doubt awaiting him. Your treacherous husband will sail to the colonies at the first convenient tide, and there will use those of Monmouth's followers who are transported to break their backs on his land.'

'You lie!' An angry flush stung Rebecca's cheeks. 'Jake is not like that.'

Ashleigh stood up, his voice scathing in her ear. 'Even now you defend that rogue you married. I was mistaken in coming. I'd rather die in a hedgerow than accept a *Masters'* hospitality.'

Sweat broke out on his wide brow as he swayed and clutched at the chair-back for support and, worried for his health, Rebecca swallowed her retort. 'You're ill, Grandsire. You must rest, and you *were* right to come here.'

'No, I should not have come.' He began to cough, his chest wheezing with a harsh, racking sound as he collapsed into the chair, his hand covering his mouth. When the seizure stopped, Rebecca was horrified to see a smear of blood across his chin.

When he attempted to rise, she gently pushed him back into the chair. 'You will stay and rest.' Her voice checked at the warm, sticky feeling seeping over her fingers and she was appalled to find her hand was crimson with his blood.

'Martha, bring hot water, towels and linen for bandages.' Ignoring her grandfather's protest, she unfastened his cloak. The shoulder of his jacket was in tatters, its plain linen collar torn and caked in dried blood. As she carefully eased back his jacket and shirt, her nose wrinkled at the smell of putrefying flesh, and her alarm grew at seeing the blackened, pulpy mass oozing blood and pus.

'A musket ball!' He answered her unspoken question. 'Skevington did his best to dig the metal out—but the wound festers. They've done for me.'

'You must not speak that way,' she said, firmly. 'It looks as though the poison has been washed from the wound by the blood. But you've lost a great deal of blood. With good food and rest, you will soon be well again.'

'You're a good child.' His head lolled against the carved back of the chair, his voice growing weaker. 'I wronged you. I should never have agreed . . . agreed you marry that—that devil Masters.'

'He's not a devil, Grandsire, but a kind, considerate husband.' She tried desperately to make him understand. 'I love Jake. Why do you hate him so? He is not like Sir Charles.'

'Is he not?' The gasping voice plunged like a stake through her heart. 'Seducer! Papist informer . . .! Where's your pride, woman . . .? The Masterses are rogues . . . scoundrels to a man. That lecher dishonoured you.'

She shook her head. 'He never laid a finger on me. Even when we were married he gave me time to accept him before he . . .' she was faltering, embarrassed at having to speak so candidly to her grandfather, but forced herself to go on '. . . before he made me truly his wife. Jake saved my reputation, but it was Tom who abused your trust. He forced his attentions on me during the journey back from Bridgwater. That's why I ran away from him.'

Oliver regarded her in silence as she took the water and cloths from Martha and began to clean his shoulder. To her relief there was no sign of any fragmented metal in the wound, and a poultice would draw any remaining poison out. When she sat back on her heels, satisfied that her grandfather's shoulder was clean and properly bandaged, he took her hand.

'Rebecca...about Tom, he——'

'You must not talk, Grandsire,' she cut across his feeble words, anxious that he save his strength. 'Tom is not important. You must rest.'

'But the fire...' Another bout of coughing left him gasping for breath.

'Hush, Grandsire. It is best forgotten. No one was harmed. Do not speak of it now.'

His eyes glazed, but he stubbornly persisted. 'Tom...' His voice faded, and she leaned closer, straining to catch at least some of his words. 'A wild youth...forgive me.'

Her eyes misted with emotion and as his eyelids drooped tiredly, she placed a finger to his lips. 'I forgave you a long time ago, Grandsire. Rest now.'

His head rolled on to his chest and in sudden panic she put her hand over his heart. It still beat weakly. She rose tiredly, and was surprised to find Skevington still in the room. 'Sir, I thank you for bringing my grandsire to me, but in view of your opinions I must ask you to leave this house.'

'Still so proud.' Skevington eyed her with distaste. 'Ashleigh deserved better than the likes of you—but he is ill, and another night in the open would kill him. Your time will come, madam. The good Lord punishes the ungodly! A certain baronet has been making enquiries about the circumstances of your marriage. There are some who will never acknowledge your wedding service as binding.'

'But you performed the ceremony,' Rebecca's hand covered her stomach protectively.

'It is binding on those of *our* persuasion,' he said, making for the door. 'But your so-called husband is not one of us.'

Rebecca stared after his departing figure with disbelief. Was it true that many would not regard Jake and herself as truly married? Would her child then be a bastard?

'Don't you pay any mind to what that preacher says,' Martha said from the doorway. 'Major Masters would not play you false.'

'I know, Martha. But if we are not truly married...'

'Don't you even think such a thing!' Martha remonstrated. 'Now we had better get your grandfather to bed.'

Simmons appeared from behind her, his voice stern. 'The Major won't be liking this—but I doubt that he would have you turn the old man out on such a night.' He bent over Ashleigh's sleeping figure to lift him, but stopped at the sound of a pistol shot. The next moment a violent banging upon the front door froze them with startled horror.

'Open in the King's name!' A gruff voice shouted above the wind and rain, and a further torrent of blows rattled the door on its hinges.

'Soldiers!' Simmons gasped. 'A pox on them—begging your pardon, ma'am. But we're done for, with a wounded Dissenter in the house.'

The outside door splintered and moments later several soldiers burst into the room. Captain Tovey was the first through the parlour door.

'Arrest that man!' He pointed to Ashleigh. 'And the rest of these curs for aiding a rebel.'

Two soldiers pulled Rebecca's hands behind her back while others grabbed Martha. Simmons put up a fight, and for his pains was punched viciously in the face and groin, and when he doubled over in agony was hauled to his feet by his hair.

'Leave my servants alone!' Rebecca demanded, her voice catching with agony as her arm was wrenched up behind her shoulders. 'They have nothing to do with this. Do you forget whose house this is?'

'Indeed I do not. Which is why it has been kept under watch this past week,' Tovey gloated. 'Harbouring traitors is treason.'

'This man is my grandfather. And if you have been watching the house, you will know he entered it less than half an hour ago. As you see, he is too ill to leave, but I ordered his companion from my husband's house.'

'The preacher is dead,' Tovey stated without remorse. 'He resisted arrest. That Ashleigh is here is evidence enough to throw you all in gaol.'

'Then you are a fool, sir.' Rebecca's anger was fuelled by the unnecessary shooting of Skevington. She conquered a stab of guilt, that if she had not turned him from the house he would still be alive. How could she have known Tovey was lying in wait and would murder him in cold blood? She faced the Captain, defiantly. 'I could not in Christian charity turn a wounded man from my door. And on a night such as this no court would expect me to send a servant to alert the militia—especially since it was obvious my grandfather was too weak to move, let alone attempt to escape. You have overstepped your duty, sir, by anticipating that I had no intention of warning the authorities.'

'It will be my word against yours,' Tovey scoffed. 'You'll not be so proud after a few days in gaol.'

Rebecca stood her ground. 'My servants are innocent. They but obeyed my orders.'

'You're all guilty and will be questioned,' Tovey snapped as he puffed out his barrel chest with self-importance. 'Who knows? We may yet learn the truth of your husband's dealings with the Dissenters while he was in Somerset and Dorset.'

'Have you lost your wits, Captain Tovey?' Rebecca flung back. 'My husband is high in favour at Court. Twice before you unjustly accused him of treason.'

'It is *Mr* Tovey now, though these soldiers are still under my command. My orders come from someone who knows I can be relied upon to serve him loyally. For now, Major Masters is beyond my reach. Not so yourself.' He strutted across the room to glare haughtily down his fleshy nose at her. 'You, madam, have know-ingly given refuge to a rebel, and before the week's end, you will know that for a woman the penalty for treason is—burning!'

Rebecca ran her tongue over suddenly parched lips. Tovey was insane if he meant to strike at Jake through her. But, as she held his malignant stare, her blood turned to ice. It was not madness which drove Tovey, but envy for all Jake was, and he could never hope to be.

A tortured groan from her grandfather, as a soldier hauled him to his feet, was more than she could bear. She could not believe that she would be condemned for what she had done this night. Jake would not let her die! But her grandfather was another matter. If he was moved from the house tonight he would perish. To save him she was prepared to humble herself.

'Please, you've killed once tonight—must you murder another? My grandfather will die if he is moved. Can you not place a guard on him, and leave him here at least for a day or two until he is stronger?'

'The devil I will!' Tovey exploded.

'My husband will not let this insult go unavenged. No one can dispute that Skevington was running from this house after I had turned him from my door, but whoever your commander is now I know my husband has re-ported your brutal conduct to the Lord Lieutenant of the county. Should my grandfather die, you may find it is yourself who is kicking your heels in prison.'

Tovey's reptilian stare swept over her as he digested her words. From his heightening colour, it was obvious she had struck upon the truth.

'It changes nothing,' he announced stiffly. 'Except that Ashleigh and your servants will be imprisoned at the nearest gaol, but you, madam, will be taken elsewhere—where your husband's influence cannot reach.' He turned to two soldiers. 'Have what horses there are saddled. We leave at once.'

'My mistress has done nothing!' Simmons shouted. 'Major Masters will have your life for this.'

A musket rammed into his stomach silenced him and Martha sobbed quietly. ''Tis the devil's work you do this night. You won't get away with it.'

Rebecca looked fearfully across at Martha, silently pleading with her to stay silent and bring no further punishment upon her head.

'I'm not dressed for riding,' Rebecca told Tovey, and was relieved that none of her terror showed in her steady voice.

'Of course you must change. I will accompany you to your room to ensure you do not attempt to escape.' Tovey's gaze travelled insultingly over her figure, lingering upon the low neck of her flowered cotton gown.

She curbed the urge to cover her breasts with her hands, the memory of his attack upon her at the inn sending a shudder of disgust through her. 'In that case, Mr Tovey, I will ride as I am. Will you allow Martha to fetch my cloak?'

He nodded, and Martha left the room.

'Major Masters will learn of every insult you have subjected his wife to,' Simmons shouted, and received another blow for his pains.

'His whore, more like,' Tovey snorted. 'Gossip has it that their wedding was no wedding at all.'

'Don't you listen to him, mistress,' Martha insisted, as she reappeared and placed a fur-lined cloak over Rebecca's shoulders. Her voice lowered. 'Keep faith. The Major will save you. He loves you. Never doubt it.'

Before she could reply, Rebecca was roughly shoved forward and from the corner of her eye she saw a soldier hoist her unconscious grandfather over his shoulder and follow her as she was taken to the waiting horses.

'Half the troop come with me,' Tovey shouted. 'The rest will take the other prisoners to Bridport.'

Shock at the rapidity of the night's events numbed Rebecca's mind. She was not aware of mounting and riding off, or that the troop soon divided. This could not be happening to her. She could do nothing to help her grandfather but pray. As the miles plodded by, she gradually became aware that she was now Tovey's only prisoner. She swallowed against the strangling threads of fear which threatened to destroy her. She was at the mercy of a brutal and vindictive man.

Hemmed in on all sides by soldiers, she had no chance of escape. But, although she could feel Tovey's cruel stare upon her, he no longer taunted or made any attempt to attack her and slowly that particular fear ebbed. She schooled herself to stay calm. Tovey did not have enough evidence to convict her, but underlying her fears of what lay ahead was the disturbing realisation that from two different sources she had been told her marriage was invalid. There was only one person she could think of who hated her enough to start those rumours. Was Sir Charles Masters behind her arrest? She would not believe Jake was party to his uncle's scheming. Once he learned she was a prisoner he would see she was freed. For a few days at the most she must be strong, and she would not shame her husband by showing any sign of her fear.

Even so, a day or two in gaol was a daunting prospect. And how would her grandfather fare—ill as he was? She tried to visualise what it would be like—a single, cold cell with poor food and just a wooden bench for a bed? It would not be pleasant, but she was strong and healthy and she would endure it with fortitude. The events of the last hour tumbled chaotically through her mind until her head reeled in confusion. Surely she would wake and find it was but a nightmare. But as the cold seeped through the thick cloak, and the rain began again and dripped under her hood to run in icy rivulets down her neck, she knew it was devastatingly real.

CHAPTER THIRTEEN

DAWN was crimsoning the horizon before Rebecca paid much heed to the direction they were taking. They should have reached a gaol hours ago, but instead they had spent the night heading north-west, the meandering, hedge-lined track taking them through darkened and unfamiliar hamlets, some with the thatch burned and the limewashed walls blackened from the soldiers' fires. Occasionally, from a ditch, the pitiful cry of a homeless young child drifted to her. This was the chilling reality of the aftermath of the rebellion. What if Jake did not learn of her fate in time to save her? The first doubts crept into her numbed mind, and she angrily cut them dead.

The troop turned off the road along a straight driveway to an ivy-hung manor house and halted. She slid to the ground, her stiff, aching legs wobbly after hours in the saddle, and, flanked by four soldiers, she was escorted into the building. The dim corridor led into a darkened, musty-smelling baronial hall where she could just make out the rows of truckle beds and scattered pieces of uniform and weapons. This then must be the militia's headquarters. As the wooden shutters were folded back, she glanced nervously round the lightening room, the dark beams of the rafters high above her head taking on the appearance of a giant spider lying in wait for its prey.

'This way,' Tovey grunted, as he led the way towards a narrow door beneath the minstrels' gallery at the far end.

Two lighted flambeaux revealed a downward staircase which disappeared into the bowels of the house. She gagged at the stench rising from within. Sweat, excrement and vomit vied with the sour smell of festering wounds and the sickly odour of death.

'Where have you brought me?' Her voice echoed dully in the confined space.

'Silence, wench!' Tovey ordered. 'You're not here to ask questions but to answer them.' He pushed her roughly down the steps. Her escort stopped before a barred door, which needed two men to lift the heavy wooden beam from its massive latch.

As they dragged the door open, Tovey turned to her with a grin of satisfaction. 'The gaols are over-full. The foundations of this house go back centuries. These old cellars serve well enough for the likes of Monmouth's gallows-meat.'

The stench from the open door was a dozen times worse than it had been upon entering the passage. Four soldiers—two bearing torches and two with levelled muskets—stepped forward into the gloom. At the sound of inhuman groans and rustlings from within, Rebecca repressed a shudder of revulsion.

'Get back, you rebel bastards,' Tovey shouted. 'Here's another of Monmouth's doxies to await His Majesty's pleasure.'

The torchlight fell upon the figures closest to the door, and sudden panic rooted Rebecca where she stood as she stared at the ragged creatures, covered in their own filth and huddled on the mildewed straw which sparsely covered the floor. 'Water,' a feeble voice cried. 'For mercy's sake—water.'

'Shut that old crone up,' Tovey commanded. There was a thud and a scream as a musket butt met its target.

'Silas Cobb is dead,' a defiant voice called out of the darkness. 'He's beginning to stink—can't you take his corpse out of here?'

'Remove it,' Tovey ordered two of the guards. His voice rose menacingly. 'And the next one who opens his mouth will find it's his turn for questioning.' He rounded on Rebecca. 'This will teach you I'm not a man to make a fool of.' He shoved her in the back, but she dug in her heels and stood firm.

'I am no common felon,' she voiced her outrage. 'My husband is a man of standing at Court. I demand the respect due to a woman of my position—a private cell with——'

Her head snapped back from a vicious slap which brought fire to her cheek. 'You're in no position to demand anything!' Tovey crowed. 'Gaoler, bring the fetters. This one's a troublemaker.'

Rebecca was pushed down on to an upturned barrel, and iron bands were clamped shut over her wrists and then her skirt and petticoats were flipped up to her knees and another set placed over her ankles and locked. Tovey ran his tongue over his fleshy lips as he stared at her slender calves before Rebecca brushed her skirts down. The angry movement of her hands, now weighted with iron, seemed to jerk her arms from their sockets and she bit her lip to cut off a cry of pain. Tovey hauled her to her feet, glowering at her as the two soldiers carried the dead man out of the cell. 'Now, Madam Rebel, your friends await you.'

She tossed back her head, her violet eyes flashing proud defiance as she refused to show the gnawing fear which made the bile rise to her throat. 'My husband will have your hide for this outrage.'

'I obey a higher authority.' Tovey gave a malicious laugh. 'Your involvement with the rebels will bring censure to his family. And the Masterses are a proud brood. It's common gossip that he only married you to cover his tracks as King James's spy. The whole sordid story will come out at your trial. That arrogant bastard, Jake Masters, is about to be humbled, and I, Tobias Tovey, will be the instrument of his downfall.'

Rebecca reined in her instinctive challenge and calmed her voice to one of quiet authority. 'You exceed your duty, Mr Tovey. I should not like to be in your shoes when Sir Charles Masters learns of the insult you have shown to a member of his family.'

To her astonishment he threw back his head and laughed. 'Prisoners, do you hear this whore's bravado?' he jeered. 'She betrayed her own grandfather in order to warm the bed of King James's spy. Her lover betrayed your leaders.' His laughter rose, the sound still carrying to her as the guards dragged her into the cell, then slammed the door shut.

The abruptness with which total darkness enclosed the cell set the hairs on Rebecca's neck prickling with fear. She stood rigid as the shufflings grew nearer. A fever mounted behind her eyes. She had never thought herself a coward, but although she was prepared to bear pain and deprivation with fortitude, nothing in her secluded life had prepared her for such squalid degradation. And more than that—the atmosphere of hostility and violence was tangible. Tovey had deliberately stirred up the prisoners against her, and they were like starving hounds after blood—her blood.

She backed away and pressed the edge of her cloak over her nose and mouth to try and blot out the appalling odours of their bodies.

'Well, now, my pretty.' A coarse voice set her flesh crawling. 'Whore to a spy, were you? Good sport for us, eh, lads?'

The wall stopped her retreat, its rough, damp surface seeping through the thickness of her cloak as the shufflings closed in around her. Close by, the ragged breathing of a couple fornicating chilled her to the marrow. In this devil's hole there was no shame. Every pore of her body was attuned to threatening danger. When a hand touched her shoulder she jumped violently. Then shock gave way to outrage when someone else squeezed her hip and seized upon her breast.

'Get away from me!' She lashed out using her chains as a weapon to keep her tormenters at bay.

'Regular wildcat, bain't thee?' a man croaked. 'And you in your fine clothes while we freeze in this hell-pit! We know how to treat a traitor's whore.'

'Strip her first,' a woman lisped, close to Rebecca's ear. 'Bain't no point in spoiling 'er fine clothes. Then the men can have their sport afore we finish the treacherous bitch.'

Rebecca struck wildly at them, the iron fetters biting cruelly into her flesh. 'I'm no traitor—or whore. My grandfather was one of your leaders.'

There was a rip of tearing linen from her skirt and the cord fastening her cloak cut into her neck as she kicked out, but, caught off balance by the sharp jerk from her short ankle chains, she toppled to the ground. 'Stay away from me!' she screamed, tremors shaking her body at the thought of being stripped naked.

'Do as the lady says,' a calm voice cut through the rabble's squabbling. 'This woman is not what Tovey said.'

The hands fell away, and Rebecca sat up, straining her eyes in the faint light from a tiny, barred window high in the wall. That voice—she knew it! In desperation she called out, 'Tom! Is that really you?'

There was a movement to her right and the shadowy forms surrounding her fell back as a man walked towards her. 'Any who dare lay a finger on this woman will answer to me,' Tom Hardwycke threatened, with a maturity and authority she had never before heard in his voice.

'You know the rules, Cap'n Hardwycke,' a gruff man's voice challenged. 'Even if Tovey lied, she has to pay her way—we're all equal here. She pays—or she strips.'

'I make the rules here, Luke Fletcher,' Tom declared. 'If you don't like them, you know what to do.'

'I bain't looking for no fight, Cap'n Hardwycke.' Fletcher surprised Rebecca by backing down. 'No, not I—not after the way you laid into Ridler.'

'Does anyone else oppose my authority here?' Tom asked as he took his place at Rebecca's side and protectively placed his arm around her shoulders. 'This is the granddaughter of one of our bravest and most ardent supporters. She will be treated with respect.'

A wary silence fell upon the prisoners. Even the couple, their lust appeased, had fallen silent, but, though the dawn brought scant light through the tiny window, Rebecca was aware of the hostile glances cast in her direction as Tom led her to a corner.

He crouched on the straw and pulled her down beside him. 'Dear God, Rebecca, you're the last person I expected to find in this accursed place.' His voice was warm and kind, but when he pulled her closer to him she stiffened, immediately wary. 'Nay, Rebecca, stay close, else you will freeze in this stinking hole. I have not forgotten you are a married woman. How could I? You will be safe while you stay at my side, and I would make amends for having failed you once before. I've changed, Rebecca. I was young and foolish then. I thought of nothing but my own desires.'

His words were so unlike the Tom of old that she could hardly believe her ears. The selfishness of youth was gone, replaced by a cool air of authority she would not have thought possible two months ago. But then war changed boys into men. Without Tom she would not have stood a chance against the other prisoners. She should be glad of his gallant protection, and that he no longer bore her a grudge.

'You must not blame yourself, Tom,' she answered, unwilling to bring up the bitterness of the past.

'I'll not harm you, Rebecca.' He kept his arm around her, the warmth of his body a comfort against the coldness of the cell, and her lingering fear. When he made no further advances, she forced herself to relax. She needed a friend now more than ever. Exhaustion sapped her strength and, grateful for his friendship, her head began to drop forward on to her chest.

She woke with a start, and was surprised to discover that the cell was lighter, the sun's rays, speckled with dust and flies, slanting through the window. She blinked, and found herself staring at a young man whose head was bandaged and who absently scratched at his body while he chanted in a low, dazed voice, 'Kill the Papist bastards. Death to James Stuart. À Monmouth. À Monmouth.'

Rebecca averted her eyes and shuddered, barely managing to resist the urge to scratch at her own itching skin. Already the fleas were biting, and within a few days she would be as lice-ridden, filthy and bedraggled as all the prisoners. Conscious that Tom's arm was still around her and that her head had been resting on his chest, she made to pull back.

'Stay as you are, Rebecca,' Tom whispered against her ear. 'It will be an hour or more before they feed us—if they remember. You will need all your strength for when they question you.'

Despite the comfort of his embrace, she drew away and saw the flash of hurt and annoyance in Tom's eyes. She had not meant to hurt him, but even here she could not forget she was a married woman and propriety must be maintained. In the morning light she saw him clearly for the first time, her shock at his appearance making her momentarily forget her own danger. His purple jacket and breeches were covered with greenish-black stains, and the once immaculate lace at his wrists was reduced to limp grey tatters as it hung over his fetters. Without the fashionable periwig, his shorn brown hair made him look younger, and his eyes . . . it was his eyes which had changed most. They were no longer sleepy with indolence; his stare cut with the hardness of flint, and showed no fear of the harsh fate which awaited him.

'Tell me how you came to be here,' Tom urged, his manner again assertive. 'It's always better to talk.'

'Grandfather came to our house,' she began, and then the words tumbled out as she told him the story of the night's events. Tom listened without interruption, merely nodding with sympathy and understanding.

'I'm glad you were reconciled with Ashleigh.' He squeezed her hand. 'What else can I say to give you ease? He's strong enough to survive his wound. He may be fortunate and be spared the gallows, but he's an old man to face transportation. I have accepted that it was a blessing my father was spared this. The Squire was killed at Sedgemoor.'

'I'm sorry, Tom.' The loss forged a link between them. Tom had changed. His actions were protective—brotherly rather than lover-like. 'How did you come to be captured, Tom?'

A flicker of hatred turned his eyes to blue ice, then, as quickly, it was gone and his voice was nonchalant. 'There's little to tell. I was knocked unconscious during the battle and when I came to I was half-drowned in one of those cursed rhines. I was able to evade capture for a time, but everyone was too scared by the persecutions to give a suspected fugitive aid. I had no horse and my sword was lost—so my capture was inevitable.'

'Modesty becomes you, Tom.' She could not resist a taunt. 'You have proved your valour—and these prisoners respect you. Such as they do not pay heed to rank or purse. But what impresses me most is that you have managed to keep your dignity in the face of such degradation.' The rattle of chains accompanied Tom's movement as he slid his arm possessively around her. She pushed it away, with a warning. 'I am grateful for your friendship, Tom, but there can be nothing more between us.'

'The laws of the outside world do not apply here.' Frustration crisped Tom's voice. 'All that awaits us is the gallows, or transportation. Why should we not steal what happiness we can in this hell-pit?'

'Because I am married, and it would be wrong. They can try and reduce me to a slattern, they can even take my life—but my honour will not bend, or my pride.'

The harsh glitter thawed in Tom's eyes. 'You're right, my dear. I've been here so damned long that I have become a defeatist. Until the noose has choked the last gasp of breath from my body, I shall not lose hope. Who knows when a chance may come and escape will be possible?'

The boom of the practice cannon echoed around the Great Court at Whitehall Palace and Jake quietened his prancing gelding before nodding to the sergeant to dismiss the troop. The empty coach rolled past and he saw the King, already surrounded by courtiers, disappear into the palace. With his duty over for the day, Jake turned his mount to walk across the sun-hardened earth towards the river bank and Whitehall Stairs, his thoughts restless. This was his last day of the duty at the Palace to which he had been posted, and tomorrow he would be free to return to Maryland. No, he corrected, not entirely free.

Jake frowned down into the Thames, his attention drawn by the arrival of a boat at the Privy Stairs to the Palace. When the guards pressed back the gathering crowd, his glance sharpened, wondering at the display of arms surrounding a shabby, gaunt figure. Recognition slammed like a battering ram through him. 'Blood and nails!' He swore with heat. 'Is this what it has come to?' Although the dark, proud head was bowed, the figure's drooping shoulders showed a man in utter despair.

Jake turned away, unable to watch the Duke of Monmouth, bound and defeated, come to plead mercy from an unrelenting uncle. Already Parliament had passed the Bill of Attainder upon him, and from here the Duke's path would take him to the scaffold. Monmouth would be remembered only for his weakness, he thought sadly, yet it was his loyalty to those who sought to use him which had brought him to this end. Jake was glad he would not be in London to witness his friend's execution.

His mood remained black as he headed back to his lodgings, for he had taken a room in an inn rather than open the London house, which had been put up for sale; now he found he was in no mood for the night of carousing his fellow aides had planned to mark his leaving the army. Instead he would journey to the coast at once, since his duties here were now at an end.

On the third morning of her captivity Rebecca was awakened by the sound of the bar being drawn, and, as the cell door opened, she realised with a start that during the night she had slept huddled against Tom for warmth. He had thrown his arm across her body and her head rested against his chest. The torchlight flickered over them as she pushed herself upright and away from Tom.

'A charming sight.' Tovey's sarcastic tone boomed across the cell. 'Masters' whore and her new paramour languishing so tenderly in each other's arms. Major

Masters will not be so damned arrogant when he learns you've presented him with a cuckold's horns.'

Rebecca scrambled to her feet, her face stinging with embarrassment at the compromising position sleep had claimed from them.

'See how she blushes with guilt?' Tovey sniggered.

It took every ounce of her will-power to stay the retort which sprang to her lips. Tovey intended to humiliate her and would use any excuse to degrade her further. His eyes narrowed as he waited for her response, and, getting none, he spat out, 'Take Mistress Masters out.' He signalled to three soldiers to obey his order.

'Where are you taking her?' Tom demanded.

Tovey swaggered forward, tapping a riding whip against his leg. 'How protective you are towards another man's wife, Hardwycke,' he provoked. 'Or was she your whore before she wed Masters?'

Tom, his chains clanking as he gathered them for a weapon, threw himself at Tovey, but he was knocked aside by a vicious blow from the riding whip. Two guards brought him down, and started to kick his hunched figure.

'For the love of God, stop it!' Rebecca cried. 'You'll kill him.'

'How forcibly the vixen defends her mate,' Tovey sneered. 'My report will make interesting reading. Major Masters will be a laughing-stock once this scandal breaks.'

'Your lies are as filthy as your mind,' Rebecca shouted as she was dragged to the door. Looking back, she saw Tom heave himself to his feet, his face bloody from the whip. 'May the good Lord watch over you, Tom,' she said. 'I shall not forget how you stood by me.'

'A touching parting,' Tovey snorted, as he fell into step with the guards behind her. 'One I am sure Sir Charles Masters will be delighted to hear. He has followed with interest the events regarding Oliver Ashleigh and yourself.'

There was no mistaking the threat behind his words and a chill ran down Rebecca's spine. Did Sir Charles know then that she was a prisoner, and yet did nothing to help her? And what lies had Tovey been spreading to take his revenge upon Jake? He was certain to have made the evidence against her blacker than it was.

Rebecca shuffled up the stairs, hampered by the chafing of the shackles around her ankles and their heavy weight. They did not enter the Great Hall of the house, but turned through an archway in a carved screen and up a flight of wooden stairs to what had once been the solar. At the entrance to the room she paused to regain her breath, and her glance fell upon a pile of knives and hatchets, pikes homemade with scythe-blades, and a scattering of muskets—the inadequate arms taken from the rebels.

'Get a move on!' Tovey shoved her through a second arch, with such force that the chains tangled with her skirts and sent her sprawling on the floor of the second room.

She bit back a cry at the pain jarring her knees as a pair of polished, silver-buckled boots stepped into her view; pushing herself upright, she looked up. Upon meeting the hatred shining in Sir Charles Masters' haughty stare, her heart thudded. Imperiously, he gestured to a soldier to help her to a stool, but she shrugged off the man's hold and, with all the grace she could muster, seated herself. For a long moment she met, and matched, Sir Charles's disdainful gaze, unconsciously straightening her shoulders and defiantly tilting her chin.

From behind her Tovey began to read out an indictment. As the words 'Traitor...harbouring enemies of the state... Dissenters' spy' penetrated her consciousness, the injustice of them brought her anger to fever-pitch.

She remained silent while Tovey's voice accusing her droned on. Before her stood one of King James's most devious and wily diplomats, and she would need a cool head to match her wits against his. Every notch in her spine set more rigidly as the charges continued, each one more outrageous than the last.

'Therefore, Mistress Masters did knowingly agree to marry her husband, whom the Dissenters suspected was King James's man, in order to spy on him,' Tovey concluded. 'To this end she set out to compromise Jake Masters and seduce him.'

Throughout the reading of the charges Sir Charles had remained impassive except for the glittering enmity in his eyes. It was the same look her grandfather always turned upon Jake, she thought bleakly, but she would not let it intimidate her. Jake had told her to keep faith in him. She must not falter. He would put an end to this madness.

The muscles in her face ached at the effort it cost her to appear serene as she regarded Sir Charles's elegant figure. Unlike her grandfather, he had changed little since she had last seen him. Though the dark, full-bottomed periwig shadowed his lean features, it emphasised the arrogant set of his nose and chin. Uncomfortably aware that her dirty and dishevelled gown made her an object of ridicule, she braced herself against the onset of his attack, and smoothed the crumpled folds of her skirts, her colour rising at the accompanying rattle of chains.

'It is all lies,' she said calmly, 'and you know it!'

A flicker of annoyance crossed Sir Charles's face as he stared at her manacled wrists as though noticing the shackles for the first time. 'How long has this prisoner been in chains?' He clipped out the words with hot anger. 'Remove them at once. This woman is no ordinary rebel—she should have been treated with the respect due to her position. You have exceeded your duty, Tovey.'

'Rebels are rebels,' Tovey muttered as he took a large key from a selection on a wooden rack. 'No matter whom they're married to.'

Tovey weaved slightly as he tried to insert the key into the lock at Rebecca's ankles. When the metal band fell away, the air hit the bleeding, raw flesh like a lead-tipped scourge, and, unable to suppress a flinch, she felt her brow glaze with moisture as she mastered the pain and flicked down her skirts to cover her legs. For some moments Tovey fumbled with the lock of her wrist shackles, until, with an impatient snarl, Sir Charles snatched the keys from him and unlocked the last of the manacles. Stepping back, he rounded on the soldier, his lips white with anger.

'Get out of my sight! You're drunk again. You have exceeded your duty in this as, from reports, you have often done in the past. Get out, before I clap you in irons myself for your incompetence. And when you leave, inform Captain Endacott to await my orders.'

Tovey paled, then flushed scarlet, his bulging eyes bright with hatred as he glared from Rebecca to Sir Charles. 'I only obeyed orders. *Your* orders.' He appeared about to say more, but Sir Charles stepped towards him, his nostrils pinched white with fury, and Tovey scurried from the chamber.

'You chose your accomplice well, Sir Charles.' Ice splintered Rebecca's voice. 'Too well. Not only does Tovey hate me—he wants to destroy Jake. Does bringing an Ashleigh down—even an Ashleigh woman—mean so much that you will sacrifice the good name of your nephew? How could you treat Jake so shabbily? He respected you.'

'Spoken like an Ashleigh!' Sir Charles mocked. 'You only married him to be your grandfather's spy.'

'You demean my husband if you believe that. Although I knew Jake was not what he claimed to be, it was obvious that he was not an informer. And then, Jake being Jake...' She sighed, her love rising up to swamp her, and continued softly, 'I could never betray him. I am innocent of those ridiculous charges. Jake knows my loyalty is to him.'

'What does an Ashleigh know of loyalty? You were caught with a rebel hiding in your home.' Sir Charles sauntered to the large desk which dominated the room. He sat down and rested his chin on his knuckles, his stare cold and assessing as he regarded her. 'It is not enough that you dishonour my nephew by harbouring rebels in his house,' he accused, in a voice that would have turned milk sour, 'but you must hold him to ridicule by consorting with your lover here.'

'You insult Jake, not myself, by your words.' Her contempt cut through the air as neither of them troubled to conceal their dislike. 'I was fortunate that Tom Hardwycke was here to protect me when I was put into a common cell.'

'But will Jake see it like that?' His eyes narrowed with calculated insult. 'Now that the rebellion is crushed, your usefulness to him is at an end. Surely you realise that your conduct forfeits your right to my nephew's protection?'

'Protection!' Rebecca almost choked on her indignation and the effort it cost her to remain calm. 'I am Jake's wife, sir.'

'By whose law? Certainly not by the Church established by law. You are his whore, madam, with no more rights than any of his other women.'

'You lie! Jake is my husband—our vows were made before a preacher and witnesses.'

'That preacher is dead, and within a week or two any surviving witness will have been hanged or transported.' The sound of his mocking laughter echoed through the room. 'Have you forgotten you were already betrothed to Thomas Hardwycke? That contract nullifies your marriage.'

'No contract was signed between the Ashleighs and the Hardwyckes. It was a misunderstanding.' To keep control of her emotions, Rebecca stared at a damp patch on the wall above Sir Charles' head. He was lying. Her marriage was valid. Dear God, her child could not be a bastard. Sir Charles lied. Lied! The words drummed through her mind until gradually the pounding in her temple lessened. Jake had told her to trust him—to keep faith. Drawing a steadying breath, she regarded her antagonist calmly.

'Until I hear those words from my husband's own lips I will not believe you. *He* is not obsessed by a stupid feud that should have ended years ago. He is an honourable man, and if he were here he would laugh at the absurdity of your suggestion.'

'Oh, he would laugh.' Sir Charles thumped the desk to emphasise each word. 'He saw it as fine sport to trick an Ashleigh so. He won you to his bed—did he not? There will always be women in Jake's life, and his interest in you has lasted longer than most. But now it's over. He leaves for the colonies in a few days. You meant nothing to him... How could you? He's still in love with his first wife. He will go to his grave loving Anne Masters.'

Rebecca was shocked to stillness, each word like a rock striking at the foundations of her love, and she felt her hold upon reality slipping. Had she really been so naïve as to believe Jake had begun to care for her?

'Do you think any Masters would wish to bind himself to an Ashleigh?' The baronet's mockery whiplashed over her. 'Jake's father may have suffered less harshly than myself during the Commonwealth, but Jake will never forget that, while Oliver Ashleigh reaped the rewards from my estate, his kinfolk starved in a garret in Holland.'

His accusations broke through her heartache, and she jumped to her feet, her knuckles whitening as she gripped the edge of the desk. She leaned forward to outface him, her body burning with the force of her anger at his injustice. 'And when King Charles came into his own again, did you return to England to find Fair Winds a ruined shell?' His eyes widened, briefly showing his astonishment at her violent attack, and, seeing her advantage, she persisted, 'It is true my grandfather was given your estate. But unlike many of his contemporaries he did not sell the land to reap a vast fortune. Fair Winds was more prosperous when you returned than during the days when your father mismanaged it and ran it to near-bankruptcy by his gambling!'

'You have an able tongue, madam. But you will not divert me from the course of justice. You were caught giving aid to a rebel. That is treason and, for a woman, the penalty could be death by fire.'

Despite her resolve to stand firm, a shudder passed through her body. The lodge fire had been a terrifying experience. Burning was a horrifying death. She was more than ever sure that Jake could not be aware of what his uncle was planning, for he would never have condoned such an atrocity merely to be free of a marriage he regretted. She tossed back her hair, drawing from her faith in her husband. 'I am no weak and foolish woman—you will not trap me with such threats.'

'Trap you to admit what?'

She felt her control sliding at the gleam in his eyes. What trickery was he up to now? She needed all her wits to keep one step ahead of this accomplished intriguer. He would distort anything she said in order to gain his own ends. 'I will never deny my marriage.'

'But I have just explained; you are not married.' He raised a brow, mocking her stubbornness, and sat back in the chair assured of her defeat. 'You defend Jake's honour—yet where is your husband now? And has he ever told you he loves you? I hardly think so... not after Anne.'

That struck her like a blow to the stomach, but she stood firm. Both Martha and Simmons were convinced Jake cared for her, and his treatment of them proved he was too honourable to abandon her. 'Jake is a soldier. He must go where he is ordered until he leaves the army.' She wished she could have spoken with more conviction, but Sir Charles's haughty self-possession was gradually breaking down her confidence, and every word he spoke cleverly played upon her own doubts and uncertainties.

Sir Charles looked at her with false sympathy. 'Madam, I see you are not aware, then, that Jake resigned his commission several days ago. Why do you insist on clinging to something which does not exist?' He was relentless in his attack. 'Jake has his land grant. He plans to start a new life in Maryland. He sails on *The Chesapeake Queen* in three days.'

Rebecca swayed. The poor food of the last days had played havoc with her pregnancy, and a bout of faintness swooped down upon her like the black wings of carrion. She gripped the desk for support to combat her weakness. For the sake of her unborn child she must be strong. She must continue to fight.

'Sit down, before you swoon,' Sir Charles said less harshly.

She obeyed, common sense overcoming her obstinacy. The crazy whirling of the room steadied, and some of the tightness lifted from her chest. 'I cannot believe Jake would abandon me and his child.'

'Admit yours was no marriage and you will be well provided for. Jake is aware of his responsibilities.' Sir Charles smiled, his condescension adding to her disquiet. 'You will find he has not been ungenerous—in the circumstances.'

He tossed a heavy leather pouch into her lap. Her hands curled over it, hatred and distrust stamping out reason and faith. She had known from their first encounter that Jake desired her. Had she been a fool to believe the practised persuasion of an accomplished rake? The cruel memory of Jake closeted with Anne Masters' portrait mocked her. Not once had Jake said he loved her—and when he had spoken of Maryland, he had never mentioned their life together. The answer was simple. He did not love her and saw no need to curtail his pleasure by rushing back. It was his way to take his pleasure where he found it. Yet she did not blame Jake: he was as he was, and she could not change that. And, loving him as she did, she would not imprison him in a marriage he did not want.

Her heart was enclosed with ice as she returned Sir Charles's hypocritical smile. 'Take what satisfaction you can from my disgrace.' As she spoke, she slowly undid the drawstrings of the pouch. 'It is the harm you have done Jake which is the greatest. You have brought a noble and very exceptional man down to your own base level.'

She held the pouch out over the floor and tipped it upside down. The sunlight caught the coins, and they fell in a shining golden shower to the floor, the hollow ringing as they hit the flagstones a fitting death-knell for her marriage.

CHAPTER FOURTEEN

As THE sound of the falling coins died away, Rebecca regarded Sir Charles with quiet dignity. 'I do not barter either my life, or my honour, for any *Masters* gold. And I know Jake better than you think. He would never send another to account for his debts.'

'The tide waits for no man. Jake's future is in Maryland, not England.' Sir Charles shrugged. 'He has much to attend to before he sets sail. I can understand your hurt at his actions, and that pride will not allow you to accept that Jake has wearied of you ... But there is your child to consider. And what of your grandsire's remains?'

'Remains?' Rebecca repeated hollowly. Was this another cruel trick? 'Are you saying he's dead?' Her eyes blazed with hatred, as Sir Charles nodded in confirmation of her worst fears. 'You killed him with your wicked persecution! He was worn out and severely wounded when your henchmen dragged him from my house.'

'But, even dead, a traitor is still a traitor,' Sir Charles informed her coldly, 'and your grandsire was one of the ringleaders of the rebellion. Such as he must be made an example.'

Rebecca gripped her hands tightly together to still the cording pain of grief which threatened to destroy her composure. The dice were loaded in Sir Charles's favour—and he knew it. She lifted her chin an inch higher, and with an effort controlled the tremor in her voice. 'Where is Grandsire's body?'

'It was taken from the gaol and drawn in an open coffin on a cart through Lyme, Axminster, Taunton and Bridgwater before it will arrive at Coombe Grange later today. It will be your choice whether he is buried in hal-

lowed ground, or rots in chains on the crossroads gibbet.'
Sir Charles leant forward, his voice lowering as he
prompted with little subtlety. 'Think well upon the consequences of your answer—a decent burial for Ashleigh,
or his body desecrated by the elements. Not an aus-
picious end, is it? Within a few days his flesh will have
become bloated with decay and crawling with maggots.
He will become a thing of horror, for mothers to point
at as a warning to defiant children, and decent men to
turn their faces from in disgust—until finally the autumn
wind will detach the rattling bones from their chains to
be carried off by scavenging dogs.'

Rebecca closed her eyes against the horror he con-
jured. Now she knew how low Sir Charles would stoop
to gain his own ends—and he was hate-riddled enough
to go through with his threat. Opening her eyes, she suppressed a shudder. For a wild moment she was tempted
to hurl her contempt in his haughty face, but upon encountering that chill, remorseless gaze she knew she was
beaten. How could she allow her grandfather's body to
be so defiled? But the alternative was to renounce her
marriage. Her mind raced to find a solution, but in her
shocked state she could find none. She needed time—
and time was the one thing Sir Charles was determined
to deny her. Her gaze dropped to the emerald ring on
her finger. If Jake was determined to sail from England
in three days without her, she could not stop him. If, on
the other hand, Sir Charles lied, she might yet buy herself
the time she needed by agreeing with his ultimatum. She
was desperate enough to try anything.

'When I have seen my grandfather decently buried,
and I have learned that Jake has left these shores without
contacting me, then I will cease to consider myself Jake
Masters' wife.'

'It is not for you to bargain.' Sir Charles remained
steadfast, but for all his stern tone a flicker of admiration passed across his grey eyes before he added, 'For
your own good you must accept that Jake has tired of
you—as he has of many women in the past. He does not
wish the unpleasantness of a scene so has no wish to see

you, and, to ensure you do not attempt to seek him out, two soldiers will accompany you to Coombe Grange. Your own mare is already saddled and waiting in the courtyard. The day Jake's ship sails, Coombe Grange, which has been sequestered, will be returned to you—though the water rights have in the meantime reverted to Fair Winds.'

'You have thought of everything.' Rebecca allowed a chink to show in her armour. 'For Jake's sake, I hope that you have not acted without his knowledge. Whether he still loves Anne is not for me to say, but we were happy together.'

She stood up, showing him she considered the interview at an end.

'Before you leave, Miss Ashleigh—the ring, if you please.'

She pulled the emerald ring from her finger and placed it on the table. 'I need no reminders that my marriage was a true one. Keep your trophy. It was given to your family as a tribute to their loyalty and honour—your deeds this day, Sir Charles, make a mockery of all that is honourable.'

He picked up the ring and pushed it on to his small finger. When it would not pass over his knuckle, he frowned. 'Did Jake have it made smaller for you?'

'What does it matter? You've got what you wanted. I knew from that first day at Fair Winds that you would do all in your power to end our marriage. Jake said I was being foolish. He never understood the hatred between you and my grandfather, any more than did I.' Her gaze slid from his pale face, feeling her misery perilously close to shaming her as she moved to the door.

With her head held high she walked out of the manor, ignoring the presence of the two guards who would be her companions for the next days. Once they were mounted and cantering south, she began to plan. She could do nothing until Oliver was buried, then somehow she must find a way to escape the guards and discover from which port Jake would sail. Deep in her heart she could not believe Jake would leave without an explanation—everything she knew of him belied that—but what frightened her was that Sir Charles could have tricked him with more lies.

She clung to her faith in Jake, but each mile they travelled her heart grew heavier. The conflict still raged between the Ashleighs and the Masterses, and if her grandfather had failed to best Sir Charles how could she, a mere woman, succeed? But, whatever the odds, she was determined that she would succeed.

Jake left the shuttered and barred cottage on the cliff in a towering fury and marched towards his horse. He looked up into Nathan's bearded face as his brother removed his plumed hat and wiped his brow.

'There's no one there,' Jake said. 'Rebecca would not have left without sending word. And where the devil are Martha and Simmons?'

'Did you send word we were coming?' Nathan reasoned, running a hand through his long reddish-brown hair before replacing his hat. 'Perhaps they've gone into town.'

'No.' Jake fought down his rising fear. 'They would not have boarded up the house if they were away for a few hours. Something's happened.'

'Who would dare harm Rebecca while she has the protection of your name?' Nathan's eyes, a shade lighter than Jake's, glowed with concern. 'Be sensible; you've been in the saddle for three days and you've got to rest. Come back to the inn with me.'

'How can I rest when my wife has disappeared?' Jake ground out, then paused with his foot in the stirrup as he prepared to mount. A soft whine came from the back of the house, and as he turned the two spaniels edged nervously forwards. The bitch was dirty and her usually plump body was honed to an unnatural sleekness. 'Becky would never have left Tess and Jasper. And Tess hasn't been fed for days.' He whistled the dogs and, picking up the pup, swung into the saddle.

'You can't take them with you!' Nathan protested.

'I'm not leaving them to starve,' Jake said with bleak finality, as he urged his horse to a canter with which Tess could keep pace. The fatigue slipped from him as his horse entered the nearest village. Seeing two dairymaids carrying their yokes and buckets into the market square, he hailed them.

'Here, wench.' He tossed a coin towards the eldest. 'Some milk for the dogs.' While the spaniels lapped from the wooden ladle, he asked, 'What news is there of the woman and servants who spent the summer at the cliff house?'

'I know you.' The dark-haired milkmaid signalled to her companion to tend the dogs as she put down her pails and sauntered forward. 'You were staying at the house. Many a time I've seen you ride out.' Her sloe-black eyes twinkled invitingly. 'She be gone, but you don' need to go wantin' for a bit of company, sir.'

Jake bit back his irritation, in no mood for flirtation. 'And pleasant company it would be, too,' he smiled, as, emboldened, the milkmaid reached up to lay her hand on his knee, 'but regrettably, dear lady, I must have news of the occupants of the house.'

She pouted, her mouth turning sulky, but she did not remove her hand. 'There'll be a cold bed awaiting you there, and that's a fact. The soldiers came. Found a Dissenter in the house, and arrested the lot of them.' She dimpled saucily, and wriggled her shoulders so that the loose neck of her blouse slipped provocatively over one bare shoulder. 'Why not spend an hour with Gila? Mary will keep your companion occupied——' she winked at Nathan who remained stoically silent '—then later I could tell you of the rumours I've since heard.'

Jake broadened his smile. 'Would that I could dally, but duty takes me elsewhere.' He took her hand and, bending low in the saddle, raised it to his lips. 'What rumours?'

She pressed her body against his leg, her eyes sultry with desire. 'That the grand lady were never your wife, for all you claimed it so.'

Jake released her abruptly, and she stepped back at the coldness narrowing his eyes. 'Who has been spreading these rumours?'

'I don' know—jes' people passing through.'

'How many days is it since the soldiers came?' Jake fired at her.

The milkmaid stiffened at his tone and, with a flounce, picked up her yoke and slipped it across her shoulders. 'What's it to me?'

No longer smiling, Jake edged his horse closer. 'How many days?'

'It be three days since the soldiers arrested them,' offered the second milkmaid, who had been fussing over Jasper.

Jake looked at the younger woman, who could not have been above fourteen summers and until now had hung back out of his and Nathan's way. 'Thank you for the information. Do you happen to know who was in charge of the soldiers?'

'That pig Tovey.' Gila spat in the dirt.

A vice seemed to clamp round Jake's chest, squeezing until he could scarcely breathe. He drew a silver coin from his pocket and tossed it to the younger girl. 'Will you look after the bitch and her pup for a few days? Another coin will be yours when they're collected.'

'They'll have to stay in the barn, for Father don' care for dogs around the place. But for two silver bits he'll hold his peace—though for not longer than a week, I reckon.'

'I'll be back before the week is out,' Jake promised. 'Stay, Tess,' he ordered, as the bitch ran towards him. 'The pup's name is Jasper.' He turned to Nathan. 'Come, brother, there's work to do, and fast.'

Jake urged his horse to a canter, his thoughts darkening with each stride. Tovey had been relieved of his rank, and the knave was too craven to act against Rebecca without being certain of success. So who had ordered him to search the house? Or had even suspected that a rebel was there? The only rebel Becky would have risked her life for was Ashleigh.

'Hey,' Nathan shouted. 'Have pity on my sore hide. Slow down, Jake. It's all right for a landlubber like yourself to spend hours in the saddle, but I haven't ridden in months.'

Jake slowed his pace and looked at his brother. 'This is not your affair. I'm sorry you've been dragged into it.'

'Nonsense,' Nathan declared. 'What are brothers for? Dammit, if you want to get this matter settled with Rebecca before we sail, then we had better split up. Two of us can cover more ground than one. But where do we start? At the local gaol?'

'That's as good a place as any, but which local gaol? With so many rebel prisoners they could be anywhere.' Jake rubbed a hand across his chin. He had come to Dorset to explain to Rebecca his reasons for leaving for America alone, but the worry of finding her gone had left him with an odd feeling of desolation. How could he leave without knowing she would be provided for? Yet he had only two days. 'At Taunton or Dorchester they should have lists of prisoners,' he continued as they approached a crossroads. His nose wrinkled at the stench of rotting flesh, carried to him by the wind from the corpse chained in the gibbet. In the last days it had seemed to him that the whole of the South of England stank from the aftermath of the rebellion. 'I'll ride to Taunton, and we'll meet halfway at St Bartholomew's churchyard, Crewkerne, midday tomorrow. If you need more time, send a messenger and I'll do likewise.'

'I'll do all I can,' Nathan responded, rubbing his hand across his bearded jaw. 'But I must be at Lyme when my ship docks from Plymouth, and with the next tide I sail to Maryland.'

Jake nodded. 'I'll be there.' He forced a bleak grin. 'It's not been much of a reunion for you, has it?'

'We've got weeks on board to make amends for that.' With a wave of his hand, Nathan turned his mount on the road to Dorchester. 'Good luck, brother. You're taking a lot of trouble over a woman you plan to leave behind.'

Jake took the Taunton road, pushing himself and his lathered mount to their limits. The thought of Becky in

Tovey's clutches filled him with fury, but as the miles sped by his rage subsided, to be replaced by a deepening fear. His name and position should have been protection enough for Becky at the cottage, even if she had been fool enough to take her dying grandfather in—and, in the name of mercy, how could she have done otherwise? His anger churned as he suspected that the house had been watched against that very eventuality. And there was only one man who hated the Ashleighs enough and would stop at nothing to bring them down. At the next crossroads he veered north instead of west—north towards Fair Winds.

It was twilight when Rebecca crested the last hill and saw the sprawling farmhouse and outbuildings of Coombe Grange snuggled in the valley below her. At first she thought the thin spiral of smoke came from the chimney, then her heart constricted as she saw the limewashed walls blackened, and the charred, broken timbers pointing skywards like gnarled fingers where the thatch should have been.

As her angry glare swept over the barns and buttery, her body flamed with outrage. All was still. Too still. The meadows were bare of cattle and sheep, and the stable doors hung open, their black, cavernous mouths bare of horses. Not even a single chicken or duck pecked in the yard or swam on the pond. All the livestock had either been taken or run off. Even the crops in the fields and garden had been trampled into the ground. So this was how Sir Charles had kept his promise! Damn his hide!

A whinny from a horse drew her attention to what had once been the herb garden to the far right of the house. Two men lounged against a cart, their horses tethered to a fence-post. As her party approached one of the men mounted and rode towards them. The flaccid figure and sneering face were all too easily recognisable.

'So you thought you could win your freedom and escape the consequences,' Tovey jeered. 'I warned you no one makes a fool of me and gets away with it. Every house in the district owned by rebels was put to the torch.

It wasn't right this one should escape—even if Sir Charles had claim to it!'

'You haven't the backbone to stand up to a man——' Rebecca poured out her scorn '—so, like all cowards and bullies, you make war on women.'

'Why, you . . .' Tovey raised his whip to strike her, but the youngest of her two escorts, and the one apparently in charge, pushed his horse between them.

'You have no authority here, Tovey,' his cultured voice clipped out. 'My orders from Sir Charles were explicit. If you stepped out of line again, you were to be arrested.'

'On what charges, Captain Endacott?' Tovey challenged.

'The charges are endless.' The loathing was obvious in the Captain's tone. 'Looting. Mistreatment of prisoners. Bribery. Need I go on?'

Rebecca looked at the Captain with renewed respect. He had spoken little during their journey, and she had been too wrapped in her misery to pay him any heed. He appeared to be in his mid-twenties and, despite his sallow skin and slight build, he was clearly no weakling. His voice was refined and educated, proclaiming him the son of a gentleman, far above Tovey's yeoman status. The strong line of his brow and jaw told her he was a man who took his duty seriously. He looked towards the other soldier by the cart. 'Rowell, tie Tovey's hands, and once the burial has taken place take him to Dorchester Gaol.'

Captain Endacott turned to Rebecca. 'I'm sorry about the house, ma'am, but Sir Charles did not intend for you to stay here—not while under escort. It was arranged you would stay with my sister who lives three miles from here. You are to remain there until Sir Charles says you are free to go as you please.'

Sir Charles had thought of everything, Rebecca fumed. Even if Jake did come to find her, he would never track her down at Endacott's sister's house. She concealed her raging emotions behind a forced smile. It would do no good to arouse Captain Endacott's suspicions. After her grandfather was buried, she would look for every opportunity to escape. 'You are very kind, Captain. From the way you stood up to Tovey, I know I shall be safe under your protection.'

When a pink flush stole up the Captain's neck and cheeks, she suspected his interest in her was more than that of a guard. It would make it easier to trick him and escape. First she had duty to attend to. She turned her attention to the cart with its plain wooden coffin, her grief rising unchecked. She bowed her head. 'Please, Captain, could the burial take place at once? It will be dark soon, and I would pay my grandsire his proper respects.'

When Tovey's hands were bound, the other soldier put a horse between the shafts of the cart and, as darkness fell, he lit two lanthorns to light their passage to the church on the far side of the valley. Before they set off, Rebecca edged her mount closer to the cart and stared down at the closed coffin. 'Could I see my grandsire before we proceed further?'

'Is that wise, ma'am?' Captain Endacott asked. 'He has been dead for three days.'

'Nevertheless, I would see him,' Rebecca insisted, needing to ensure that in this, at least, Sir Charles Masters had not tricked her. As the coffin lid was raised and a lanthorn held aloft, she felt her misery swirl up like an icy mist around her. With the life and the fanatical fire gone out of him, Oliver Ashleigh looked wizened and frail, smaller in body and build than she remembered. But such was his forceful personality that it had given him a strength and stature which had made him the equal of any man. Though he had dissented from the church of bishops and Prayer Book, in its ground he could lie at rest. She started as a hand touched her shoulder.

'Are you ready to leave?' Captain Endacott asked, as Rowell nailed down the coffin lid. She looked up at Endacott, the dim light slendering the contours of his face. He was distinguished-looking rather than handsome, with a hooked nose, but his eyes, reflecting the lanthorn light, were sapphire-bright and held both kindness and a deepening interest in her as a woman.

'Yes, I am ready to leave. You are kinder than I deserve,' she answered, as she self-consciously dragged her fingers through her snarled ringlets, glad it was a stranger and not Jake seeing her dirty and reeking from the prison cell.

'Then we best get the burial over with.' Captain Endacott smiled. 'I cannot understand how a lovely woman like you came to be in prison. Was it your loyalty to the rebel in the coffin which brought you so low?'

'He was my grandsire, and, if you do not mind, Captain Endacott, I would rather not talk about it.'

The procession moved slowly along the valley to the churchyard, where it halted under the yew trees. Rebecca dismounted and leant against the cart as the coffin was lowered to the ground and the soldiers began digging the grave. To the accompaniment of shovelling earth and the occasional grunt from a soldier, she offered prayers for her grandsire's soul. Her tears dried. Her grandsire had died for a cause he believed in, and she knew he would have had no regrets. At least Oliver had been spared the gibbet, the heartbreak of seeing Coombe Grange a burnt-out shell, and the livestock plundered. It was small comfort in her lonely sorrow. For despite his death the feud had not died, nor had Sir Charles's hatred.

She looked heavenwards, gazing up at the clear, bright moon against the black taffeta sky. Where was Jake? Her heart ached with a loss more profound than her grief for her grandfather. Soon her duty to Oliver would be done. The burning of Coombe Grange had released her from any word she had given Sir Charles Masters, and she was not about to give up Jake without a fight. First, though, she must escape her guards.

The sound of digging ceased, the yellow light from the lanthorns conjuring the soldiers' tired figures into a macabre image as they began to lower the coffin into the blackness. Her quietly spoken prayers were the only sound other than the creak of the ropes. Ashleigh was spared the rites he'd despised.

As the first of the earth fell on to the wooden lid, she turned away, moving out of the light. 'Rest in peace, Grandsire. Forgive me——' Her voice broke off, but she finished the sentence in her mind with a passionate avowal. Forgive me for what I must do. I cannot forsake Jake. The clink of a spur warned her that Captain Endacott was close behind her, foiling her instinct to flee into the night. Even so, she moved deeper into the shadows, her mind racing for a solution.

Then, suddenly, everything happened at once. There was a shot, followed by a thud, and she spun round in time to see Captain Endacott crumple to the ground. Behind him, outlined against the moon, was Tovey, his upraised arm with the rope still dangling from his wrist clearly visible as he brandished a stout stick. The other soldier who had escorted her from the gaol lay writhing on the grass, shot in the stomach. With a cruel laugh Tovey threw aside his weapon and lunged at Rebecca. 'Now that the fine Captain is out of the way, it's time for the reckoning between us!'

Rebecca didn't wait to hear more. Picking up her skirts, she ran into the cover of the yew trees. This was her home ground and she knew every hiding place and hollow. She leapt across a dry ditch, stumbling as she came upon uneven, bramble-covered ground. A muffled curse told her Tovey had fallen, and further behind him were the faltering steps of the second soldier, pursuing them both. Darting to the left, she scrambled over the low churchyard wall and, keeping to the shadows, skirted its perimeter as she made for a nearby wood. Already Tovey's heavy tread carried to her.

'You'll not escape, bitch,' Tovey panted, closer than she had reckoned. 'There's two of us—you can't escape us both.'

That was how Tovey had got loose—the other soldier was his accomplice! There would be no help or rescue from him, if Tovey caught her. She ran on. The wood was still some distance away, and she began to flag, each step beginning to feel as though she were pushing against an invisible barrier. Her steps were slowing, she had no reserves of energy left to go faster. Ice coated her spine, for it was obvious that a second man was crashing through the undergrowth on her right and cutting off her path to the wood. Others, too, seemed to be joining in the chase, for a horse was being ridden hard and closing fast upon her.

Just as an arm circled her waist and the weight of her attacker felled her to the ground, she heard a second shot. Instinctively, she rolled on to her side and kicked against Tovey's bulky shape, but the shot had also taken Tovey by surprise. He squatted on his haunches, the moonlight showing his face drawn with fear as he stared wildly about him. Seizing her chance, she wriggled free of his hold. A flash of yellow caught her eye, and another pistol fired.

Rebecca scrambled to her knees, unable to take her eyes from Tovey's menacing presence. She checked, gasped, seeing the hole appear in Tovey's temple. His eyes rounded with shock, then he toppled forward on to the grass.

'Rebecca!' a breathless voice cried out.

She shook her head, convinced she was dreaming, as she rose shakily to her feet. How, in heaven's name, had Tom got here?

CHAPTER FIFTEEN

BEFORE Jake crossed the land belonging to Fair Winds he detoured towards Coombe Grange, hoping for a miracle and that Rebecca was there. The blackened walls revealed by the moonlight and the devastation of the farmyard were a bitter blow. Everywhere was deserted. As he turned his horse towards the boundary of the Fair Winds estate, he caught a glimpse of two lanthorns moving through the distant trees. Yet another burial procession, or homeless rebel family travelling on the road, he thought absently, too preoccupied to pay them much heed. He had passed so many these last few days he had lost count.

In contrast to the ruins at Coombe Grange, nearly every window of the sandstone Elizabethan manor was ablaze with light. Jake inwardly groaned. Sir Charles was entertaining, and he was in no mood to face his uncle's guests.

He dismounted, and when a servant came out of the house to take his horse he snapped, 'Have a fresh horse saddled and waiting. My visit will not last long.'

Striding through the brightly lit hall, he called out to a liveried footman, 'Kindly inform Sir Charles that I await him in the library.'

For twenty minutes he was left to kick his heels, his mood blackening, until, losing patience, he marched to the door and flung it wide, just as Sir Charles appeared from the marbled hall.

'Jake, my dear man, your pardon for keeping you waiting.' Sir Charles frowned as his sharp glance swept over Jake's travel-stained figure. 'By the devil, you look like a vagabond! What do you mean by coming to my house in such a state?'

'I've been on the road for three days. When I arrived at the house I had taken on the coast it was to find Rebecca gone. But I believe you know that!' There was none of his usual courtesy in his voice, and Sir Charles's eyes narrowed as Jake plunged angrily on, 'Where is my wife? And why the devil was I not informed that Ashleigh had gone to my house?'

Sir Charles crossed the room and filled two goblets from a silver flagon on a table. He held one out to Jake. 'Drink this; you will need it.' He took his own goblet, his finger tracing the pattern of vine leaves on its stem, before adding, 'I only learned of the events which led to Rebecca's arrest last night, when I received a list of all prisoners taken. Your servants, by the way, were also arrested, but rather strangely were taken to a different gaol than Rebecca. They were released this morning and are being tended upstairs. Simmons suffered rather badly from the questioning—his crippled hand—but he will recover.'

Jake moved to the door, his voice catching in his throat. 'And, Becky—is she upstairs?'

'She is not!' The coldness in Sir Charles's voice stopped Jake in his tracks. 'And after the shame she has brought to our family you are well rid of her.'

Jake spun on his heel. 'What in Hades do you mean by that? She's my wife!'

'Not by the laws of our church,' Sir Charles said with feeling, 'and you should be glad she is not. Especially after what I discovered she got up to in that prison.' He checked at seeing the rigid set of Jake's beard-shadowed face, and his voice mellowed with commiseration. 'You've enemies in Dorset. Especially a man called Tovey. For reasons of his own, he kept watch on your house and when he saw Ashleigh given shelter he arrested the household. When I arrived at Rebecca's gaol this morning I discovered, to my horror, she had been put in a common cell.'

Jake stiffened with outrage, his hands clenching as he took a grip upon his mounting temper and fear. 'Did they not know who she was? When I discover who's responsible, I'll——'

'Jake—Jake! Calm yourself.' Sir Charles came to his side and sympathetically put his hand on Jake's shoulder. 'It pains me to have to say this, but I must. She was not worthy of you. Tom Hardwycke was in the same cell— they became lovers. Several prisoners have sworn statements that it was so.'

'Lies fabricated by Tovey—and the prisoners signed under duress,' Jake declared, white-hot anger spreading through his veins. 'I know Rebecca better than that.'

'She tricked you with her false innocence. She only married you because Ashleigh wanted a spy in your household.' Sir Charles's voice rose. 'But then you out-witted Ashleigh by agreeing to that ridiculous ceremony. Being married to his granddaughter won you the Dissenters' trust, did it not?'

'So it may have done, but you know me not at all if you think I married her for that reason.' Jake dropped his voice to a low, dangerous tone. 'Rebecca was loyal to me. And she despised Hardwycke.'

'A woman will do many things to gain a few creature comforts. Hardwycke was her protector in the gaol—her lover. Can't you see that to such a woman you have no further obligation?' Meeting Jake's volcanic stare, Sir Charles tempered his attack. 'You sail tomorrow. You are free of her, Jake. Free!'

'She is carrying my child and she *is* my wife.' Jake rapped out in harsh staccato. 'When I sail, she will come with me.'

Momentarily, Sir Charles looked taken aback at Jake's vehemence, then his expression became grave. 'Your sense of duty is a credit to you. But I have Hardwycke's sworn statement, which in the circumstances is best de-stroyed. You see, Jake, no matter how nobly you defend this woman, it makes no difference. You are still free. She died in the cell, of gaol-fever.'

Jake's knees gave way and he collapsed into the chair. He passed a hand across his eyes and down over his stubbled chin. Becky could not be dead. Not *his* Becky!

'Where is her body?' His voice seemed to come from a great distance.

'She was buried in a common grave with others from the gaol.'

'Where?'

'I did not ask.' Sir Charles continued to study him with a frown. 'I had no idea you would take it so badly. I shall find out, of course, but your ship sails so soon that there will be no time for you to visit the grave.'

'I cannot believe she's dead.' Jake stared unseeingly across the room. 'She had so much strength, so much life and vitality—and so much courage.'

'You must accept it, Jake.' Sir Charles held out the emerald ring. 'This was taken from her finger before they buried her. She had sold it to buy food for herself and her lover while they were in the gaol.'

Jake rose unsteadily to his feet and put the ring in his pocket. He did not believe Rebecca had betrayed him. Nor would she have sold the ring for food. Only if she were dead could it have been taken from her finger.

'I will find out the truth behind this.' He fixed his uncle with a harrowed stare. 'And when I do, God help those responsible. Tovey and Hardwycke are weak men. Even Tovey, bent upon revenge as he was, would never have arrested Rebecca unless he knew himself safe from prosecution. And Hardwycke would sell his own mother to the devil to save his worthless hide.' Through his shock Jake looked with contempt upon his uncle, the years of respect withering as he measured Sir Charles's hatred against his own incalculable loss. 'Rebecca was right. You did hate her enough to destroy her. But you've destroyed me, too. I would never have left England without her. She was my salvation—my future. God damn you to hell, Charles...I loved her!'

Jake stormed from the room.

'Jake, wait!'

He ignored Sir Charles's shout. He had to get away before his rage and pain turned against his own kin. At that moment he wanted to kill Sir Charles Masters.

'Have Martha and Simmons taken to Lyme where Nathan's ship will dock,' he managed to grind out before he slammed the door of the manor firmly shut behind him.

'Thank God I got here in time.' Tom leant down from his horse and held out a hand to Rebecca. 'Make haste and mount behind me. There's another soldier coming from the churchyard.'

'That will be Captain Endacott,' she replied, relieved that the kindly Captain had not been mortally injured. She took Tom's hand without hesitation. Here was her chance of escape.

'Hold tight,' Tom ordered as he kicked his horse to a canter. 'Best to get as much distance from here as possible before we stop.'

When the horse veered north, Rebecca shouted, 'No, Tom, not north! Go south. If the soldiers are after you, your only chance is to find a ship to take you to safety.'

After the barest pause Tom turned the horse south. At least they were travelling towards the coast. But by what miracle had Tom so opportunely arrived at the churchyard? With difficulty, she contained her curiosity. Time enough for talk once they were safely away from the district. But, despite her relief at Tom's rescue, she felt uneasy, and caution had stopped her adding that Jake would be on the coast. But which port? She knew that after Nathan Masters had landed at Plymouth, his ship would put in at Lyme. Yet Jake was in London— what if he took Jake on board there?

Her fears grew with every passing thought. Don't think that way, she rebuked herself. Have faith—didn't Jake ask you to trust him? She had to believe that, or her resolve would fail. If Jake intended to take her to Maryland, he would have arranged for the ship to be docked at Lyme. She prayed she was right. And also that Jake had not heeded any lies Sir Charles had concocted. Her blood chilled at the prospect. Sir Charles would have had his story well devised. *What if Jake did believe his uncle?*

She ruthlessly quashed such thoughts. If she began to think that way she would lose hope, and with it the strength she needed to push herself to her limits in the next day or so, if she was to find Jake before he sailed.

As the miles sped by Rebecca felt her eyelids starting to droop, and her fight to stay awake became harder. 'Tom, is it not safe to stop? I know we must reach the coast for safety, but I'm so tired.'

Tom stopped the horse at once, all concern as he dismounted and helped her from the saddle. 'Of course, my dear, you must be exhausted. Look, there's a woodcutter's hut just ahead. If it's empty we'll rest a few hours there—or you will. We won't get far in daylight in the clothes we're wearing. Especially me—in this.' Tom plucked at his dirty jacket which carried Monmouth's colours. 'Wait here while I check the hut.'

Moments later Tom was back. 'We're in luck. It's empty.'

Rebecca had never felt so weary as she entered the hut, the poor food in the gaol and her pregnancy sapping her energy. The moonlight streaming through the open door revealed a pallet bed in a corner and a roughly fashioned table against a wall. It was primitive, but to Rebecca it was a blessed haven. She sank on to the pallet, too tired to care that the straw which stuffed the mattress smelt fusty.

'Get some sleep,' Tom continued to take charge, with the new confidence he had shown at the prison. 'I'll have to leave you for a while. There must be a house nearby. I'll get us some food and clothes.'

'Have you money, Tom?' Her voice was drowned by a yawn.

'I'll come by the clothes and food the same way I came by my horse and pistols. Steal them.'

'But, Tom——' she began to protest, but it was too late for he had already left. Rebecca had no energy left to call him back, and as her head hit the mattress she was already asleep.

A rustling startled her awake, and she stifled a scream as she felt a soft, furry body run across her legs. It took a moment for her eyes to grow accustomed to the darkness, and in the path of the dawn light shafting through a crack in the roof she saw the rats. Still dazed from sleep, she drew herself up smaller, thinking she was still in prison. Then with a rush, her memory returned and she sat up. Where was Tom? She swung her legs to the floor and winced. Every muscle in her body ached as she stretched to ease the kinks from her tortured limbs, and as her arms lowered she spotted a broken knife lying on the ground. She picked it up and tested the short, broken-off blade with her finger. It was not a very adequate weapon, but it was better than no weapon at all and she slipped it into the pocket of her gown before walking outside.

She guessed she had slept for about four hours, but there was no sign of Tom or his horse. Rubbing the sleep from her eyes, she peered about the small clearing, her tongue running across her parched lips and her hand touching her stomach as it rumbled with hunger. Low overhead two mallard flew past and, as she frowned with distaste at the dirt ingrained into her hands, there was the sound of a splash. The ducks had landed in water which was close by. Thirsty, she hurried in that direction, and discovered a clear stream lined with willow trees. The water was cold but wonderfully refreshing as she cupped it into her hands and drank.

When she sat back the only sound for miles was the occasional rustle of a foraging animal. It was a strange feeling to be so alone after three days in a cramped cell, but it was welcome. As she scratched at her itching body, she looked around, craving privacy which would allow her to wash the stench and filth of the prison cell from her body. Surely there would be time before Tom returned, if she was quick?

Taking cover behind a hawthorn bush, she pulled off her soiled gown and petticoats, and, using one of them as a cloth, soaked it in the stream, which was no more than a few inches deep. The water was icy and, even by rubbing vigorously, she could not stop her flesh rising in goose-bumps; before she had finished her teeth were rattling together and her skin had begun to mottle with blue. Discarding her wet petticoat, she gave the rest of her clothes a good shake, and, finding some wild mint, rubbed it into the inside of her gown and petticoats to freshen them. Even so, the thought of having to wear them again made her flesh crawl, but, smothering disgust, she pulled them over her head, having no choice. As she fastened the buttons of her bodice, she heard a horse approaching.

Cautiously, Rebecca hid behind a stout oak trunk, lest it be a soldier or stranger. The rider leapt to the ground and proceeded to the hut.

'Odsbones, she's gone.' Tom's angry voice carried to her. Relieved at his return she ran from her hiding place as he emerged from the hut, his face working with fury. The moment he saw her he relaxed. 'Good God, you gave me a fright,' he said, with a shaky laugh. 'I thought you had been taken by the soldiers.'

She thrust aside the notion that Tom had looked angry, not worried, when he came out of the hut—in the circumstances, could not either emotion stem from his fear for her safety? 'I took the opportunity to bathe as best I could. There's a stream over there.'

'A sure sign you're feeling better.' Tom grinned. 'And what I've brought should cheer you.' As he spoke he moved to his horse, rummaged in a sack slung over its back and drew out a plain linen petticoat, russet wool skirt and bodice which he tossed into her arms. 'They're not very grand, and probably too large, but beggars can't be choosers, as they say.'

She saw that he had also changed, and now wore plain black breeches, a rough linen shirt and a battered leather jerkin.

'There's more,' he added, with an air of pride. 'The farmhouse I broke into was well stocked from a day's baking. There's a loaf, some cheese and a large slice of mutton pie.'

Rebecca looked at the clothes with concern. 'No matter how much we need these, Tom, it's not right to take them from others who can ill afford to lose them. This skirt and bodice must be the woman's Sunday best.'

'There's gratitude for you.' Tom shot her a sullen look. 'I risked my life to get those. That farmer had a musket. Damned nearly creased my hide as I rode away. If you want to play the martyr and starve, that's your affair. We'd not have got two miles without attracting attention dressed as we were. I suppose it has not crossed your mind that there'll be warrants out for both our arrests? At least in these clothes we look like any other couple journeying to market.'

'I suppose you're right, Tom. I just wish there was some way we could repay the farmer.'

'And get them hanged for aiding fugitives?' Tom scoffed. 'Odsbones, Rebecca. These are dangerous times. You either live by your wits, or you die.'

Although she could follow his reasoning, it still did not sit easily upon her conscience. But the stained flowered dress she was wearing would attract suspicion. 'I'll change,' she gave in, salving her conscience with her need to stay free and see Jake. If there was any way she could repay the farmer and his wife, she would do so, but that must wait for now. She paused by the door of the hut, still troubled. 'You were gone a long time, Tom.'

'I had much to attend to. Despite the persecutions of our men, there are still those who are willing to help Monmouth's followers. I was given the name of a fisherman at Charmouth who may take us to France.'

'But I . . .' she began and stopped at seeing Tom tense. She had no intention of going to France with him, but since Charmouth was only a mile or so from Lyme, where she hoped to find Jake, there was no point in antagonising him now. Clearly Tom knew nothing of her home on the cliff. 'I'll change, and after we have eaten we had better move on. Or do you need some sleep?'

'I doubt if your devil-spawned husband would rest while danger is all around.' The resentment was back in Tom's voice. 'Do you take me for a lesser man?'

'You have proved your bravery, Tom, by coming to my aid. I make no comparisons between you and Jake.'

Her unease increased as Tom reverted to the sullen ways of old. 'If you will wait outside the hut I will change.'

Tom unfastened the food sack from his horse, slung it over his shoulder and grinned. 'Come now, Rebecca, there's no need to be coy. Not after all we shared in the prison. We can spare an hour before we move on.'

'No, Tom.' Rebecca stepped back, her hand going to the knife in her pocket. 'I know what you are about to suggest, and you can forget it. Nothing has changed. I'm married to Jake, and I will not play him false.'

'Who's to know?' He sauntered confidently forward. 'I can understand your embarrassment in the cell, but here . . . such delicacy is misplaced—we are alone.'

She brandished the knife before her. 'I said no, Tom. And I meant it. Lay a finger on me and I'll use this.'

'Always the vixen.' To her surprise Tom backed off, but there was an ugly glitter in his eyes. 'I can wait. You'll come to me in the end, for you'll have no other choice. And isn't that how it was meant to be—you and me?'

'Tom, you must accept that that was over long ago.' His change of mood puzzled and not a little frightened her.

'Go and get changed, Rebecca, my dear.' He laughed carelessly. 'I am not the impatient youth you fell in love with—but a worldly man now. I have learned that anything worth winning is worth waiting for. And I have but to wait for it all to be mine.'

She ran into the hut, his confident laughter unsettling her further. Tom had changed, but there was something very odd about his manner. She must tread warily and be on her guard. Perhaps Tom's opportune rescue had been just that—too opportune.

CHAPTER SIXTEEN

THREE hours later Rebecca and Tom rode through the narrow main street of Charmouth and halted by the fifteenth-century inn, the Queen's Arms. Throughout their hard ride south, speech had been impossible as Tom pushed their mount at a furious pace, and during the times when they had been forced to take cover from the militia still scouring the district, silence was needful to avoid detection.

At once Tom took charge, throwing the reins to the ostler and, lifting Rebecca to the ground, led her into the inn.

'A private parlour, if you will, landlord,' Tom ordered.

'Do you just require a meal?' the rosy-faced landlord enquired as he led them to the parlour.

'Food for now, and an hour or two's privacy while my wife rests.'

Rebecca stilled her protest that Tom had referred to her as his wife. By creating a scene she would only arouse the landlord's suspicions that they were fugitives. What if he became apprehensive and alerted the militia? With the county still in turmoil after the rebellion it was not safe to trust any stranger.

'Have you travelled far?' The landlord's apparently innocent words sounded like the inquisition to Rebecca's strained nerves, especially since he was looking at her closely.

'From Taunton,' Tom lied, and, apart from refusing to look the landlord squarely in the eye, showed no other sign that he was ill at ease. 'We are travelling to visit my aunt. Her son was caught up in that damned rebellion and she's suffered badly. Lost her home, so I believe. Terrible business. But my cousin has paid his price. Died at Sedgemoor for his folly, and brought shame upon us all.'

'It were an ill day for these parts when Monmouth landed.' The landlord eyed them narrowly. 'Not that we haven't played our part in the past. It were in this very inn that young Charles Stuart hid in disguise. That was after he fled Worcester and failed to regain his father's throne. He were waiting for a ship to take him overseas. But there were no ship and he rode on. Had he been caught he would have shared the same fate as his son Monmouth.' The landlord drew his finger significantly across his neck. 'Executed, Monmouth was. Took five cuts of the axe to take off his head, God rest his soul. But then you would have heard that.'

Rebecca again felt subjected to the landlord's assessing stare, and stopped herself from wiping her sweating palms on her skirts.

'Indeed, landlord.' Tom casually shrugged off the news, but Rebecca saw he was pale and shaken. 'A flagon of your best wine, if you will.'

'Poor Monmouth,' Rebecca said softly, once the landlord had left. 'He did not deserve such an end.' She sat down on the settle and stared down at her hand, her thumb seeking the reassurance of her wedding ring and, finding it gone, the pain covering her heart increased. Jake would feel Monmouth's death acutely. Her arms ached to comfort him, and be comforted in return for the death of her grandfather. She hugged her arms about her chest to combat the wave of loneliness, the craving to have Jake at her side, to hold her—to smile—in that devastating way of his, and chase the shadows from her mind.

'Save your sympathy for the living.' Tom's voice hardened. 'If Monmouth had stayed in The Hague, we would not be in this mess.

'Tom, that's a callous thing to say. It was because men like my grandfather, and your father, were prepared to support him—and thereby end the intolerance of a Catholic monarch—that he landed at all.'

'What would you, a woman, know of politics?' Tom responded sourly.

Again Rebecca stifled her retort. It was characteristic of Tom to be embittered by the failure of the rebellion, and she was too tired to quarrel with him. A serving-maid brought them the wine, and once Tom had downed his first goblet he looked happier.

'I did not mean what I said about Monmouth,' he said at last. 'But through him I've lost everything. Hardwycke Hall has been confiscated, and if I stay in England—my only future is swinging from the gallows.'

'Do not think that way,' she encouraged, watching him closely. Her unease grew as she noted the bulge at his waistband where the two pistols and a dagger were hidden beneath his leather jerkin. She added, 'You could be on a ship tonight heading for the Continent.'

He downed his second goblet, and, as he sipped more leisurely at a third, his mood mellowed enough for her to probe gently.

'Fortune smiled on you, Tom. Not only did you escape prison, but you are well mounted and armed.'

'The dagger and pistol I took from the two guards I overcame to make my escape. The horse, as I said before, I stole.'

'You never said how you escaped.' She forced a light laugh. 'It's not like you to be so modest, Tom.'

Tom contemplated the depths of his wine goblet before answering. 'Shortly after they took you from the cell, I too was taken for questioning. As I was being led through the Great Hall, I heard that oaf Tovey bragging to another soldier.' Tom swaggered across the room, his voice throbbing with outrage. 'My blood boiled when I heard what Tovey planned. That he meant first to burn Coombe Grange and then, when you attended Ashleigh's funeral, he would even his score with Masters. He meant to abduct you.' Tom swigged back the dregs from his goblet and banged it down on to the table. 'Dear God, if I wasn't already nearly out of my mind with worry for you! To hear that made me ripe for Bedlam. I lashed at the guard with my chains and knocked him out cold.

From him I took a pistol…after evading several guards, I encountered the sentry at the outer door and clubbed him with its handle. Then I took his pistol and dagger.'

'You were lucky your chains did not betray your presence to him,' Rebecca said, without thinking, and Tom shot her an affronted look.

'I took him by surprise. Though the chains hampered my flight across the courtyard as the alarm was raised. Odsfish, I don't mind admitting I was scared! I expected a musket-ball in my back as I ran into the garden and scaled the wall. It was then Dame Fortune smiled on me. Not fifty yards outside was an old parson, dozing, as his horse plodded homewards. Before even the first guards had reached the wall I had the old man out of the saddle, and I was galloping to freedom!'

'Your bravery served you well.' She hoped her scepticism was not obvious in her voice. It sounded too easy—too convenient. Had it been part of Sir Charles's plan that he had allowed Tom to escape, suspecting he would come after her? A cold finger of dread grazed down her spine. Had Sir Charles outmanoeuvred her yet again?

'How did you rid yourself of your chains?'

'I went to Badger Farm, one of the tenants of Hardwycke Hall. I knew I could trust them not to betray me. Once the chains were hammered off, I made straight for the church.'

'Just in time to save me from Tovey.' Rebecca smiled thinly, unsure how much of Tom's story she could believe. That did not alter the debt she owed him, and, guilty lest she might have wronged him, she added, 'I will miss you when you are in France, Tom.'

'Miss me!' He caught her to him, his eyes flashing with a fervent light. 'Why, my love, you'll be coming with me.'

Rebecca strained away from him, her body rigid in his arms. 'Have you forgotten my condition?'

'You think I could forget that!' His voice stung her by its coldness. 'It should be my child you're carrying—not his. But there'll be others.'

She stared at him, incredulous. 'I have no intention of sailing with you to France. My place is with Jake.'

'He doesn't want you. Where was *he* when you needed him?' His lips twisted with anger, and his hold tightened when she tried to push him away.

'Let me go, Tom. You're hurting me.'

His eyes glazed, seeing not herself but the tool of his vengeance against Jake.

'Jake never betrayed me,' she went on fiercely, trying to make him see reason. 'You have your freedom, Tom. Flee while you can. It's Sir Charles who continues the feud and seeks to end my marriage. He knew you were a prisoner, from the lists he receives as a Justice of the Peace. All he had to do was place a watch on my house, and my grandfather played into his hands when he sought shelter. By ensuring we shared the same cell, our past relationship was bound to become known and gossip would spread. He planned it with great care. Without demeaning the bravery of your escape, I am sure Sir Charles contrived that you were not too closely followed.'

'That's absurd!' Tom protested, his face yellowing with ugly humour. 'What of Tovey?'

'Tovey hated Jake enough to be Sir Charles's accomplice and arrest me. But Tovey angered Sir Charles by going too far when I was put in chains. Which is why Tovey was at the church and Coombe Grange was burnt. All Sir Charles wanted was proof that we were lovers so he could confront Jake—your escape gave credit to his lies. Now everyone will think that I escaped with my lover, which is what Sir Charles intends Jake to believe.'

'And what if he does?' Tom pouted, his voice ringing with spite. 'The man is a rake. Good Lord, Rebecca, he's a Masters—a scoundrel to the bone!' His fingers bruised her shoulders as his anger mounted. 'It was me you were plighted to marry. Not him!'

Unable to free herself from his punishing hold, she sought to reason with him. 'Tom, I have no wish to cause you pain, but you know that is not strictly true.'

'What does it matter? It's me you love—not Jake Masters,' Tom declared, sending a shiver of alarm through her. 'He stole you from me. Have I not proved myself worthy of your love? Come with me. Forget Masters.'

'You rave, Tom.' Her fists struck against his chest, her eyes blazing as she fought to wrench free of his hold, while her fear grew at the glitter frosting his eyes. 'You are a dear friend, but that is all our relationship can ever be. I'm married, and I will not disavow my marriage. I have to find Jake.'

'You'll go to the devil first,' Tom snarled through bared teeth, and he shook her roughly. 'Willing or no, it is the Continent for you, and in the guise of my wife. I've not come this far to lose all now.'

Rebecca stared at him, wide-eyed, as realisation broke over her with the suddenness of a summer storm. Her suspicions had not been ill-founded. Tom had not changed. 'You're in league with Sir Charles Masters!' she spat. 'I suppose he promised you your freedom for this infamy?'

'That, and much more,' Tom crowed his triumph. 'Once it is known you are my mistress, Masters will renounce the marriage. He's too proud to be ridiculed for a cuckold—probably he is already at sea. Besides, he never intended to take you back with him to the colonies.'

'That is what Sir Charles wishes to believe. I have more faith in Jake.' Her mind raced to reason with him. 'How can you trust Sir Charles? Help me find Jake! He's a just man. When he knows how you protected me in prison, he will reward you. I'll ask him to give you passage on his brother's ship, and you could start a new life in the colonies as a free man.'

'Do you think I'll tug my forelock to Jake Masters?' Tom scoffed. 'Or that money can repay the humiliation you forced upon me? You and I have a score to settle. I courted you for months and you never let me lay a hand upon you, but you jumped into bed with Jake Masters quick enough. Vengeance is sweeter, especially since Sir Charles has promised that after a year I can return to England, pardoned, and my lands will be returned to me. A short exile beats being hanged for a lost cause.'

'I'll not come with you.' She pushed against his hold and, when he held firm, kicked his shin.

'Bitch!' he grunted through his pain. Her head reeled at the impact of his slap, blood filling her mouth from the cut on her lip. 'I shall enjoy breaking your spirit, and with it Jake Masters' pride. To think I once thought burning a fitting end to you both.'

'*You* burned the lodge, not grandfather?' Rebecca lashed out at him with renewed fury.

'That old fool tried to stop me,' Tom gloated as he ducked his head aside from her clawing nails.

Rebecca fought him like a demon. 'You're insane if you think I would let Jake believe I forsook him for you!'

Tom grabbed her wrists with one hand, his face demonic with hatred. 'You could have had it easy, Rebecca. But you're too damned clever for your own good. There was no escape. Sir Charles gave me my freedom provided I took you with me to France.' He struck her again, knocking her backwards. 'I said you would come, willing or no.'

A sharp pain exploded through the side of her head as she fell against the table. Momentarily, stars spangled her vision—then blackness.

Jake paced the deck of *The Chesapeake Queen*, his face a bleak mask as he listened to Nathan.

'You have to accept that Rebecca is dead,' his brother persisted. 'Besides, why should Sir Charles lie? Good God, Jake, he loves you like a son. He would not put you through this torment.'

'Once I would have believed that,' Jake dragged out, his voice strained with exhaustion. He had not slept for two days. 'But Becca was right. Sir Charles is eaten up with hatred for Ashleigh and his family. He, who is always so clear-headed and rational, is totally irrational where the Ashleighs are concerned.' He rubbed his thumb along the cleft of his chin, staring past his brother and across the harbour at Lyme. 'If Rebecca is dead, then I am as much responsible for her death as I was for Anne's. Blood and nails! I've lived ten years in that particular hell.'

'When will you accept you were not responsible for Anne's death?' Nathan's hazel eyes were shadowed with concern. 'Unfortunately, women die in childbirth every day. It is a risk they take.'

'But Anne never wanted a child.' Jake unburdened himself for the first time to anyone. 'She was a child herself. That side of marriage terrified her. God knows I was patient, but I was never cut out to be a monk. And it was Anne I wanted, not other women then. For a year I managed to restrain my needs. I knew she hated Maryland. She called it barbarous and uncouth, where no gentlewoman could bear to live. Yet I made allowances. She was so very young—so very innocent, and, dear God, absolutely frigid with horror whenever I touched her. Then, one night, my restraint broke. I could not stand the wanting any longer. I virtually raped her. The result of that night was her pregnancy.'

'You were within your rights!' Nathan exclaimed. 'I only wonder you restrained yourself so long. From the first moment you met her you were in love with her. You're only human, Jake.'

'And when she died I had only pity for her.' His voice rustled with the dryness of dead leaves. 'With Becky it was different. She brought me peace, and a contentment I had thought lost forever. But she too is a gentlewoman. What life could Maryland offer her? Especially the uncleared land deeded to me by King James. In five or seven years the land can be cleared and a decent house built, fit for a wife. I thought I was being noble in sparing her the hardship.'

'I had not realised you loved her so much.' Nathan regarded him sadly.

'Neither had I.' Jake gripped the ship's rail tightly and stared down into the sea. 'The land grant means nothing to me now.'

'But it will,' Nathan said gently. 'It will be a new beginning. It's time you came home, Jake. There's nothing for you in England now.'

A cry from a narrow-boat pulling aside drew their attention, and Jake turned away at the sight of Sir Charles Masters climbing the rope to come aboard.

'I've no wish to see him,' Jake said bitterly. 'He was responsible for Becky's arrest and I'll never forgive him for that. But he's my father's brother—that alone spares him from answering to my sword. Since the tide is almost full, you had best make your own farewells brief.'

'Mistress Masters!' An urgent voice called from far off.

Rebecca stirred, aware first of a hammering in her skull, then of the lesser pains in her arms and legs and a tightness across her mouth. She made to raise a hand to her head, and found she could not move. Her eyes blinked open with alarm, her blurred vision clearing as she recognised the landlord of the Queen's Arms bending over her feet.

'Thank God, you've come round,' he said, as he continued to untie the rope which bound her hands and ankles. 'That knave who called himself your husband left some minutes ago—with orders you were not to be disturbed.'

As the blood rushed back into her wrists and ankles, Rebecca groaned, the sound muffled behind the gag still over her mouth. She struggled to sit up from her prone position on the wooden settle, wrenching the gag free as she did so.

'He's not my husband,' she croaked.

'I know. Which is why I took the liberty of disobeying his instructions,' the landlord said, holding out a mug of ale to her. 'I've seen you riding with Mr Masters. So I knew it for a lie.'

After a few mouthfuls, she pushed it away. 'I have to get to Lyme. I must leave before that man returns. Have you a horse?' Her eyes widened in distress. 'I have nothing with which to pay you, but my husband should be in Lyme and he will settle my account.'

The landlord frowned. 'There's been strange rumours about you. Some say you're one of Monmouth's rebels. I even heard you had run off with a lover. And there was Mr Masters asking after you in the village two days past.'

'It's a long story,' Rebecca said, rising determinedly, her wits and strength recovering with the knowledge that Jake had been seeking her. 'Too long to explain now. But I must get to Lyme. There's been a grave misunderstanding, and I know my husband has been misinformed. I can only guess at the lies concocted. I fear now he may sail before I can see him and explain.'

The landlord hesitated. 'How do I know you bain't an escaping rebel?' He looked at her hard and, seeing the anguish and plea in her eyes, his expression softened. 'Nay, you're never that. Your face is too honest. A mare will be saddled at once. Go quickly before your companion returns. 'Tisn't safe for you to ride to Lyme alone. An ostler will accompany you and he can return the horse.'

'God bless and keep you,' Rebecca said, hurrying to the door. 'The man I was travelling with is the rebel, not I. I was his hostage to safety.'

Minutes later she was galloping headlong through the streets and along the harbour wall. At discovering the fullness of the tide, fear clutched at her heart. She sped onwards, her glance darting from side to side with the dread of meeting Tom. When she saw him talking to a fisherman who was mending his nets her spine stung with alarm, but mercifully his back was to her. And then she saw the four soldiers, their muskets drawn as they prepared to surround him.

She did not pause to see Tom taken but, fearing they would recognise her as a fugitive, too, urged her mare to lengthen its stride as they passed the last of the houses and began to climb the cliff to follow the coastal track to Lyme.

A stiff breeze buffeted her from the sea and forced her to crouch low in the saddle, while the boy with her cautioned her to slow her pace. She ignored him. All she could think of was that the tide would soon turn, and that with it the ship could take Jake away. A sixth sense screamed at her that this was the day Jake was to sail. The wind stung her face and tore at her hair, stripping the breath from her already aching lungs as the long arm of the Cobb came into view. She bit back an anguished cry. There, with her sails straining full-bellied with the wind, was a merchantman making fast out to sea.

Agony scored like a plough through her, and her mind and body were frozen with dread as the mare proceeded down the cliff to the seaport. The ship was little more than a diminishing dot in the distance as she dismounted, knowing with an inner certainty that it was Nathan's ship.

Her legs stiff and wooden, she hailed a youth stacking lobster pots. 'What ship has just sailed?'

'*The Chesapeake Queen*,' he replied. 'A fine ship bound for the Americas.'

Rebecca swayed. It wasn't fair. To be so close and yet to fail. Defeated, her hands clenched over the mare's mane as misery engulfed her. 'Jake, oh, Jake—my love.' The salt of tears ran into her mouth and her shoulders shook. 'How could you let this happen?'

A seagull screeched, mocking her plea, the sound of the wind and sea fading to become a bitter lament for all she had lost.

'Did you truly believe I would leave you?' The husky voice directly behind her held a catch of relief and amusement. She whirled, heart pounding, fearing her ears had betrayed her. A lopsided grin split Jake's handsome face. 'Now, isn't that just like an Ashleigh to think ill of a Masters? I shall have to teach you your place, dear wife.'

'Jake!' Her cry was filled with wonder and, oblivious of the crowd forming on the quay, she ran into his arms. For a long moment she clung to him, drinking in the scent of his warm skin which was more heady than any seductive perfume, and her heart thumped against her breastbone as she revelled in the thrill of his arms tightening around her.

'Temptress mine——' his low, throaty chuckle against her ear was the sweetest sound she had ever heard '—I never knew the joy you had brought me until I thought I had lost you.' His hands slid up to caress her wet cheeks, and his thumb rubbed the tears away. There was a mistiness about his own jade and golden gaze which sent her pulse racing. 'They told me you were dead.'

'And the lies spread about Tom and myself?' she asked with trepidation. 'You did not believe them, did you?'

'My darling, I never doubted your fidelity. But if you knew how close I came to leaving on that ship.' A shudder passed through his body.

'I can imagine the lies Sir Charles spread,' she forced out, through a throat constricted with love and happiness. 'He was determined to end our marriage. I'm glad you didn't listen to him.'

'Oh, but I did.' Jake looked grave, but a light danced behind his eyes. 'Had it not been for Sir Charles I would still be on my brother's ship. He told me you were dead, you see—but then he repented after I'd stormed out.' His mouth tilted with self-mockery. 'It seems he realised how much I truly loved you before even I did. He came to the ship and told me everything.'

Rebecca felt her hatred for Sir Charles recede. Locked in her husband's arms, she could forgive his kinsman anything. 'I'm glad he healed the breach between you. You were once close. And this feud is long outdated.'

'You can say that, my love, after he caused you such hardship and grief?' Jake looked at her with tenderness and admiration. 'I could not stand to face him after what he had done.'

It was the second time he had spoken of love, and she knew her own heart was shining in her eyes as she smiled up at him. 'I love you, Jake. To me that is all that matters now. Sir Charles believed he acted in your best interests. You must forgive him,' she urged, wanting no further barriers to mar their future. 'He's a proud man, and he humbled himself to come to you. His love for you was greater than his hatred for my family.'

A discreet cough dragged their attention from each other, but Jake kept his arm about Rebecca's shoulders as they turned to face Sir Charles.

'I deeply wronged you both,' the baronet said with stiff formality. 'Your wife proved her courage at the prison. And after Oliver Ashleigh turned his back on her she still risked her life to help him, showing a nobility of spirit, and a great capacity for loyalty and love.' His gaze fell upon Rebecca, regret obvious in his unblinking stare. 'I was too stubborn to acknowledge the happiness you had brought Jake. Now I would right that wrong. Tovey is dead, and from Captain Endacott's report he met a deserving fate. Hardwycke will also be dealt with.'

Rebecca experienced a qualm at Tom's fate. 'What will happen to Tom? He acted on your orders, Sir Charles, and, in truth, had he not been in the cell when Tovey arrested me, I would have suffered the most appalling degradation. He saved me from that, and from Tovey's attempted rape. Apart from tying me up at the inn at Charmouth, he treated me with respect.'

'You have a forgiving heart, Rebecca,' Sir Charles said. 'Hardwycke has been guilty of grievous crimes. He must pay the penalty.'

'But not for the way you used him.' She was aware that Jake was watching her with a frown. She would have to risk his displeasure, for she owed Tom some debt for having saved her from Tovey. 'Tom is selfish and avaricious, but his treatment of me proves he is not totally lacking in honour.'

Sir Charles regarded her levelly and nodded. 'It will take months for all the rebels to come to trial, and, though I believe Judge Jeffreys has been appointed by King James to preside over most of them, I will have some jurisdiction. I will see that Hardwycke is transported, not hanged.' He cleared his throat and shifted uncomfortably. 'I do not expect your forgiveness, but I give you and Jake my blessing and as a wedding present the deeds of Coombe Grange, with funds to rebuild the house.'

'You are generous, Sir Charles.' In acknowledgement of the sacrifice he had made to his pride, she left Jake's side and curtsied respectfully, her voice lowering. 'But my life is in Maryland, not at Coombe Grange. Since Jake will need all the money he can raise to stock his land and build a house, with his permission, I would ask you to act as our agent and obtain the best price you can for the Grange. Though I can think of no better owner than yourself. What better way to end the feud?'

Sir Charles bowed to her and, putting his hand in the pocket of his full-skirted jacket, held out the emerald ring. 'This is yours. And you are worthy to wear it. As for the property, the money will be in Jake's hands in two days. In time for *The Chesapeake Queen*'s return.'

Rebecca took the ring, but did not put it on her finger as she voiced her surprise. 'Nathan's ship did not sail for Maryland?'

'Indeed not.' Jake chuckled softly, again at her side. 'Nathan has embarked on another wild-goose chase on my account. He was putting into every port between here and Portsmouth as we had no idea which route Hardwycke would take. I was to have ridden to Plymouth. He will return in two days.'

'But how would Nathan have recognised me? We have never met.'

Sir Charles laughed, his earlier discomfort turning to amusement as he regarded his nephew good-naturedly. 'How could Nathan fail to recognise you after Jake so poetically described you? What were your words—hair like burnished rosewood, eyes lustrous as polished amethysts, a figure tall but graceful and a beauty comparable with the sultry promise of a siren!'

A tinge of colour spread across Jake's high cheekbones.

'Did you truly describe me like that?' Rebecca gazed up at him, her eyes bright with devilment.'

'That and much more, temptress mine,' he said, leading her out of hearing of Sir Charles. 'And when we are alone I will leave you in no doubt of my admiration.' He drew her close, his lips hovering tantalisingly above her own. 'But first there is a serious matter to remedy. The legality of our marriage. Though I regard our vows as binding, I would have us properly wed in the eyes of the legally established church before we sail.' He took her hand and, retrieving the emerald, slipped it over her third finger and raised her hand to his lips. 'There is no one more worthy than you to wear this ring. To think I had thought myself done with love... Trust an Ashleigh to shatter my conceited illusions!'

'You are not just saying that, because of the baby?' she asked, needing to end a last, nagging doubt. 'You did not seem very pleased when I told you I was with child.'

Jake tightened his hold, his hazel eyes clouding with pain. 'Because Anne's death still haunted me. But, not as you think, because I loved her. Because she died in childbirth—she died cursing Maryland and everything I care for, because she thought it primitive and uncivilised. The first years will be hard.'

'If we are together they will be happy, fulfilling years, Jake.' She placed her hands against his chest, delighting in the quickening beat of his heart. 'My grandfather was a gentleman, but he was also a farmer. It is a life I am used to. It was the shallowness of Court life which was abhorrent to me.' There was determination in her violet eyes as she pressed her body closer and heard him catch his breath. 'I am not as Anne. Maryland sounds an exciting place, and with you by my side what more could make my happiness complete?'

Jake kissed her long and hard, passion and tenderness mingling in the ecstasy of his restrained embrace. He drew back with reluctance as a ribald comment carried to them from a passing fisherman. But the smile in his eyes promised her heaven.

'We will take a room at the inn,' he said with urgency as he impatiently propelled her in that direction. She saw Martha and Simmons, his arm in a sling, standing by the door, and at their feet Tess and Jasper.

Jake gave her no time for more than the briefest of greetings, and her curiosity would have to wait to learn how they had come to Lyme, for Jake had taken her hand and was bounding up the stairs to the privacy of their room. The moment the door shut behind them she was captured in his arms, his lips claiming hers with a wild and possessive passion.

'Becky, my love, my heart—my life.' His words were muffled by his kisses, deep and urgent, drawing her into a world where only he existed.

Her hunger matched his, inflamed by his words of love, which she had yearned for with such intensity and which were now endless upon his lips, as their bodies moulded, hearts and minds shared in a love which would span to eternity.

GIFT OF GOLD   *Jayne Ann Krentz*   £3.50

One dark night in Mexico, Verity Ames tantalized a knight in shining armour – Jonas Quarrel. To release himself from a tormenting nightmare, he was compelled to track her down and discover all her secrets...

A WILD WIND   *Evelyn A. Crowe*   £2.99

Ten years ago, Shannon Reed and Ash Bartlet had planned to marry, but disaster struck. Now they have been given a second chance, until Shannon is accused of murder...

SHARE MY TOMORROW   *Connie Bennett*   £2.75

It was a dream come true for marine biologist, Lillian Lockwood – not only working with the renowned submarine pilot, Neal Grant, but finding such happiness together. But only by confronting his ghosts could Neal bury the memories which were crippling their love.

These three new titles will be out in bookshops from April 1990

W⬤RLDWIDE

2 Historical Romances and 2 Gifts FREE!

Experience the excitement and romance of the past by accepting two **FREE** Masquerade Romances plus a pair of glass oyster dishes and a special MYSTERY GIFT...Then, if you choose, you can go on to enjoy 4 more exciting Masquerades every two months, for just £1.75 each! Send the coupon below at once to-

Reader Service, FREEPOST, P.O. Box 236, Croydon, Surrey CR9 9EL.

------✂------------------No stamp required ----------------------

YES! Please rush me my **2 Free Masquerade Romances and 2 FREE gifts** ! Please also reserve me a Reader Service Subscription. If I decide to subscribe, I can look forward to receiving 4 Masquerade Romances every two months, for just £7.00 delivered direct to my door. Post and packing is free, and there's a free Mills & Boon Newsletter. If I choose not to subscribe I shall write to you within 10 days - I can keep the books and gifts whatever I decide and I can cancel or suspend my subscription at any time, I am over 18 years of age.

EP66M

NAME _____

ADDRESS _____

_____

_____ POSTCODE _____

SIGNATURE _____

The right is reserved to refuse an application and change the terms of this offer. You may be mailed with other offers as a result of this application. Offer expires Dec 31st 1989 and is limited to one per household. offer applies in the UK and Eire only. Overseas send for details